POWERA

Josephine Ronk

First published by Josephine Ronk 2022

Cover design by: Latte Goldstein

ISBN: 978-1-7397140-1-7

Contents

Chapter One: Fred Demson

The doors to the secret headquarters are locked. Inside, the seven deputies assigned the task of managing each continent are gathered.

'I am proud of you all, but more must be done. We need powerful men and women; more presidents, prime ministers, the billionaires of the world and all those who will serve our purpose. The real work is about to begin, and each member must fulfil their task without delay.

'We must take over e-commerce in all sectors; transportation, aviation, farming, medical facilities, mining, politics and, of course, positions of power. You need to be meticulous about managing everything we control.'

'Sir, we have chosen Campbell as the new president after the late president refused to listen. Do we need to worry about him?' Andrew Hughes of Blue Gama asks.

I burst into laughter. 'We know everything about him, even the colour of the underwear he is wearing today. He will dare not turn against us; he saw what happened to his predecessor.'

Andrew smirks. 'Yes, sir!'

'I have a question as well; what about Mohammed Pir? You chose him for the organisation, but now he is drunk on power. He might destroy the world; he is very unpredictable,' Hussain Atta asks.

I lift my wine glass. 'The world will be destroyed but not by a nuclear bomb. Your job is not only to look after Mohammed; you have twenty-four other countries assigned to you. I want to incite anger and resentment from the Muslim nations toward the Western world. I want people to live in fear, with more terrorist attacks, then the governments of the West will respond by sending troops to destroy them. There will be no peace; we will profit from selling weapons to both parties. It's a win-win situation.

'I need to see results from all of you. You have been given the greatest weapon; information. Use it wisely. No man is more powerful than us. We have made money, but we need to control each continent. I want to see discrimination and division that leads to hate, selfishness, maliciousness, and anger among the people.

We thrive in chaos, not unity. We need political parties to turn against other political parties, without consideration for their citizens. Political leaders should be fighting each other. There must be strife in every nation.

'We will obtain all contracts in all fields. Don't feel compassion for the masses. It is not your fault they are useless. Anyone who is not with us must be eliminated. We take and take until there is nothing left to take. Do you understand? We cannot fail; we have access to all technologies and everything people are thinking about.

'I want children to turn against their parents. I want more death. I want businesses destroyed; I want our people to take over the media; we can brainwash the common man into believing anything. I want homes divided, burglary, violent crime and rape on the rise. Police killing innocent people, and judges sentencing the wrong people. I want lies and deception to be the norm.

'In front of each of you is a file; you all have individual goals. The world must be conquered in six months. Each continent has its strengths, and every member of your hub must fulfil their personal goal within a specific time. If they disappoint you, eliminate them. The world is full of people; nobody is irreplaceable. I need this done at the stipulated time.

'Do you know why I chose each of you? James Cooper for Red Gama, Andrew Hughes for Blue Gama, Lekan Gbada for Green Gama, Hussain Atta for Yellow Gama_1, Sophia Richardson for White Gama, Adriano Cardoso for Purple Gama and, finally, Ping Wu for Yellow Gama_2? I saw something in all of you that no one else had; the desire to succeed no matter what it takes. You were ready to squash anyone in your way; not even your family could hold you down. That is an exemplary quality. You need to prove to me that I chose correctly. After all, I have deposited billions of dollars into your bank accounts. Make me proud; the world is your playground – go out there and take control.

'One last point, once we leave this room, no business must be discussed at the dining table; everyone from the waiters to the chef is my trusted employee, but what we have discussed here is top secret. These goals are given to the selected few; to you. No one else must know, except for the small part they will play.'

I stand up. 'It's been a long day. Let's celebrate.'

We move into another room where waiters are ready with wine and cigars. The dining table is filled with food from all over the world, featuring delicacies from each continent, and no money has been spared in preparing this feast. There is laughter and jubilation, while the world waits in ignorance, not knowing what is about to knock on its door.

Chapter Two: London

Jude

I have to find a way to get out of Red Gama before I lose my life. The situation in Europe is getting worse; people are turning against one another, all sense of community has gone and desperation has taken hold.

Imagine having money and not being able to buy food. I have seen people break into stores, hoping they might find something, but the shelves are empty. My restaurant remains closed and is now a base for distribution of the drug Demalon, and more and more people are turning to this type of drug to soothe their worries.

A small quantity of food will be released to the public at a higher price tomorrow. What choice do they have? People are dying from starvation and lack of medical care. More people are committing suicide. Most are forced to fast or give what little they can to those who need it most. I watch hopelessly, as little children on television cry from hunger, their parents begging the government to help them, but to no avail.

But not in my household. My mother looks at me with her eyebrows raised questioningly whenever I come home with bags of food, and I tell her constantly that no one must know. I am not allowed to help others or share what I have with anyone outside of the house.

The only person who can help me is Sergeant Roger Smith whom I saw at the gala. Maybe he wants to get out of this sickening hub as well?

I watched on TV as Sarah Philips left her father's company. She is trending on all media platforms announcing that her father was innocent. She wants to find a way to revive her father's company, 'Sam Wholesale', supplying foodstuffs to the continent. I've been given the assignment of planting myself in her life; all information about her has been shown to me. I know everything about her; her daily routine, her favourite toothpaste, and the private meeting she had yesterday with investors.

I look at my watch as I alight from my car at precisely 5.14 pm. On her way to her car, Sarah will be attacked by one of our men pretending to rob her while I come in like some kind of superhero to save her.

Everything happens as planned, and I rush to her aid when she starts shouting for help. I kick her attacker in the stomach, and he drops her bag, holding his stomach as he runs away.

'Jesus!' I rush towards her. 'Are you OK?'

'Yes, thanks to you,' she replies.

I pick up her bag and return it to her. 'I hope he didn't hurt you?'

'I'm just a bit shaken up. I'll be fine.'

I give her my best smile. 'I think I should escort you home to be on the safe side. I'll drive my car behind yours.'

'Thanks, but I don't want you to go out of your way for me.'

'It's no trouble. We have to be careful. Nowhere is safe anymore. I'm Jude Williams, by the way.'

'Hi! I'm sorry; didn't mean to be rude. I'm Sarah Philips.'

'Nice to meet you.'

I help her into her car. 'Wait while I get behind your car before you start driving.'

I shake my head as I enter my vehicle. Jesus! I hate my life! This poor woman has no idea that I am the worst thing to ever happen to her.

I follow behind her until she reaches home; I know she is staying at her father's house in Knightsbridge. When she has parked her car, I get out of my vehicle and walk up to her.

'Thank you again,' she says. 'Today is already a shitty day, but it would have been worse if you hadn't stepped in.'

'I am happy to help.'

'I've seen you somewhere before. Are you that celebrity chef from the television?'

'I used to be but with the way things are going, who knows?'

She nods. 'I am trying my best to help people. The only way to do that is to revive my father's failing company, but banks keep turning me down.'

I can see sadness written on her face. 'It has been nice meeting you.,' I say. 'Can I have your number? So I can check up on you and make sure you are OK.'

She laughs shyly as she gives me her mobile number. I have it already, so I pretend to store the number on my phone. I smile at her and promise to be in touch as I walk away.

Back in my car, I place my head on the steering wheel and sigh heavily. I hope they won't kill this woman; but the only way she can get out alive is for me to put an end to her dream of reviving her dad's company.

***

The trucks leave various warehouses to distribute food all around Europe. I have never before seen a stampede in supermarkets and local markets. People rush to grab anything they can lay their hands on.

Inevitably, it turns violent. People fight each other to get the last carton of milk or loaf of bread, blood streaming down their faces in the struggle for food. The few who are able to get something are robbed and wounded by the desperate. Cars are vandalised as people try to steal food from vehicles.

I am going to hell! I sit in my house with my mum, as I prepare my best pasta with prawns and pour her a glass of her favourite red wine. She is not allowed to ask questions.

'Eat up, Mum. Don't overthink the situation. Just enjoy your meal and be thankful.'

Chapter Three: New York

Martin

How can I be homeless? I was asked to leave three motels and I am told they are fully booked whenever I give my name. Why is this happening to me? I have been forced to sleep in the back of my car, but how long can I continue to live like this?

The death rate in the country has quadrupled; hundreds of thousands have lost their lives in the past two weeks after the president's death, and no further explanation has come from the White House. Roads and bridges are blocked. More people have come out to protest, and to mourn the death of their sister, mother, father, and children. The police have come out in full force, arresting protesters, or murdering them. People are dragged to the ground by their hair for daring to complain. Every state is locked down. It has been announced that anyone found protesting will be killed; this has led to increased violence between the public and the police. I don't understand what is happening.

I visit an ATM to withdraw some money, and I am told I have insufficient funds. I check my bank balance only to find that I have just twenty dollars in my account. What the hell? I have worked in the force for many years, and I am prudent with my spending. This particular account is not even a joint account.

I enter USA Bank, not caring how unkempt I look. I am desperate. How can I survive on just twenty dollars? The woman behind the counter looks at me warily after providing me with my account statement.

'I'm sorry, sir, this is the printout of your expenses. It clearly shows you have only twenty dollars.'

'That is impossible. I should have $5,049 in my account.' I bring out my chequebook and show her how I have spent my money, and the balance remaining.

'I'm sorry, sir, I can't help. It appears you are mistaken; you never had such an amount of money.'

'Can I speak to the manager?' I ask.

I see two security guards pulling out their guns.

They warn me to leave the bank quietly. I walk out of the bank in frustration. What am I going to do now?

Dan Campbell

'Mr President, we have successfully dumped the chemical waste into the central water system. The good news is that no one knows what is causing the illness and death. We informed the public that the water pollution problem has been resolved, and anyone who raised a complaint was eliminated. The public is anxious; we need to tell them something.'

'Don't worry; we will give them something. Blame it on the African American people, no! The Europeans, better yet, blame it on a country. Yes, I don't like the president of Mexico; blame it on him, call it 'Mexican Death' brought into the country by their people. The big boss wants to remove the Mexican president, so let's direct people's anger at their people. We need more violence and killing.'

Martin

I sit on the ground in front of the bank. How can all my money have just disappeared? I will not last a day without food and fuel for my car.

They gave a contradictory statement. The late president blamed the water pollution on an oil spill from tankers that resulted in deaths and a rise in fuel costs. The current president blames the spike in fuel prices on oil tankers being sabotaged by unknown people, leading to the country's oil shortage.

I get up and dust myself down watched by the security guards. I walk for a short distance, get into my car, and sit inside. I didn't know where to go. The only person who can help me is Edward; he is the only person who can make sense of my predicament. 'Gama, call Edward!'

I call multiple times but get no response. What should I do now? I know the answers lie with my former partner and boss, but I can't tail them without money to buy food and fuel.

A message pings on my phone: 'Come to 10th Street, Brooklyn, now!' I look at the gas meter. The tank is almost empty; I think it would get me to Brooklyn, but I won't be able to leave. I have to trust my instinct that this message is from Edward or I am finished. I need to find a way to get to Brooklyn. Many roads are blocked, and damage has been done to shops, houses and vehicles. I can see fires burning on the street, people making firebombs and throwing them at the police as the police open fire. *God!* My car must not die on the road because I've had to take an alternative route to avoid the violence in the city.

I arrive safely at the street. Where exactly am I going? Another text arrives. 'Get down from your car and start walking straight for the next five minutes, then turn left. You will see an abandoned underground station, take the staircase down.'

I follow the instructions and enter a dark station. I feel someone touch me. 'Follow me!' I hear Edward's voice, but I can't see him at first.

He switches on his torch and I follow him until we reach a door. He enters a code, and the door opens. I have never seen so much technology in one place; computer systems, monitors, some I don't even know.

I look at Edward and ask, 'What is this place?'

'My hideout from the world. You are in deep trouble; your name has been flagged. You are now the most wanted man in the USA. I was able to protect you in the bank; I prevented the federal alert from being triggered. You have gone up against some dangerous people.'

Chapter Four: Lagos

Lola

I did not leave my house after being robbed, and my car magically reappeared in my compound. The country's security has gotten worse. People are being kidnapped in their houses and children disappearing on their way to school. Nowhere is safe anymore. I have decided that I will no longer drive my Range Rover; I will drive my trusted old Toyota to be safe. All the opposing parties have been strangely murdered. Now we have only one party running for the presidency, and everyone is too afraid to talk.

People are angry because the government is not saying or doing anything. They turn on themselves. How can you kidnap and murder your fellow humans without any guilt? Hoodlums are free to terrorise people, destroy property, steal and kill. Even the police are afraid of them.

My father has instructed me to start work, at a time when nowhere is safe and people live in fear of their lives. I walk into the office, looking around in fear of being followed; I summon the elevator to take me to the second floor. Someone stands beside me and says hello. It is Segun, my helper.

'What are you doing here?'

'I work here now. The name of the company is BankYemo Oil & Gas that is both our parents' names. I was given no choice. My father forced my landlord to cancel my lease, and I lost my job.'

We walk in silence to the conference room where a meeting has been set up with some of the staff, by our parents, to discuss the year's business forecast.

Lekan Gbada

'Congratulations are in order, all the opposition party leaders have been eliminated. Our party is now in charge and will rule for years to come.' The men and women of Green Gama raise their glasses.

'We must never be defeated. We are taking over the whole of Africa. No more democracy; people will not be allowed to vote anymore. Their voices must be silenced; we will take over with force. I want armies everywhere, on the streets, no more hiding; we need to oppress them or others will rise, and we cannot have that.'

Lola

My doorbell rings. I look at the time; 7.00 pm.

Armies carrying submachine guns are parading the streets. People are hiding in their houses, afraid to come out. We don't know why they are here. I was hoping they were here to help with security, but I doubt it. They go to people's houses, beat the inhabitants and burn down their homes.

I check my peephole before opening the door,

'Segun, what are you doing here? It's not safe!'

'I need to talk to you before returning to my hotel. I refuse to stay in that man's house.'

'Why?'

'I told you that he had a hand in my brother's death. I confronted him before I started working for him, and he laughed in my face. He said that he sent me to the best school. I live an opulent lifestyle that people could only dream of. Do I think the world is fair? He needed to make certain sacrifices to get to the highest position. He toiled day and night to bring his family out of poverty to this position of wealth we now enjoy. Do I like my life, or do I want to go the way my brother did? We have to work together to find a way to bring down him and his cohorts.'

'Ha! That includes my father.'

'These people are evil. The unrest happening in Africa has something to do with them, I'm sure of it. I went through my father's documents. He and other influential people have contracts to mine mineral resources all over Africa; gold, diamond, copper, iron ore, the list goes on. They are taking over the continent, and no one can stop them. The more money they make, the more powerful they become. The opposition parties that can question them have all been eliminated; it has become a dictatorship.'

'What can we do?' I ask.

He thinks for a moment. 'We have to find a way. I don't think your father is a bad person, but my father is scum. All he cares about is money! He already sold his family for it, and he will not stop.

'We need to dig deeper; how can they get these vast contracts? The secret meetings they go to regularly; whom do they meet? We need answers, this is just the beginning, and it will get worse. I can't sleep in luxury when others suffer because of it. Did you know that leader of the opposition party was murdered, and his whole family was wiped out? When you sleep in your mansion, think about that,' he says, as he opens the door and walks away.

Chapter Five: Kabul

Ahmed

Mohammed behaves unpredictably. One minute he talks to me calmly, the next minute, he is shouting angrily. His behaviour is erratic, and I don't know where I stand with him. I have been working for him for months now. He doesn't trust anyone. I suspect some of the answers I seek lie with that key he wears constantly, on a chain around his neck, but how do I take it off him, and what does it open?

I can hear him shouting in his office as I stand behind the closed door. I know this has to do with millions of dollars that weren't transferred into his Union Bank of Afghanistan account last week. The situation in Afghanistan is bad. He has imposed taxes on everyone; 40% of your income belongs to the government, and people can hardly eat, but what is 40% of nothing? Someone else is pulling the strings; the question is, who?

There is a loud noise outside. Mohammed opens the door and tells me to check what is happening. I walk outside to see over fifty malnourished men, their clothes in tatters. I call one of the security team over. 'What is going on?'

'Mohammed has given us a directive to go to certain homes to collect their taxes, but these people have nothing of value to take.'

I look at the men, forced to lay flat in the dirt. I am sure these people have not eaten in days.

Mohammed appears by my side and addresses the men who have rounded up the miscreants. 'I was told these people have nothing. Explain!'

'In the few homes we went to, most didn't have any means of livelihood, and many had no food – nothing! We raided homes; we collected the little money they had.'

The money collected was brought forward for Mohammed to see.

'We were only able to get twenty thousand afghani from a hundred homes. Still, we took any valuables that we could find from their homes.'

Clothes were thrown on the floor, and a few pieces of gold

jewellery were placed on it.

'From some we collected their animals.' He pointed at a few sheep, cattle and goats.

Mohammed looked at his men and shouted, 'What nonsense is this? This is all you could get? Don't you understand that I have a target I must reach by next month. This won't do. What about these men?' He points to the wretched men lying on the ground.

'Sir, they don't have anything, some live on the road, their houses are empty, they have nothing of value to take. So we brought them to you. I don't know what you want us to do with them?'

'Bring them to me!'

The men are kicked and spat on and told to crawl on their knees towards Mohammed. They are warned to keep their heads down.

Mohammed points at one of the men in front. The security man strokes the man's face, telling him to lift his head. He holds the stroked side of his face as he begs to be spared.

'What do you do?' asks Mohammed.

'I was a farmer. The crops have all died because of the severe drought. We can't afford to eat. I have sold everything I have to survive. Please, if I had money, I would give it to you, but I don't have anything.'

'They are useless; killing them is a waste of time,' says Mohammed. 'You have two weeks to find a way to pay your taxes.'

He turns to leave but hesitates. 'Give them fifty strokes of the cane as a lesson not to default in paying my taxes.'

I follow behind him to his office. I can see the men already being roughed up by the laughing security guards.

Mohammed enters the conference room with his right-hand men behind him. I watch him as he paces the floor angrily. He looks at his trusted men and says, 'We need to get them to pay taxes with good money, not animals, but how do we get money from poor people?'

'We could take away their lands and houses whenever they default,' says Nader. 'Eventually, the whole country will belong to us, and they will have to rent from us. For example, they will be given farmland to cultivate, but all profit comes to us, and we will pay stipends for their labour.'

'That's a good idea, but there is a drought; how can we profit from this?'

'This drought provides an opportunity to take over everything that they own. In the next couple of months, more and more people will default, and the ones with nothing of value become our slaves. When things get better, they will take care of the lands and the animals with no pay; it is a win for us. Just imagine, in the next couple of months the people of Afghanistan will be at your mercy, working for you for free.'

'I like that idea; get it done!'

***

Hussain Atta looks at the task placed in front of him by the big boss: 'The world needs to be fearful.' He picks up his voice changer phone and calls Mohammed. 'I want you to threaten some nations for me with your nuclear bomb!'

Chapter Six: Sydney

Henry

News is streaming worldwide about the possible war declared by the Islamic nation Afghanistan. World leaders would hold an emergency meeting, discussing protection for their citizens, sanctions and the next steps to stop a possible world war.

China is pretending to back Afghanistan; the leaders are accusing each other of the mess that is happening presently. This has caused great fear among the people of Australia; all parties that opposed nuclear plants being built in the country have been silent.

Witnessing how easily people can be manipulated to believe that war will happen is the most painful thing. Parliament has approved a contract worth billions of dollars for weapons for both air and sea. I cringe, knowing the contract was given to White Gama, who staged the whole thing. I can only watch as people start to build bunkers in their homes, preparing for war. As Minister for Defence, I stood in front of the world's press to lie about how dangerous the situation is and how we had been in talks with our allies, but nothing looked good. How shocked we are to learn that a country like Afghanistan could have a nuclear weapon, when we, as a nation, do not have one. That should be rectified immediately!

***

I go to see Carl at Moreland Mental Hospital. Part of his treatment is talking with his parents in front of a counsellor to air grievances.

I blink away the tears when I see my son after a month apart.

'Where is Mum?' he asks nervously.

'She is seriously ill, but I wanted to see you, so I came on my own.'

How can I tell my son that I don't know where his mother is? I don't know if she is dead or alive!

The only good thing in my life right now is that my son seems to be getting better, and for the first time in a long time, he told me how angry he was about my working habits. With everything happening, I struggle daily to go to work, knowing the country's situation will worsen because of greedy people whose only concerns are money and power.

I reflect on my life as I drive to my parents' house after visiting Carl. My mother has assured me that she will help me to find my wife. I had a meeting with the head of her security, Tom, who promised to do his best to look for Mia. It has been weeks, and he has found nothing. None of her family has seen her. The police told us that their investigation shows she ran away. I can't go back to my noiseless house; I will drown in guilt, so I am staying with my parents temporarily.

Arriving, I notice another car parked outside. I can't deal with a guest today. I am fed up and frustrated by everything that is happening, and my mum seems not to be bothered.

I walk into the house, trying to escape to my room when I hear my mother call my name. I force myself to smile and approach her.

'Hello, Mother. I am exhausted; I need to sleep.'

'I know, honey, but I would like you to meet Cynthia Coleman. Do you remember her? You grew up together before she travelled to America for work, and now she is back.'

I follow my mother to the dining room, where I see an elegant woman. My mother always liked her, but I think she is pretentious. She smiles widely as she gets up and hugs me.

'It's been a long time, Henry; you never called.'

'How are you, Cynthia?' I look at her more closely; everything is perfect, from the perfectly styled red hair to her figure-hugging dress.

'I am doing well, I just wanted to say hello to your folks, and I was told you were around.'

'It's nice meeting you, but like I told my mum I'm drained, I need to rest.'

'Henry, don't be rude!' My mum chastises me, as if I was still a child.

'I'm sorry,' I say, walking away angrily. I know exactly what my mother is up to.

Mia

I look around the room I am forced to stay in – in virtual darkness. Food and water are brought in twice daily; I don't know by whom. The food is dropped in the dark; when the person leaves, the light comes on. When I finish eating, the light goes off immediately afterwards.

I was sleeping in my room when a hand was placed over my mouth. I couldn't see their face. I was forced into a car and brought here. 'Why am I here?' I yelled at the top of my lungs. 'Please talk to me, someone…' but all I could hear was the echo of my own voice.

I have been here for about a month now and not seen or heard from my son or my husband. Is no one looking for me? How long will I be forced to remain here? I cover my mouth to stifle a sob, as grief engulfs me.

Chapter Seven: Rio de Janeiro

Ana

I have been working on various spreadsheets, moving figures to different continents worldwide. How are these people able to amass billions of dollars? They are involved in everything from mining, farming, e-commerce, telecommunications, and artificial intelligence to cocaine smuggling and prostitution; the list is endless. The economy is deteriorating, and the number of low-income families in the country has increased significantly. People can't eat three decent meals a day, and beggars line the streets. Homelessness and prostitution have increased across the nation. People are willing to do anything to survive. I heard on the news that people are even selling their kidneys and organs.

The government has scrapped free public education, so many people can no longer afford to send their children to school. The line for jobseekers has increased, but there are no jobs. People now engage in illegal activities like poaching wild animals, and the crime rate is alarming.

I look around my spacious office on the fourth floor. A couple of months back, I was just an accountant, oblivious to what was happening around me. Now I have more money than I need, and I am miserable. I saved all the incriminating files onto my flash drive when I was in the toilet at home; I know I am being monitored in the house and the office.

I walk into the meeting room. The assembled individuals don't work in this office, but I have seen their faces in the photographs Antonio sent me. What is happening here? I don't belong among them. I turn to leave, but my boss calls me back.

'Ana, where are you going?'

'I thought I was in the wrong meeting.'

'No, you are not.' He smiles. 'This meeting is for the privileged, and you're lucky to be one of them.'

A man walks in, and everyone is immediately quiet. My boss whispers to me that is the big boss. The big boss walks up to me and extends his hand. I shake it.

'Welcome, Ana,' he says. 'I insisted on meeting you personally, since it is you that handles the books. I have been told you are trustworthy and not particularly interested in money.' He stares directly at me. 'Whatever we do here must be discreet; no record must be made of any transaction. You understand?'

'Yes, sir!'

'So what do you hope to gain by keeping a record?'

I start to shake, as I reply, 'It is essential to keep a record for accountability.'

'Your boss instructed you to delete all copies of completed transactions.' He snaps his fingers, and my brother-in-law Pedro is brought in front of me. 'You are having problems with him, are you not? You issued his death sentence.'

'Please don't kill him; I will do anything you ask.' Pedro is blindfolded and gagged.

'Do you know why I brought him here? For you to see him being executed. I want to teach you and every member here a lesson. We have goals, and our targets for the year must be reached.

'We have taken over the continent's mining sector. We have discovered that the poaching of animals is lucrative and have engaged in that business. The world wants a scapegoat for the extinction of rare animals, so we manipulated some records, and the crime was pointed towards someone we hate.

'You have the spreadsheet of all our activities; this is sensitive information. More than any member, you have intricate details of how we operate. All the flash drives have now been destroyed, the one you opened in your sister's name and the one you kept in your house.'

One of the security men pulls off the gag, and Pedro starts to beg for his life. His mouth is forced open, a pill is placed inside, and he is forced to swallow it. I quickly wipe away a tear with the back of my hand.

'Please spare his life,' I say. 'He has four children with my sister.'

'Yes, I know. They will be next.'

'No, please, I will do everything you tell me to do.' A heavy blow lands on my face, and I fall to the ground.

'Do you think we cannot do without you? You're an imbecile! No one,' he says, looking around the room, 'is indispensable.'

I roll on the floor in pain and see my brother-in-law slump to the ground. He starts convulsing and foaming at the mouth.

'Listen, I am not your direct boss. In the next hour, police will arrest your sister for the crime of murdering her husband, and your nieces and nephews will be sold to the highest bidder.'

'I made a mistake; I was stupid! Please don't harm my only family. I promise I'll never do anything stupid again.'

'From now on, every job you do, you will not do it alone; you will be closely monitored. I know everything about you, from what you had for breakfast this morning to the pretend toilet breaks you take to compose yourself. Be very careful! This is your last chance, and believe me when I say, mess up; you die!'

I watch helplessly as Pedro's lifeless body is carried out of the room.

'Get up!' he says.

I stand up holding the side of my face that has swollen.

'Your sister will not be arrested, but she will be informed that you caused her husband's death. You will lose the only family you have. We are your family now. No one is more important than us.'

***

I rush back to my office with everyone staring at me. I sit on the floor, crying uncontrollably; this was worse than prison. Whom can I turn to? I have no one.

Gama connects a call from my sister. 'You killed my Pedro,' she wails at me. 'I'll make you pay for this.' The call disconnects. My stomach lurches and my heart beats wildly as I wrap my arms around myself. *I have no one!* I repeat to myself.

Chapter Eight: Hong Kong

Huan

I sit in an armchair in my room, rocking back and forth, completely numb. How do we get out of this increasingly deadly situation? Blue-collar people are being paid peanuts for their work. Major companies stopping the manufacture of products for just a month has led to many people dying. They are only allowed to sell products to specific individuals and countries working for this horrible group. I know that the prices have gone up tremendously for consumers. There is no law and order; the police do whatever the organisation tells them.

My biggest concern is that they can make me and my husband disappear without a trace, and the technology they have access to makes this possible.

My husband enters the room, watching me closely. 'Are you OK?' he asks.

'Look at our situation! We must find a way out of this, or we will die. I have been tasked with monitoring certain people. It is scary the power these people wield. You are just recovering; I am paranoid, constantly looking around my house for bugs. Cheung Wu pretended to be your loyal friend to use me to find Feng. Tell me, how do we get out of this?'

'They are afraid of exposure. That is why they were so desperate to get that information. They work behind the scenes, and anonymity is their greatest weapon. We need to use that against them.'

How? They have all the power. How can we bring down such a giant?'

'Wisdom; we know they are connected to all technology using Gamaplug, a unique technology that allows us to get things done through our minds. First, you need to stop using your Gamaplug; but do use it sporadically, or they will be suspicious.'

***

When I arrive at the office the next day, my secretary informs me that the CEO wants to see me immediately, and I take the lift to the seventh floor. His personal assistant directs me to go in, having announced my arrival through the intercom. I knock on the door as I open it and enter.

'Take a seat,' I hear without him lifting his head.

'I am sorry, Mrs Huan Li, but we have to let you go.'

'But I have worked for this company for many years. Why would they want to get rid of me now?'

'You have done a tremendous job. The new generation of telecommunication came into effect because of you but employing a woman whose husband has been all over the news for murder is bad for business.'

'I don't understand. When my husband was in prison, you supported me. Now that he has been cleared of all crimes, you are firing me?'

'I am afraid you must leave the premises immediately. You will not be allowed to return to your office, and your severance pay will not be paid.'

The door to the office opens, and two security officers stand by the entrance and lead me out of the building like a criminal.

'What the hell is going on?' I protest. 'What did I do wrong?'

I am escorted out of the building, where a cab is waiting. I am told I will no longer be allowed to use the company car. My purse is handed to me as I get in the cab, and the door is closed by one of the security officers. I am then driven out of the large parking lot. *What is happening to me?*

I arrive at my home to see several police cars. My husband is being rearrested.

'You will not need a lawyer,' one of the officers tells me as I hastily alight from the taxi. 'As a directive, your husband has been charged with the murder of his mistress and children. He will be taken to a high-security prison. He will not be allowed visiting rights because of the gravity of his crime, and he will be given life imprisonment.'

'How can this happen? He has not even appeared in court yet.'

'According to our records, he was tried in court a month ago, and we don't know how he was able to escape prison.'

'Something is wrong; this is a mistake!' I scream.

'There is no mistake, Mrs Li.'

Chun looks at me and says, 'I am going to die in prison. This has something to do with the discussion we had yesterday.'

I watch helplessly as he is led away. 'Be careful, they are watching,' he whispers before he is pushed into the back seat of a police car.'

They all drive away, leaving me alone. 'I'll find a way to destroy you even if I have to die trying,' I yell at the empty driveway. I enter my house, reluctantly. I won't show any emotion for their satisfaction, but I will give them a show. They are messing with the wrong woman. If you think taking away my access to the telecommunications network I built will hinder me from bringing you down, you're mistaken. You have taken away everything important to me; now, I'll find a way to take everything away from you. You will all be exposed, one after the other.

The first thing I need to do is find an ally because they will come for me next.

Ping Wu

The CEO of Yamson Telecommunications, Mr Hunan, stands before me.

'Do you think removing her from Yellow Gama is a good idea, ma'am? She is the best in the field of telecoms.'

'That is why we need to remove her; if she turns against us, it will be easy for her to bring us down. She designed and built the technology, and even though it is part of the many technologies we use, it is still the most important.'

'So, what next?'

'We watch, and then we eliminate her.'

Chapter Nine: London

Jude

I walk into my closed restaurant. I have scheduled a meeting with the newly promoted inspector, Roger Smith. I know he hates me, but I can't do this alone; I need his help. I sit in the restaurant and wait. I hope he will come. I look at the time; he is thirty minutes late. I am just getting up to leave when he strolls into my restaurant, looking angry.

'What do you want? How did you get my number?'

I smile at him. 'Hello, Roger! We work for the same group, it's not hard to find out.'

'So, why do you want to see me?'

'I need your help. I hope I'm not making a mistake coming to you, but I don't know who I can trust. We were forced to join this group. No option was given; you either join or die, and I am tired of it.'

'Are you pulling my leg? Aren't you exactly like them; the greedy rich restaurateur for whom nothing is ever enough?'

I shake my head. 'I never wanted this; I was content with what I had. The situation in the country will continue to deteriorate; they have taken over every sector, from politics to business. The goal is to take from the poor and give it to the rich. Anyone who opposes them is eliminated. I don't know what to do!'

Roger sighs heavily and nods. 'I am now chief inspector; all this has happened in a month. By next month I will be made superintendent. I have been moved to a four-bedroom house in Mayfair – to my wife's delight. I manipulate reports, falsify testaments, and arrest the innocent. I can't look at myself in the mirror. I constantly ask myself, how did it get to this?'

'Gamaplug! We must be cautious even though we have disconnected it for this meeting; they see and know everything.'

'They do! I will do what I can. I will carry out the necessary investigations from my side; I need you to do the same. I will be in touch with you later this week.'

With that, he gets up and leaves the restaurant.

***

I knock on the door of Sarah Philips. The door opens and I walk into an opulent home decorated to the tiniest detail. I force myself to smile when I see her. I know her days are numbered, and I have to find a way to save her.

The death of Sam Philips is trending on all news platforms. The greedy millionaire who did not think about the lives of others. The government is claiming that he is liable for the deaths of six people. The families of the deceased must be paid at least one hundred million pounds.

'Where am I going to get that kind of money?' she asks me. 'The company has filed for bankruptcy, and the shareholders have pulled out. I went to the bank to ask for my father's bank statement, and they told me he only has about fifty thousand pounds in his account; all his millions have magically disappeared. I argued, but they showed me bank statements for over three months. How can my father be broke?'

I shake my head and signal to her to disconnect her Gamaplug. She removes it, reluctantly, and I hold both of her hands in mine. 'I need you to trust me,' I say. 'Don't ask questions.' I give her a new phone. 'Don't download any applications on it, and under no circumstances connect it to your Gamaplug. I'll call you on this number, don't tell anyone!'

***

The big boss looks at his enforcer.

'I want the chef disgraced and the policeman implicated in criminal acts. Fools! They know that we hear and see everything, and they dare to hold a meeting to bring down this group. I want them both destroyed by tomorrow.'

Chapter Ten: New York

Martin

I look around the massive, abandoned underground station. 'Edward, how did you find this place?'

'As one of the best hackers globally, the Federal Bureau of Investigation (FBI) has been trying to find the hacker known as "the snake" for a long time. I come here from time to time to hide, but I have never encountered such powerful people as those after you.

'I was able to get into the secret gala they held. Everyone was there, the Secretary of State, the Vice President who is now the President, the Governor of New York, not to talk of the business juggernauts, the list is endless. They are after me for a reason, and it all started when I was assigned to investigate the death of the late Mayor's daughter.

'I am trying to enter their security network without them noticing, replies Edward. The code is peeling through their security little by little because, if they should find out, there is nowhere else to hide, they will find us.

'You can't leave here, Martin; as I told you before, you're now one of the most wanted men on the FBI list. I disconnected your phone and Gamaplug the minute you got my text because you are being traced.'

'What the hell, man,' I say, running my fingers through my hair. 'My wife, my children! These despicable people took all my money; how will I survive?'

'You will stay here with me, and we will find these motherfuckers so that you can get your life back.'

Edward points to a massive computer screen on the wall. 'I have put a trace on your ex-partner, Bobby's phone. He is getting close to your wife, seeing her every day.'

'The bastard!' I shout. 'If I get my hands on him, I'll kill him.'

'Hold your horses; nothing is happening from what I can see, at least on your wife's side. All your missing money has been transferred to your wife's account with extras.' He shows me my wife's bank statement. I looked at the figures and I see one million dollars.'

'Where did she get that kind of money?'

'I don't know; I'm also wondering; so many unanswered questions. The starting point is Bobby. We need to find out what he knows that will help us to bring down these people.

'The death rate in the country has increased more than fivefold, and the number of racial attacks has increased. People are killing Mexicans for polluting the country's water. President Dan Campbell has declared war against Mexico; people are being deported, both young and old, and it doesn't matter whether or not they have papers. The police have been given carte blanche to decide on any case. The world is crumbling in our faces, and people are unaware of what is happening. The announcement made by the Afghanistan ruler has taken over the global news where all political leaders had emergency meetings is all a hoax. It is a scare tactic; the government has opened a new sector, and a new contract has been awarded in billions for more arms. People are buying more guns. Guess who is heading the new sector? Your former Captain, Marcus, has taken the realm.'

'The number one question is, how do they get all this information?'

'I'll find out soon once I can chip away at their security network, but I know it has something to do with Gamaplug. Now, you need to rest.' Edward points to the bed.

'Thank you,' I say. 'I don't know what I would have done without your help.'

Chapter Eleven: Lagos

Segun

I am not safe.

I booked the hotel room myself, knowing I might be closely watched. I get into the lift, and push the button to the first floor. I have come from my room on the seventh floor, but decide to play safe and take the staircase the rest of the way.

I see a member of staff and give him 1,000 naira to take me through their back door. I am shown the way out and race out of the hotel. I knew this day would come. My father murdered my brother, and he would not hesitate to kill me. I stop a cab and give the address of a room I have rented in the slums of Lagos; they would never look for me there.

I keep looking behind me to make sure I am not being followed. I know what led to this; my father demanded to see me after I left Lola's house. I knew it couldn't be anything good. I entered the house I used to call my home; a cold and soulless place in all its architectural grandeur. I knocked on the door of my father's office, and waited for him to say, 'Come in.' When I entered, without looking up, he said, 'You will be flying to Congo tomorrow; we have taken over oil extraction in the country.'

'I'm not going anywhere,' I replied.

It is bad enough that I am forced to work in a company I hate, but the country has security problems; kidnapping, killings, the army destroying properties and confiscating homes. The government is taking over everything, and no one can oppose them. The worst part is that the same is happening in Africa.

My father got up from his chair, and one of his bodyguards entered the room and stood in front of me. The next thing I knew, he had wrapped his hand around my neck in a chokehold.

'I tell you to do something; you do it! No questions asked; you have no choice, or the big boss will kill you. We are taking over Africa. The most powerful method is fear. When people don't know who to turn to, they turn to religion. So we have got ourselves involved in that area as well. You are my only son; we will work side by side to take over the wealth of Africa that the big boss has given us.'

'I will never work for you or your big boss.' I struggled to talk as the bodyguard tightened his hold.

'If you leave here, I will not be able to protect you anymore, you will be on your own. You will be killed.'

'I don't care!'

'Release him!'

I held my neck as I tried to breathe.

'Get out of my house! I don't have a son anymore. You will die soon, and I'll have to bury you.'

I raced out of the house, jumped into my car and drove to the hotel, refusing to submit to my fear. But my father wasn't joking; they will come for me.

Chapter Twelve: Kabul

Ahmed

We sit down to watch the news as the world leaders threaten sanctions on Afghanistan for threatening to wage war against the Western nations with nuclear weapons. I don't understand Mohammed. Why would he do this? The people are not only impoverished but broken in spirit; the heavy tax placed upon the citizens has made many lose their lands, homes and source of livelihood. Every night I find it difficult to close my eyes, protecting the vilest person I have ever met. He rejoices in people's pain and suffering.

I have been monitoring his night-time routine. We have a rota for his daily protection; but the bodyguard on night duty doesn't work during the day. Mohammed insists that I protect him during the day; he is very paranoid and believes everyone wants him dead. I have convinced him to allow me to work extra hours, to ensure his safety. I'll seize that opportunity to get his key chain. First of all, I need access to his office, which is constantly locked and he keeps the keys in the pocket of his trousers. I'll put my plan in motion tomorrow, and will have a ten-minute window to obtain his keys.

I have to act now; I don't know how long I can last before reaching breaking point. We have lost countless citizens, murdered daily in this compound. There is no mercy! He places a heavy weight on his people's shoulders, then has them killed for not having the strength to carry it. People are turning against each other; fathers against mothers, daughters against brothers. Crime has increased, and people selling food in the market are being robbed in broad daylight. The economy was terrible before, now it's worse. Mohammed controls everything from the nation's finances to the media coverage. Now, his people are enslaved, working for him without pay, and he only gives them food maybe once a day.

I look at the time. Mohammed will be leaving his office at precisely 9.30 p.m. I need to pick his pocket. He opens his office door, turns the key, and locks it again, giving me his files to carry. He places the keys in the right pocket of his trousers, and his tunic covers the pocket. I walk him to the door of his room, he turns to retrieve the files, and they fall on the floor, papers scattering everywhere.

Mohammed looks at me and shouts, 'You are an idiot!'

'I am sorry, sir,' I say, as I bend down to pick up the documents from the floor.

'Don't touch anything,' he yells as he stoops down to get them himself.

I fall to my knees. 'Please, sir, I'm sorry, this will never happen again.'

'I would have you killed for this, if I didn't need your skills. Imbecile!'

He is distracted, picking up the scattered papers and trying very hard to prevent me from seeing what his file contains. He pulls up his tunic to prevent it from touching the floor while he picks up the documents. Without noticing, I slip my hand into his pocket and take the keys.

'Can I help, sir?' I ask.

He scoops up the last of the papers as I slip the keys into my pocket. He opens the door to his room and enters, locking the door firmly behind him.

I race to the corner of the building; Mohammed will notice his keys are missing; I have five minutes or so before he opens his door to see if he has dropped the keys. If he doesn't find them, I am dead.

I place the office key into the clay in the key casting mould.

I have instructed the night bodyguard to resume his duties – I look at the time – in two minutes. I race back and drop the keys in front of Mohammed's door and run as fast as my legs can carry me. I hear Mohammed's door open and watched from my hiding place as he looks around and discovers his keys on the floor. He curses, picks them up and goes inside, locking the door.

Thank Allah for sparing my life; now I need to find out what Mohammed is hiding.

Chapter Thirteen: Sydney

Henry

I return to my room, fuming; my mother is so manipulative and controlling. Now I understand why my father separated from her for five years before they got back together when she became prime minister. She knows how distraught I am over my missing wife, and she has brought that bitch Cynthia Coleman into my life; she is exactly like her, and that's why she loves her so much. I hear the door of my room open, and my mother strolls into the room.

'How could you behave that way towards our guest? That was very rude.'

'Mum, I'm leaving this house first thing tomorrow morning; I don't want to see you for some time to come.'

'What do you mean by that? I have done nothing wrong. I look for ways to make you a better man.'

'That is the problem!' I say. 'I am tired of your controlling ways. I am not a puppet you can manipulate; you think I didn't know that you invited that cold bitch to the house to try and set us up?'

'I did no such thing; why would you think that? She came willingly; I didn't invite her. I wouldn't do that; after all, we don't know where Mia is.'

'I am tired of being manipulated by the organisation, dictating everything I should do because I am in line to be the next minister. I don't want to be prime minister anymore, not under their control. I am done! I'm letting you know now that I'm resigning tomorrow.'

'Don't you dare! Look at me! Do you want to die?'

'I don't care anymore; death is looking good; just look at what is happening around us; the economy is in tatters, and White Gama has replaced everyone in a position of authority. They have taken over every sector; nothing is free anymore. People pay through their noses for the newly privatised hospitals, taxes, and food costs. The only free thing is the air we breathe; soon, that will be privatised. Look at the unnecessary fear they invoke. The suicide rate and murders have gone up and people are rushing to buy guns that our members are selling. The gun laws have become more lenient and now people are armed. I am done!'

'You can't be done! I don't want to lose you; if you go to that office tomorrow to resign, you will not leave there alive. I'm begging you, don't be stupid.'

'I guess I am stupid then, be prepared to lose your son.'

Mrs Graham

I enter my home office. This boy will be the death of me; he is just like his father – weak! I can't lose him. I have to prevent him from resigning.

The task the big boss has given me is to find him another wife who is a White Gama member, which is why I introduced him to Cynthia. I have told her to do whatever needs to be done to get him to fall for her; I'm not against manipulating him.

Tonight, I will give him the date rape drug to make him sleep; he will wake up and find Cynthia naked beside him.

Henry

I have just finished taking a shower. I am lying on the bed, when I hear a knock on the door and my mother enters again. A heavy sigh engulfs me. 'What do you want now?'

'Nothing, honey,' she replies, carrying a wine glass filled with red wine on a tray.

'Mum, why are you bringing me wine?'

I watch as a tear escapes from my mother's eye, and she stares at me with great sadness.

'You see me as a bad mother, I don't know what I did wrong, so I'm bringing you this wine myself to plead forgiveness and to help you relax.'

'Mum, there's no need, OK, I don't hate you.'

'If you don't hate me, just drink the wine, honey, to show that you forgive me.'

I shrug, take the glass of wine from the tray and drink it. The liquid slides down my throat; she's right I can feel the tension leaving my body.

'Thank you, honey; now go to sleep; I hope we can talk more when you're well-rested.'

She leaves the room. I lay down in bed; my head feels heavy, and everything looks blurry. *Am I hallucinating? I think someone just entered my room. Let me close my eyes; everything will be better tomorrow.*

Chapter Fourteen: Rio de Janeiro

Ana

I arrive home completely drained of energy; they murdered Pedro. I wouldn't say I liked the way he manipulated my sister, but I never wanted him dead. I have gone through hell since I was forced to join this sadistic Purple Gama. Turning my only living relative against me is the final straw. I'm done with these people; what is left to live for? I'll find a way to stop them and If I have to die in the process, so be it.

They have destroyed all the copies I made of their transactions. There has to be an alternative way to expose them, but I can't win this battle if they think I'm against them. I must gain their trust; that is the only way. They will see the new Ana Santos, who does everything they tell her to do without hesitation.

***

I arrive at my office at 7.00 am. I know my direct boss will want to talk to me after yesterday's debacle. They must see the new Ana. I dress the way they want me to; in four-inch heels and a designer skirt suit.

I am being watched closely, as I walk confidently into my office with my head raised. I enter my office to see Carlos sitting on a chair, waiting for me. 'Well, well, look what the cat dragged in!' he says. 'I've been given double work because of your stupidity. I've been assigned to babysit you for all sensitive accounting data.'

I smile and look at Carlos confidently; he seems surprised as I usually cower when he's around. 'That will not be a problem,' I reply. 'You are welcome to join me; I'll no longer be doing anything stupid. The price is too high for me to pay.'

'Then, why arrive in the office at 7.00 am when it doesn't open until 8.30? Are you trying to hide something?' he says.

'I'm not an idiot; I know I'm being followed and monitored closely. I'm not going to make the same mistake twice!'

'These are new accounting figures, we need a certain percentage distributed around different hubs as before, the assigned money for this will be further broken down to fund certain activities, pay the members, etc.' He turns his computer to face me. 'You can see the numbers, but your work must be completed on my laptop.'

'As you wish.' I force a smile. I wish I could jump across the desk and slap the smirk off his face.

'Good, I'm glad we understand each other. I'll not bother sitting to watch you; I'll do that in my office.' He points to the left corner of the ceiling and I see a camera pointing directly at my desk. 'We have more than one camera in your office, so you're being watched closely since you rarely use your Gamaplug.'

He saunters out of the office. One day I'll have the last laugh.

I look at the spreadsheet in front of me; I can see that the numbers have increased more than before. They have invested vast sums of money in satellites, the police force and the justice system.

They are running most of South America's banks, including Central Bank. The interest rate has increased to 60% annually, making it impossible for most people to pay back. Why would they take over the police force and justice system? To arrest people and imprison the innocent? They don't know that I have a photographic memory; I don't need to store the information to remember it. The tentacles of the Purple Gama spread wide. They are in all sectors; I see the members' names and how much each is being paid. The big boss has a big boss! Wow! I didn't know he reported to someone. They never give a name on the sheets, but he is being paid the highest amount. My big boss is being paid a billion dollars while he's paid twenty billion dollars. I already know the names of each member and the businesses they run. Now I just need to think of a way to bring down the most powerful organisation in the world.

Carlos

'Sir, she seems different somehow. I think she has resigned herself to her fate. For months she has looked reluctant to do anything, but today, I saw another side to her, a more confident, determined person.'

'Carlos, continue to monitor her. No more slip-ups; the big boss has warned of the consequences of any more mistakes from her. We all face the same fate,' Mr Montes replies.

Chapter Fifteen: Hong Kong

Huan

I know the power they wield using the smallest earplug in the world that reads your minds without having to talk; it has taken the world by storm. Now they know our thoughts. Gamaplug was approved worldwide and integrated into all equipment, applications, telecommunication networks, satellites, and digital networks. Gama are now the most powerful people in the world. They can destroy anyone without lifting a finger, wipe out your accounts, change your medical reports, and declare you dead when you are still alive. I have spent the past two weeks researching everything I know about Gamaplug. They don't know who they are messing with; I built the network they are using.

My husband has been sentenced to life imprisonment for a crime he never committed. He was not given the right to an attorney, and I am not allowed to see him. I don't know if he is dead or alive, but I am no longer ignorant. I'll personally bring them down.

I am going to the one-bedroom apartment I bought in a different name ages ago; they are not the only ones that can play this game. I know that my house has been bugged with secret listening devices; that's how they knew about my conversation with Chun.

For two weeks, I sat in my mansion and planned how to leave my house without being noticed. I didn't use my laptop or phones because they were all being monitored. I got up each day and pretended that everything was fine. Then on the fifteenth day, I took action.

In complete darkness, at exactly 3.30 am, I left my house and gave all my staff an extended vacation. I took nothing with me, only the clothes on my back; joggers, and a hoodie. I jogged for about a mile; I used a burner phone to call a taxi that took me to my new home.

I knew they would take away my money to render me useless. That fateful day my husband was arrested, I wrote a program to move my money without anyone knowing and made it look like the bank did it.

I don't want to draw attention to myself in my new secret

location, so I order equipment in bits. I need to build a virus that can penetrate the telecommunications network and bring it down. That is just one part; I will need help to bring down the other systems they use.

Ping Wu

'What do you mean you can't find her?' I yell at Cheung Wu.

'Ma'am, as you instructed, we went to her house today to eliminate her. The whole place was empty. We traced some of her staff, but she gave them paid vacation a week ago.'

'I don't like having incompetent people around me. The instruction was to monitor her; why didn't you notice these things?'

'Ma'am, we monitored the listening devices and the secret cameras, but nothing was out of place.'

'I want her found today or it's on your head. Is her husband still alive?'

'Yes, ma'am!'

'I want him killed. Take everything away from her. Did you seize her money?'

'The bank said her accounts are empty.'

'What do you mean by "empty"?'

Cheung visibly trembles.' Someone emptied her account, but they don't know who. The money cannot be traced.'

'I want her face all over the news and every police officer in the country looking for her. She has won many awards. She is a certified genius; I don't want her working against us. She must be found and eliminated. Don't come back without her head, or I'll have yours instead. Now, get out of my sight!'

***

Cheung wipes the sweat on his brow. I'm dead if I don't find her, he thinks. She is not using her phone or computer, we tried using satellite to track her, but it is impossible without her using any equipment. What am I going to do now?

I signal for Chyou, the female bodyguard who worked for Huan. I need to speak to the Commissioner of Police. I want Huan's face splattered in every newspaper and television broadcast. She must

I have put a trace on her credit cards, but none have been used in two weeks. How is she surviving? I should have killed her months ago when I had the chance.

Huan

My face is all over the news; I knew this would happen. My name and reputation are being sullied. According to new evidence, I'm now an accomplice working closely with my husband to kill an innocent woman and her children.

It will not be easy to remain hidden; but I'm taking precautions. I look at the four wigs I have bought and the thick, transparent framed glasses that cover half my face. I've cut my hair short and I never leave the apartment without my trusted hoodie with my head facing the ground.

Chapter Sixteen: London

Jude

I hear my mother scream, 'Run, Jude! Run!' I jump out of the window, my heart pounding. *Jesus! What is going on?*

I keep running, and looking behind me; I don't see anyone. After running for some time, completely exhausted, I decide to stop. When I get going again, there is a severe pain in my left leg as I try to walk, so I hop on one leg. My room is on the first floor, and I jumped down without thinking about the danger I was escaping from. God! I hope my mother is alright. I am such a stupid son; I can't even protect my mother. I look around, seeing a street sign in the quiet area of Chelsea; maybe I should go back? I need to get home and ensure my mum is OK.

Tentatively, I enter the house to find two men in police uniform sitting on the three-seater sofa waiting for me. My mother's lifeless body lies on the ground. I run up to her; and see that she has been shot in the head. I look up; the men are smiling at me. 'We thought you wouldn't be back after your mother yelled at you to run, but you're stupid enough to return. Anyway, you are under arrest for the murder of your mother.'

I sit on the floor speechless, uncontrollable tears running down my face. The gun used to kill my mother is placed in my hand by one of the men, who is wearing gloves. 'We need your fingerprints on the weapon.' I am dragged up, handcuffed and led into an unmarked car.

I don't utter a word, and shut my eyes in anguish. *I killed my mother; how can I live with myself?* I think to myself.

One of the police officers drives the car, the other sits beside me. 'Do you know why you're in this situation, chef?' he says. I don't bother answering. They both started chuckling uncontrollably. 'You thought you could bring down the big boss; you are such an idiot for having a meeting in your restaurant, when it's being monitored 24/7. You brought this on yourself; they offered you wealth, fame and power; instead you now get disgrace, poverty and life imprisonment.'

Tears drip down my face. How do I get out of this?

We drive for a long time before the car stops, and I am taken to a police station in Drayton. The police station appears to be empty. I try not to put pressure on my left leg; I'm not sure if it's broken. I am forced to sit beside Roger; who is already in the station. His eyes are swollen and he has a burst lip.

James Cooper, the big boss walks in, and says, 'Roger! I'm not going to send you to prison. That would be too easy. You killed two of my men.'

'They murdered my wife and son,' he replies angrily.

James Cooper starts laughing. 'That was their assignment in which they would have failed if they did not plan for you being a policeman with certain skills. Listen, it's not just your wife and son; your daughter was killed also.'

Roger jumps up from his seat, trying to reach his tormentor, but a heavy punch lands on his face, and he falls to the ground. The big boss is handed a gun and he shoots Roger in his right arm. He screams as the wound starts to bleed profusely.

'Fool! Take care of them!' James Copper instructs, before walking out of the police station.

'You will be sentenced tomorrow,' says one of the men that came to my house. 'News of your arrest is already trending all over social media. How the mighty has fallen. You were hailed some months back as a hero; now you're a criminal, malicious enough to murder his mother.'

I am placed in a cell with Roger. He looks pale; he is losing a lot of blood. No one cares; he will bleed to death if nothing is done. I call over to one of the men. 'Please, he needs treatment. He seems so weak.'

The man looks at Roger, shakes his head and walks away. 'We are dying here!' I yell after him. The pain in my leg is worse; it's bruised and swollen. I must have twisted it, but I am sure it's not broken. I try massaging it, but it's not helping. I sit beside Roger. His shirt is soaked with blood; the bullet needs to be taken out and the wound treated, but I don't know how to help him.

I can't sleep, although the police station is tranquil, and the cell is in darkness. I hear the sound of my cell door opening and a voice says, 'Don't make any sound. You need to follow me.'

I glance behind me at Roger. 'He needs help,' I say.

'I can't do anything for him; he is going to die, but I can save you. We don't have much time.' The cell door is locked, and Roger is lying on the wooden bench, completely weak.

'Not all of us agree with the big boss,' the stranger whispers.

I force myself to walk, trying to block out the pain in my leg, and follow behind him. The stranger seems to know his way around and leads me to the back of the station. The door is opened with a key, and he says, 'Go, as fast as you can, and don't look back!'

I feel the cold rush of air as I run for my life, thanking the angel who saved me. I need money. After running for some time, I stop, trying not to think about the pain from my twisted leg. I see an ATM, and withdraw the maximum amount I can. Then I force myself to move again, because I know they will catch me if I stay any longer. I have to get to a train station and leave London. I flag down a black cab to take me to Euston railway station. I quickly buy a ticket for the first train leaving London; to Manchester.

I don't know how I'm going to survive. I can't use my account anymore. Europe is in chaos now; with food scarcity and a high death rate, everything has collapsed because of these evil people. I have to find a way out, but first I need to hide my face; it's all over social media. I have to reach Manchester without being caught, and then I need to survive.

Chapter Seventeen: New York

Dan Campbell

I smile to myself. I've just received a phone call from the big boss congratulating me on the billions of dollars I have generated in the short period since becoming president of the USA.

I have never seen a country so gullible; they will believe anything. We told them that the Mexicans caused hundreds of thousands of deaths in the country. And they believed it! People are looking for someone to blame, so we give them scapegoats.

Citizens used that as an excuse to turn on one another, and the number of people massacred daily has increased tenfold. When people are angry, all you need to do is bait them. They don't know that we have made billions dumping toxic waste into the sea, which led to much damage. Crops are dying and drinking water is poisonous. More people will die because we have taken over everything. They will have to face higher rent costs, and increased taxes, medical care, transportation and defence. I am even contemplating that we even need to start charging for the air they breathe.

Martin

I watch as my face is plastered all over the news; there is a five-million-dollar reward for any information about my whereabouts. Apparently, I murdered more than twenty people when I worked as a police officer. I see pictures of people I supposedly killed; all African Americans. Now I am a racist policeman murdering minority people. My wife gave a statement disassociating herself from me, stating that she had already filed for a divorce months before the news broke.

Edward switches off the TV. 'Stop looking at that! They are just desperate to find you, that's all. You already know they used Gamaplug to get all that information about you. As you know, it is connected to all networks and applications in all countries. You went to the gala, you met some of the people there, and wrote down their names. These people have amassed more wealth than you can imagine in the last two months and become more powerful. The only way to destroy a strong organisation is to find who their leader is.'

'When I was at the gala, a man spoke to us; he was the leader of the North America hub. What if they have hubs on other continents?'

'That's right! If we watch the global news, other countries are facing similar problems; food scarcity, a rise in the cost of living, and a rise in criminal activities; the world has been torn apart in a few months. We need to reach out to people like us, in other parts of the world, who are tired of being oppressed and terrorised by these people.'

'How do we do that? Locate others from different parts of the world?'

'It can be done. I'll write a program that can't be traced; it will be like an SOS code to find people like us.'

'The big question who is the boss, the man in the shadows who controlling the world?'

'It has to be the inventor of Gamaplug since it is his invention that caused this problem.'

'I doubt it's him. Have you seen Fred Demson in the news? His company is worth a trillion dollars. What does he need all that money and power for? I was at the gala; if he is the boss, he should have been there.'

'Well, we need to find out. The most important thing is, how do we bring down Gamaplug? Fred Demson is the wealthiest man in the world and the most influential. It is being used by billions of people all over the world.'

Chapter Eighteen: Lagos

Lola

A text pings on my phone telling me to come to Oshodi; what? That's a dangerous place to go to, especially at 7.00 pm. This message cannot be from Segun. What would he be doing in such a place? I look out of the window and see the three men assigned to protect me patrolling the compound. They have strict instructions to follow me everywhere. With the amount of commotion in Africa and the high death rate, I'm surprised the continent is still functioning. I look at the time; I have to go now; as the 'stop and search' order by the government means it might take longer to get to my destination. I dress entirely in black; jeans, a T-shirt, a cap with my hair hidden under it and trainers.

I open the door of my car, and one of the security team walks up to me. 'Madam, I'm sorry but you can't leave the house.'

'What do you mean I can't leave the house?'

'We have instructions from your father not to let you go out at night.'

'What do you mean night? It is only 5.30 pm, and I need to go to the supermarket.'

'Madam, I'm sorry, you can't leave. It's not safe outside. If anything should happen to you, we're finished.'

'Open the gate! If you want to follow me, you can with your car, but you cannot keep me here.'

I get into my car and drive towards the gate, but they refuse to open it. I open the car door and shout, 'Open this gate, or you lose your job!'

One of the security men reluctantly opens the gate as the other two get in their patrol car to follow me. I have to find a way out of this. They must not follow me to my destination.

As I drive, I can see the aftereffects of the riot that happened a few days; tyres were set on fire to create roadblocks, and the army fired tear gases and rubber bullets, but it got to a point when they started shooting live ammunition. Many lost their lives.

I am at a three-way junction with my car in the left lane, signalling left, when I abruptly turn right when the traffic light turns red. There is a deafening sound of car horns as people shake their fists at me, mouthing 'mad woman'. Trying to avoid cars going straight on, I shriek when my car is almost hit by oncoming vehicles. Somehow I manage to avoid a collision; changing lanes, until I can turn right. Most importantly, when I looked back, I see that the car following me is stuck in the commotion I have caused.

I speed away; hoping I have made the right decision. Or am I walking into a trap?

As I get out of my car in complete darkness; I feel a hand tap my shoulder. I turn around and scream.

'It's me, Segun! Switch off your phone and Gamaplug immediately. I don't want you to be traced if they have not traced you already.'

I do as he says.

'Now, get in the car,' he tells me, jumping into the driver's seat. 'I'm taking you somewhere else; I know they will be here within minutes.'

'What is going on, Segun? Why are you in this horrible place?'

'This is the only safe place; the police and the army can't come here. They know they are putting their lives at risk. They are trying to kill me for opposing my father. I have been doing much research, and a lovely family has taken me in. I helped them many years ago; they don't have much, but I can eat once daily. My father took everything away; my house, finances and freedom. I need your help!'

We go to a quiet and isolated bungalow that looks incomplete. The house has been built but not painted; I can still see building materials on the untarred driveway.

'Follow me! I've something to show you.'

I follow him to a room with a tiny bed and his laptop.

'Segun, you can't live like this.' I look around the windowless room in disgust.

'I would rather live like this than in a beautiful home, knowing it comes from the sweat and death of other people. I don't know much, but from the information I was able to obtain from my father, he answers to a higher man. They have taken over Africa by extorting people. I keep asking myself, how do I stop these people from doing more damage? I've been spying on one of their networks; I have to be very careful because they have the best people working for them and they monitor the network daily. One thing I was able to find out is that Gamaplug is what they use to manipulate people. It is a very powerful device. One out of three people uses it, and it is connected to all the systems in the world.'

'Gamaplug!' I start laughing. 'Come on, how is that possible?'

'It reads your thoughts and turns them into action; it's that simple.'

'What can we do? These people are too powerful for us.'

'Yes, they are powerful people, but I still believe your family is one of the good ones; Lola, we can use your father.'

'Use him for what?'

'Information! He knows the people he works for and how they operate. That is the only way we can bring down this organisation.'

Lekan Gbada

'Mr Adeyemo, where is your daughter?' I ask. 'I hear she is very close to Segun Gerald, and we have been trying to find him for over two weeks now.'

'I don't know, sir! The security men assigned to her lost sight of her.'

'Then you have one hour to find your daughter, or you will be killed.'

Chapter Nineteen: Kabul

Ahmed

I know the routine of the security men that patrol the compound daily. We have about twenty men in total who watch the different buildings and the main gate, including those who monitor the cameras. There is a direct camera facing Mohammed's office, and I have to enter his office without anyone knowing. I've got to find Jabar, the only ally I have here in this house. He must find a way to tamper with the camera without anyone noticing.

I return to my room. This plan must be carried out by midnight tomorrow. This is the only way to get into Mohammed's office and have enough time to be thorough in my search. I need to ensure that everything is back in the right place. Mohammed is a perfectionist. Everything in his office has to be in order. If you touch anything, he will notice. During the little time I have spent in his office, I have seen the order in which he arranges his files. The labels are on the top right corner and the files are arranged according to their importance. The most important would always be on top.

I have been in this place for months; I have only spoken to my wife once. I only text because it breaks my heart whenever I talk to them. I have to keep use of my phone minimal; I know they come into the room when no one is there to search the place.

I go to look for Jabar. I'll resume my station in an hour. I know that he works in the Surveillance Department. I enter the office and see him looking directly at the monitor. One of the men comes up to me. 'Can I help you?' he asks.

'You know who I am; I want to know how a threat is communicated?'

'If we notice any problem, we inform Mohammed directly and it is a direct order,' he replies.

I notice that everyone is watching me; I just need one person's attention. I glance at him quickly and signal with my head that I would like to see him, and he nods.

'Thank you very much,' I tell the man.

I step out of the office and head back to my room, taking the staircase, knowing that most people would use the elevator. I feel someone tap me; I knew it was Jabar.

'What do you want? I don't have much time,' he says.

'I'm going to go into Mohammed's office at midnight; I need you to alter the feeds. He has one facing his office directly and two others hidden in two secret corners. Can you do that?'

'I'll see what I can do.'

I shake my head. 'That won't work. I need confirmation from you; if I'm caught, I am dead. You know that.'

'We have people monitoring us, so I need to be careful. I will send you a text to confirm whether it can be done.' With that, he turns and walks swiftly down the stairs.

My heart is pounding fast; this is one of the most dangerous missions I have ever carried out. Mohammed is the most cautious man I have ever known. I know he sets traps for people; his office will not be an exception. I know he doesn't have a secret camera in his office, monitored by the surveillance team, because he doesn't want anyone to know what he does in his office, but I wouldn't be surprised if he has installed one that he monitors himself. I have tried to check for hidden cameras whenever I enter his office, but I haven't noticed anything.

All the security lights are on and, even though it is dark, everywhere is bright, and you can see clearly. I hide behind buildings when the security men come in my direction. I cover my face so only my eyes can be seen. Jabar gives me the all-clear. I have a twenty-minute window to get in and out. I look at the time as I open Mohammed's door, ensuring no one is around, and set a timer on my phone.

Today is Wednesday; and women are sent to the men for fun. Earlier, I allowed Moska into my room, as usual, and told her to pretend I was still in bed when I snuck out. I didn't switch on the light; I had a small torchlight. I tiptoed out so as not to leave footprints.

Inside his office, I approach Mohammed's desk, where some files have been left out. I open the top file and see that some money has just been transferred into his account, the sum of two million dollars, and his net worth was over fifty million dollars. Where did he get all this money from? It shows it's from an offshore account. Who is sponsoring this man?

I look through the other documents. I need to find where he keeps those nuclear weapons. I glance at the shelf. It's filled with books; Mohammed doesn't have time for reading. This shelf is hiding something. I take a picture of his books with my phone; maybe I'll be able to find the one that opens a secret door. But, right now, I need to get out of here.

✳✳✳

'Someone entered my office at exactly midnight. I set a timer on my door. When the door opens, it clocks it. Get me the people working in the Surveillance Department yesterday. I need videos of the one monitoring my office,' Mohammed says to me directly.

Allah! How did he know? I'm in trouble. I was cautious. I made sure everything was in place. The surveillance videos were watched, and nothing was out of the ordinary.

'You have a traitor in your midst,' Mohammed is told.

The surveillance team and the security men who worked the night shift are brought before Mohammed. I sigh with relief when Jabar is not one of the people standing in front of Mohammed, but it is short-lived.

'You have thirty minutes to find the culprit among you,' he says. 'Or you all die!'

Chapter Twenty: Sydney

Henry

I try to get out of bed. Why does my mouth taste bitter? I felt like I have slept for days and can't remember what happened yesterday. I feel my mattress move; I turn my head to see a naked Cynthia getting out of my bed, reaching for her clothes.

'What the hell are you doing in my bed?' I yell.

She looks at me in surprise. 'Don't you remember? You called me over and apologised for being rude. One thing led to another. We ended up in your bed,' she says, continuing to get dressed.

'No! That's impossible! I would never do such a thing.'

'I tried to stop you yesterday, but you were insistent. I knew you would deny it today,' she says, tears rolling down her face. 'Why do you mistreat me? What have I ever done to you?' She begins sobbing loudly.

I stand up, shaking my head. This is ridiculous. I hate Cynthia! She repulses even my subconscious. *I would never touch her;* my mind keeps telling me.

There is a knock on the door and my mother enters the room. 'What is going on? I heard crying. Your father is resting; please don't wake him up, you lovebirds. Why are you crying, Cynthia?' She rushes over to comfort her.

'Your son denies what happened yesterday,' she sobs on my mother's shoulder.

'How could you, Henry? I raised you better than that!' my mother scolds me.

'I don't know what's going on. My memory is foggy, and I can't remember what happened yesterday.'

'Henry, you asked me to give you Cynthia's number, which I did. To be honest, I was surprised myself. I am shocked you can't remember how you sat down together to talk about old times growing up together before I left you to go to bed.'

I look at Cynthia. 'I'm sorry for whatever happened yesterday. I need to think; maybe we can talk later?' I walk into my bathroom and lock the door. I lean against the door. *What the hell have I done?* I let the devil into my life; I've got to get rid of her.

Mrs Graham

I urge Cynthia to follow me to my home office, where I give her a warm hug after closing the door.

'That was an excellent performance,' I say. 'But you should leave now.'

'What do I do next?' asks Cynthia.

'You know the plan. Henry will never welcome you into his life willingly. You will wait two weeks, then call him to say you are pregnant; I'll handle the rest.'

'Won't Henry take me to the hospital to confirm the pregnancy?'

'Don't worry about that. Everything will be handled, just play your role, or we will all be dead. Remember the warning of the big boss.'

Henry

I go to my office, still trying to remember what happened. It's like I've lost twenty-four hours of my life.

I have to find a way out of this situation; the only reason I have not resigned yet is Carl. I can't take it anymore! I'm going crazy!

My assistant calls to tell me that Tom wants to see me. Why does my mum's security man wish to see me? 'Send him in.'

'Hello, Tom, what does my mother want this time?'

He enters my office and hands me a note. It states that my mum doesn't know about his visit, and I need to disconnect my Gamaplug before he can talk to me.

'Why?' I whisper.

'Just do it!' he mouths.

I disconnect my Gamaplug, watching Tom closely as he inspects the office.

'What's going on?' I ask. He places his finger over his mouth, telling me to be quiet.

He has brought a bug sweeper, and points out that there is a listening device under my desk. He gives me another piece of paper and walks out of my office. I read the note: 'If you want to see your wife again, you will fly back to Sydney and go to this address in Guildford.'

***

I follow his instructions and arrive at the bungalow in Guildford. I am met by Tom and follow him into a sparsely furnished house.

'What is going on, Tom?'

'I brought you here because either you don't know what is happening or choose to be ignorant of what is going on. What I'm about to tell you, I don't want you to react because you will be putting all our lives in danger. Your mum instructed me to kill your wife. She did it only because you had twenty-four hours to get it done, or you would be destroyed.'

'You murdered Mia,' I shout.

'Slow down! I said that she instructed me to kill her, I didn't say I had done so. I did not kill Mia, but you can't see her. I can show you the camera monitoring her.'

'I want to see her now,' I say, rushing towards him.

'Do you want to die? I need you to answer me now, and I'll kill you myself. I would blame myself for being stupid enough to talk to a moron like you. It would help if you calmed down. Don't you know the kind of people you are dealing with? They will wipe out your whole family in one day. There is so much I need to tell you, so prepare your mind. It's going to get worse before it gets better.'

Chapter Twenty-one: Rio de Janeiro

Ana

I know one thing, they have links all around the world. The spreadsheet shows that they are operating in different continents. I've never been more determined to bring down this group; but my previous approach made me an easy target. Now, I am working non-stop. I go to work and come home to continue what I was doing. For the past two weeks, I have given them a show like they have never seen. I pretend I am dedicated in moving the organisation forward, and even my boss has commented on my new and improved attitude.

I have managed to buy a new laptop by paying a stranger to pick it up. I offered him money; people are desperate and they will do anything to survive. I am developing a code to access their network. I know the financial system they use is CIXCA 10.5 to move their money secretly and without delay without anyone being the wiser. Once I have access, I can see how it is done in other continents, but I will need help from people living there to ultimately bring down their financial arrangements.

I have developed a security code that allows me to surf the dark web, without being noticed, to see whether anyone out there is having the same problems. I saw an SOS code from New York a few days ago; I finally responded, stating I am facing similar issues in Rio de Janeiro and need their help.

Chapter Twenty-two: Hong Kong

Huan

I watch the news. It states that my husband committed suicide in prison because he couldn't handle the shame. The news presenter shows my face and encourages the public to help find me. According to the news report, I'm the mastermind behind the death of my husband's lover and children because I could not handle the public disgrace. I feel my throat closing up with emotion. *Chun! You were a good husband. You wanted to do the right thing; look at the price we have had to pay.*

I have been hiding in this apartment for over two weeks, I hardly go out only to buy groceries, and I don't associate with any of the other tenants. I have cut my hair and, today, it is dyed red.

I have been working non-stop developing software that will shut down access to telecommunication networks, but I can only do that for Hong Kong. I know they are using Gamaplug worldwide, and I need help from people across the globe for this to work. I have access to the dark web and have answered the cryptic SOS message I picked up from New York, where they are experiencing the same thing as me.

These people have taken everything from me. I was one of the most respected women in the world, and now I'm the most wanted criminal in Hong Kong.

Ping Wu

'Have you been able to trace where her money went?'

'No, ma'am!'

'How is that possible? This woman is worth millions of dollars; that kind of money doesn't just disappear without a trace.'

'Ma'am, she is a genius. She has won many awards for advanced technology; she would have been one of the best people to have on our side, Mr Hunan states.'

I glance at one of my men; and the CEO of Yamson Telecommunications is immediately punched in the face. He screams and holds his face in pain.

'How dare you question my decision? She would never work for us; giving her access to the network would make it easier for her to bring us down. Did she contact her husband before he died?'

'No, ma'am, her mobile phone and Gamaplug have been switched off for over two weeks, and there has been no sighting of her in her house.'

I turn to Cheung Wu. 'I gave you a simple instruction "Find Huan!" How difficult is that?'

Shaking with fear, and stammering at the same time, Cheung Wu replies, 'She went underground, ma'am!'

'"She went underground!" I scream. 'I own this continent; why do I have incompetent people working for me? Why have the satellites not been able to find her? We are connected to all technologies; there must be a way. Why are you still looking at me? Have you checked everything?'

'There is no stone unturned; we still came up empty!'

I stretch out my hand. A gun is placed in it. 'You're of no use to me anymore.'

'Please, ma'am, give me till the end of today; I'll find something.'

'You have eight hours, or I'll destroy you and your family. You cannot escape me.'

Huan

An encrypted message flashes up on my computer. It looks like gibberish, and I will need to break it down into layers to understand.

The little I can decode for now shows that others are facing the same predicament and hiding somewhere in New York. They are the most wanted criminals in their country because they found out about an organisation called Blue Gama.

This is good, I tell myself. I knew they were powerful. They must be all over the world. I need to finish decoding and reply to them by sending an encrypted message in a secured network. They are tracing all networks, trying to find me, but I can create a firewall preventing them from locating me. I still need to be very careful.

Chapter Twenty-three: London

Jude

I sit on the deserted train; and the emotion of everything that just happened to me hits me hard. I quickly wipe my eyes. I've lost my mother. I was a rich man. I didn't need these people, but they imposed themselves into my life. Now, look at me. My shirt is stained with the blood of an innocent man, Roger, and I have only £145.35 to my name. How am I going to survive? I need to find a way to access my money, but I doubt it is possible. I know how they operate; the first thing they take is your money, then your freedom. I was under pressure for months to join them, and I lost everything in the end. Now, I'm sneaking out of London like a thief. No more! I have nothing else to lose. I have to destroy this nasty organisation, and I don't care if I die in the process.

I arrive in Manchester with nowhere to go. I have nothing with me. I was lucky they didn't take my wallet. I need help, but who can I turn to now? The only person in a similar position as me is Sarah Philips. I hope they have not eliminated her. I look like a homeless man, limping badly, hobbling on one leg with a blood-stained shirt. I have to contact Sarah, but I am sure her phone is being monitored.

It is early in the morning; I can see night workers going home looking very tired. I walk up to a woman who is trying desperately to avoid me. 'Please, can I borrow your mobile phone? I've just been robbed. I need to contact my sister.'

The woman is torn. She doesn't know whether to believe me, but I see sympathy in her face, when she sees me I am close to tears.

'I'm so sorry,' she says. 'I think you should call the police, but you can use my phone to contact your sister.'

'Thank you very much,' I say.

The pain in my leg is excruciating. I can't stand up anymore, so I collapse on the pavement.

'Oh my goodness! Are you OK?'

'I just need to rest my leg; please bear with me.'

I'm grateful that I still have my wallet. I take out the card where

I wrote the new number I gave Sarah and dial it. God! Let her pick it up.

It is 6.43 in the morning. I look at the mobile phone, as it rings several times, but then I hear her drowsy voice. 'Hello, who is this?'

'Hello, Sarah, it's Jude. I can't talk for too long; so please listen. Your life is in danger, and you need a hiding place. Now!'

'Where are you?'

'I'm not in London; we need to meet somewhere.' I send her the address of my grandmother's house in Hackney in London and say to meet me there at 7.00 pm. I tell her to dispose of her old mobile phone and Gamaplug immediately. *How do I get back to London when everywhere is being monitored? I have to find a way out.*

I look up at the lovely lady, who is trying to give me some privacy while I talk. 'Thank you very much. I appreciate this,' I say, handing back her mobile phone.

She glances at me. 'Are you sure I shouldn't call 999 or take you to the hospital?'

'I'm going to be OK. My sister will pick me up. I appreciate your kindness.'

James Cooper

The five police officers working the night shift are lying flat on the floor in Drayton Police Station. The door of the station is locked from the inside.

'Where is Jude Williams? You had one task; to keep him in the cell until this morning before his hearing today. Now you are telling me you don't know where he is? Who opened the cell door? Who let him out without anyone knowing?'

'We don't know, sir. We went to check on the prisoners and found the lifeless body of Roger Smith, but Jude Williams was not there. We have been searching for him for hours, the whole of London is being combed.'

'Kill them all!' I instruct my men. 'Then find him!'

'He used an ATM at 3.20 am, but he could only withdraw £500. There has been no activity after that,' one of my men responds.

'Have you now ensured that he is penniless? That should have been done days ago; incompetent fools!'

'Yes, sir, he doesn't have access to his money anymore. His

face is already over the news and social media. There is nowhere to hide; we will find him.'

Jude

I spot a closed charity shop with bags of clothes outside. I go through the bags, hoping to find a shirt and a cap. Today is my lucky day. I find a shirt; it's a little tight, but it is better than the one I was wearing. I also discover a winter cap and sunglasses. The store needs to open so I can quickly buy what I need before people start to notice me.

I know my face is all over the news; I am being portrayed as a disgraced chef who killed his mother. Women I don't know have come out to say that I molested them. Police are asking for information on my whereabouts. I hope that the stranger who helped me doesn't recognise me. It was still quite dark when I asked for her mobile phone, and I kept my head down as much as possible.

I hide behind a car, wearing the hoodie that I was able to buy in the store, while I figure out what to do. I look like a homeless man, and no one is giving me a second look. People are too sad and broken by their own problems to worry about me. I force myself to walk properly through the pain. I have so many things weighing on my shoulders. I have to find a way to get back to London. I walk to the underground station to buy a ticket. I keep looking around trying to be inconspicuous. *Keep your head down!* rings in my head.

The carriage is empty, only a few can afford train tickets with unemployment and homelessness on the rise. I sit on the train, and the ticket inspector asks for my ticket, studying me intently. I keep my head down not looking at him directly. *Jesus! I hope he doesn't recognise me and decide to be a hero.* He inspects my ticket closely then returns it to me.

'You look familiar,' he says.

'I have that sort of face,' I reply, not lifting my head.

I heave a sigh of relief as he walks away. When you force people to work for you there are bound to be slip-ups.

***

When I reach London, I go straight to my grandmother's road. I know they will be watching the house, so I have to try and stop Sarah before she gets there.

I see her walking in the direction of my grandmother's place. I am glad that she has dressed inconspicuously but I can see she is being followed by two people. She knocks on the door to the house, but there is no response. She picks up her phone and tries to call several times, I can see her frustration. They watch her as she crosses the road, trying to reach her as she turns abruptly into the side road where I am hiding.

I tap Sarah on the shoulder, startling her. 'Follow me,' I whisper. 'You are being followed; we need to get out of here.'

We lay on the floor to blend in with the homeless who are all around us. 'Cover yourself with this blanket,' I say. We hear footsteps, but they don't stop as they pass the rows of faceless homeless people.

We need to escape as soon as they leave. They will come back and they will not be alone.

We enter the cheap motel I was able to rent for the night. It is cash only, which should have raised questions about how horrible the room is, but I'm out of options.

'We have a lot to talk about,' I tell Sarah. 'And I need your help. There is a group called Red Gama that set your father up and killed my mother. We have to find a way to stop them.'

Chapter Twenty-four: New York

Martin

'I ran the names of all the people you identified from the gala. It is incredible how their money and assets have increased tremendously in the past couple of months. They now sit in the most powerful positions in North America.'

Edward displays their names, showing their net worth, assets and appointments on the screen.

'Last time, I told you your ex-partner was worth twenty-five million dollars. Look at how much he is worth now.' I look at his name, moving closer to the screen to be sure. 'How can he be worth a hundred million dollars in so short a time?'

'They are involved in all kinds of activities; they don't care if it adversely affects people or the environment. I had to hack into their system slowly because they have the best people on the ground monitoring everything. The good news is that I got responses from Rio de Janeiro and Hong Kong. They are going through the same thing that is happening to you. They can access the deep dark web and communicate with me without anyone knowing which means they are smart, maybe geniuses.'

'We must be careful; we need to be sure they are real,' I say to Edward.

'I know they are also careful, but we need them; we cannot bring down this organisation without assistance from others. This means there are people everywhere, not just on this continent, experiencing similar problems. We know that the world economy is deteriorating every day. Crime has increased, homelessness, hate, and every evil thing you can think of is happening.

'I am developing an algorithm that will penetrate their system and bring it down, but I haven't completely figured it out yet. That is why I need people from the other continents to help me. This way, I can access the systems used in their countries easily. We need to do this, and we need to do it quickly. I don't know how long we can hide here, with you being the most wanted man in America.'

'I know, man, and now I am a racist too.'

They have just announced that I murdered the Mayor's

daughter, leading to his suicide. My family is being targeted. On the news, I can see people camping outside my home, hurling abuse and throwing stones at the windows even after my wife announced that we are getting divorced.

'I'm getting frustrated; I need to help my family.'

'That is their strategy. They know you cannot watch your family being assaulted without wanting to help. If you leave this building, you will be arrested, and you still won't be able to help them.'

I sigh heavily. 'So, damned if I do, damned if I don't!'

'I'm sorry.'

Edward switches off the television, but not before I see my children crying as the police try to send the mob of protesters away from my house.

Bobby

'Where can he be hiding? The Martin I know would be out in full force to help his family.'

'Maybe he doesn't have access to television,' one of my FBI agents responds.

My phone has been ringing non-stop, and I know that Martin's wife, Leah, is trying to reach me. Unfortunately, she is being used for collateral damage.

'Let us arrest his wife publicly; if he doesn't come out from hiding, then we know he doesn't have access to a phone or television,' suggests another agent.

'Arrest them immediately! Make sure it is all over the news, papers and internet. We will detain them in one of our safe houses. Most importantly, I don't want him to have access to his family. Let his wife plead in front of the world for him to surrender himself.'

Martin

Edward is trying to hold me back. 'I don't care if I die,' I yell.

I can see my daughters holding on tightly to my wife, crying uncontrollably, while cameras flash around them. They made my wife stand in front of the press to plead for me to surrender. They are being arrested for aiding and abetting. I know Bobby is behind all this, that bastard!

'What are you going to do?' shouts Edward, pulling me back. 'When you get outside, what exactly are you going to do? Tell me!'

'They have destroyed my life. I thought my family was safe after my wife gave that statement about our divorce. They will not stop until they have taken everything away from me. Edward, you need to find out where they are keeping my family, they will be killed, for sure, after appearing on live TV.'

'I'll do everything in my power to find them, but you might not like what I discover.'

'I need to know! That will determine how slowly I kill Bobby.'

Chapter Twenty-five: Lagos

Segun

We are not the only ones in this predicament; I was able to decode an SOS from New York. I haven't responded because I want to ensure it's not a set-up. I know a global organisation is behind all of this because of the kind of influence and power they exercise. It can't just be Africa.

'You need to leave now,' I tell Lola. 'Your father will be looking for you here also.' I give her a new SIM card. This is your new phone number; don't connect your Gamaplug to it. Don't tell them anything about me; even if you do, you will not find me here again. The most important thing is to be careful!

Lola

'Dad, please, why are you doing this?'

'I'm doing this for your own good. I warned you not to get involved, but you never listen. Maybe you will learn to obey when you are homeless and without money.'

He gets into the passenger seat of his Bentley and is driven away with a police escort following.

One of his men stays behind and walks over to me. 'You need to leave. I've been instructed to lock the gate when you go.'

I get into my car, but where can I go? I'm homeless. I hope I still have money in my account. I take out my phone and log into my bank account. I see a zero balance. I need to go back to Segun.

Mr Adeyemo

'Follow her car.'

The only way to save my life and my daughter is to give them Segun. He brainwashed her into believing that she could save the world.

'You must not fail me this time! Find him before the big boss kills us all.'

Lola

Where is Segun? I sent him a text on the new number, but he is not responding. I explained to him what happened to me but still nothing. It is midnight. It's dark. I am outside the house, it's empty. Where did he disappear to? I'm scared out of my mind. I look around; everywhere appears to be quiet.

A hand covers my mouth; I can't scream. I feel something pierce my skin and everything goes black.

***

A bucket of water is poured over me, and I am forced to open my eyes. Where am I? I am strapped to a chair; my hands and feet are bounded as I struggle to free myself.

I hear laughter. 'Why are you fighting? You can't get free.' A man enters the room, followed closely by another.

'Where is Segun? What are you two up to?'

Tears sting my eyes. I have been cheating death for months, and today might be my last day on earth. A fist catches my eye. I scream, just as my dad is hurled into the room.

'I repeat, where is Segun, and what are you up to?'

'Please, I don't know. I went looking for him, but I couldn't find him. I don't know anything.'

'I have spared your life all these months because of your father. Look at him! Your father has been beaten because of you.'

'Please don't hurt him; he has done nothing wrong.'

'He tried to protect you by taking everything away from you. He thought you would be intelligent enough to disappear or find your partner in crime, Segun, but you are useless, not even street smart. The instruction I gave him was to bring you to me. Now, where is your partner?'

'I honestly don't know; the last place I saw him was where you found me.'

'What did he tell you?'

'He said that he was running away from his father and some people were trying to kill him; that is all I know.'

'Look at me, lady!'

I have a throbbing headache; I can't open my eyes, but I force myself to look up.

My father is thrown on the dusty floor in front of me. 'You caused this, you have a choice. You will find a way to reach Segun and give us his location. If you don't do as I say, your father will be killed, not only him; your mother and brothers also.'

'Please! Please! He knows you are looking for him. He is not going to show himself.'

'That is too bad! Then, say goodbye to your family.'

A tear rolls down my father's face, in humiliation. He has been severely beaten, he has a swollen face, there is blood on his head and his clothes are torn.

'Please, I'll do whatever you want, spare my family.'

'Good! I always knew you were clever; you have thirty-six hours to find Segun in whatever hellhole he is hiding and bring him to me. Lock him up,' he orders, and my dad is dragged away.

'What's going to happen to him?'

'That depends on you. Your father did everything he could to protect you, even joining our organisation, because of his spoilt child. Now, what are you willing to do for your father? Are you going to continue to be the selfish brat I know you are, or do everything to protect your family? Even if it means sleeping with the devil himself?'

Chapter Twenty-six: Kabul

Ahmed

'You were given specific instructions to protect me!' says Mohammed. 'How can someone enter my office and the cameras not show anything? It tells me that someone altered the cameras from the surveillance room. Check their rooms, someone here is working for the enemy, and I want answers now!'

The men lay on the ground pleading for their lives. *How could I be so stupid!* I knew something was wrong; I didn't realise he had set a trap to catch anyone entering his office. This incident will make things more difficult for me. I know for a fact that there is a hidden room behind the bookshelves. This holds the key to the answers I am looking for. I need to leave this hellhole and return to my family.

The security men rush back after checking the rooms of the nineteen men pleading for their lives.

'We found nothing, sir!' they say. 'We checked everywhere.'

'That means we have more traitors; I don't trust anyone anymore. It could be any one of you. You need to understand that I'm infallible! I will bring you down if you think you can betray me. I want every room on this premises checked. The men must be paired in two, and no one must enter a room alone. Most importantly, they must not know each other.'

My heart starts beating fast. I changed the hiding place of my mobile phone yesterday after switching off the light in my room. I lifted the mattress, and at the edge of the bed, I made a clean cut, placed my mobile phone and charger inside, and sewed it back up again – all in complete darkness.

Mohammed turns to me. 'I need your protection more. You will be allowed to rest only in the evenings when I return to my room. The others can protect the door, but you need to be alert. I can call on you at any time.'

I stand behind Mohammed while the men are divided into groups to check the premises.

It takes about four hours before the search is finished. Five other men are added to the men on the ground; they find contraband in their rooms such as like mobile phones, cameras, and books.

'Why do you have a mobile phone when it is prohibited?' Mohammed asks.

'I just wanted to talk to my family; I've been here for two years.'

'Yes, you have been here for two years, and you miss your family. Don't worry, they will join you soon.'

The camera contains nude pictures and videos of the girls he slept with, grotesque pictures of the girls being brutally beaten, and the sadist laughing at their pain. I'm glad Mohammed is ending that idiot's life. Weirdly, Mohammed doesn't allow reading on the premises. Is he afraid his men will be wiser than him?

'Kill them all,' he says. 'And their families.'

Hussain

Hussain looks at the text from Jabar; this is good news. Mohammed Pir is my puppet. I control him, and he does what I tell him to do by invoking fear in the people. I sent Ahmed into his midst to cause a bit of commotion; I didn't want him to be too comfortable. Jabar has done an excellent job of messing up the recordings and implicating others. We knew Mohammed would be aware when someone enters his office.

'What do we do about Ahmed? He is getting closer. He might find out about us,' asks Yusuf.

'We have his family. Take them away from the house to one of the slave houses and put them to work. He will call his family, trying to reach them, but he will get nothing. He will start to panic. He will reach out to us, and he will get no response. Then we will tell Mohammed that he is the traitor. Let's see him escape from that. His death is imminent, be patient. I don't just want him; I want to eliminate Mohammed also.'

Ahmed

It's been a long day; I had to do a double shift. Mohammed is getting increasingly paranoid, and I honestly don't know what he will do next. Two cameras have been installed in his office that transmit directly to his phone. I am under my blanket going through the pictures I took in his office; some of the books have gathered dust and still look new. Apart from him, no one is allowed in his office, but I noticed that five books look worn and have no dust. Could these books answer my questions?

How do I get into his office now with the newly installed cameras in operation? I'll talk with Jabar tomorrow about how he managed not to get caught. I am elated that I will be leaving here soon. Hussain will get the answers he is looking for, and I'll be able to see my family again.

I have been trying to reach them for over an hour now. I usually send a text, but I haven't got any response. I decide to call, but Aisha is not picking up the phone. What is going on? I hope nothing has happened to my family. I text Yusuf to help me check on them, but I haven't had anything back from him. I need to get a response from them by tomorrow, or I'll be forced to leave this compound to search for them.

Chapter Twenty-seven: Sydney

Henry

I am livid; my mother gave the order for my wife to be killed! I don't care about her intention; all she cares about is her legacy. I need to stay calm to understand everything Tom is saying to me.

'You attended a gala with your mother, weren't you paying attention? Everyone was given an assignment they needed to carry out; yours was your wife. The big boss disapproves of her; she thinks she is too weak to be the wife of a prime minister; it's bad enough that you are considered a weak man.'

'What does this all mean?'

'I'm trying to tell you that. I have carried out my investigation, and I'm sure you're frustrated with their control over you. I told you to disconnect your Gamaplug because it is used to trace you and get information about your thoughts. They have a wide range of things they use, like satellite and your mobile phone. Their applications are downloaded to almost all technologies, they are very powerful.'

'Why are you helping me?'

'I'm not helping you; this is about me. I want revenge. They took everything from me; they killed my son. When they give an instruction, you have to do it. Your mother protected you; they would have murdered you and your family. We have to work together in order to destroy them. I require your help.'

'Can I see Mia?' He opens a laptop, and I see my wife sitting in a basement, looking very frightened and fragile. 'Is she going to be OK?'

'She will be fine. But if anyone should find out, we are all dead. You need to go home and pretend everything is normal; don't take your anger out on your mother.'

'Where do we go from here?'

'Their tentacles are everywhere; we have to take them apart little by little. We need to bring down all the technologies they are using. That is the tricky part; I don't have the singular expertise to do that. I have sought help from people outside this continent experiencing the same thing as us.

'You need to keep your ears close to the ground; you are already in the organisation, so you can find out what they are doing and how they are doing it. Your role is to play along and not make any mistakes. Be careful of your mum!'

He escorts me out of the bungalow. 'Go home to your mother, and pretend you don't know anything. She was also given an assignment. Find out what it is. I'll get in touch with you regularly, don't use your Gamaplug anymore.'

***

I enter my mum's house with a perfect smile on my face. 'Hello, Mother!'

'Where have you been? I was told you left your office early and no one could reach you.'

'I just needed time to think about this Cynthia situation.'

'Honey! Don't overthink it; these things happen.'

'I have a question, Mum. You know how I feel about Cynthia, yet you allowed her into the house. You said I called her, yet I have no record on my phone. Let's say I deleted it. I took her to my room; I must have been drunk to do such a thing. You saw all this and did nothing?'

'You're a grown man! Cynthia and I tried to stop you, but you wouldn't listen.'

'OK. So why didn't you call Dad or your many security men to help you?'

'I told you, you overthink! You constantly blame others for your mistakes. You need to own it.'

'Of course, Mum, I know it is my fault for trusting you; that will never happen again.' I give her a peck on the cheek and walk away.

'What does that mean?' she calls after me.

'I need to sleep, don't follow me, or I'll leave this house tonight.'

I lock the door to my room to be safe. I would pack out today, but I need to know what is happening. I can't do that in my house. I know my mother; she will panic and try to dissect my statement. I know she has a plan with Cynthia; I woke up and couldn't remember anything. The smartest thing I did this morning was pee in a container. I'll send it to the hospital for a test. I'll get the confirmation of what I already know – I was drugged. Whatever her

73

plans are, it will not work!

I hear a knock on my door, then my father's voice. She has sent my father.

'Dad, can I talk to you tomorrow? I'm so tired; I've had a long day.'

'No problem, son, I'll talk to you tomorrow.'

Mrs Graham

'What did he say?' I ask.

'That he was tired and he will talk to me tomorrow.'

'God! I gave you a simple job, and you couldn't do that right.'

'I'm tired. So is he. Leave our son alone,' he says, walking away in the direction of our bedroom.

What kind of a husband do I have? He is such a weakling. My son is angry with me; I hope he hasn't discovered the truth.

I must call Cynthia. We need to go to plan B. A fake pregnancy will not work. We have to find a way for him to marry her; I'll falsify their marriage licence. I have less than fifty-six hours to complete this task.

Chapter Twenty-eight: Rio de Janeiro

Ana

I received a coded response from Hong Kong and New York; this cements what I already know from the transaction details I worked on. This organisation is established worldwide, and there is someone overseeing everything. I shared the knowledge of what I have discovered with them, but it is integrated into other codes, so if you don't analyse it carefully, it will look like nonsense. We are trying to get help from other continents. I am working to bring down their system in my country, but we can't do this alone.

I have not seen the news in two weeks. It constantly breaks my heart to watch the demise of my country. Purple Gama are getting richer, and the people are getting poorer. They have taken over every sector, and the amount of money they make daily is astronomical, from legal to illegal deals. In the next year, the Amazon rainforest will be destroyed. Every plant, animal, and natural resource that they are so focused on will lead us closer to the destruction of the world.

I called Maria, my sister. As much as she hates me, I cannot abandon her. Unfortunately, her mobile phone is switched off. Where can she be? I've been calling for days using different numbers, but she is not picking up; now, it is switched off. I hope nothing has happened to her and the children.

I went to her house. It has been sealed off. I asked the neighbours what has happened, but no one will talk to me, saying I am a disgrace. I've all this money, and I can't help my sister, who stood by me, and her children.

Chapter Twenty-nine: Hong Kong

Ping Wu

'Where is she?' I yell. 'I am tired of asking you the same question. It's been days now.'

'Ma'am, there is no trace of her; I think she must be dead,' says Cheung Wu.

'You're an idiot!' I pull out my gun and place it against Cheung Wu's forehead. 'Your time is up.'

'Please, ma'am, we have talked to her co-workers, we have been to her house, the slum, everywhere, and found nothing.'

'Do you think she is still in Hong Kong? She could be anywhere by now.'

'She can't travel. How can she survive? We can trace her money; it's still in her account. The bank made a mistake.'

'Really! The bank made a mistake; a lump sum of money disappeared and reappeared again. Don't you think that is fishy? I'll not have incompetent people working for me; we have all the resources in the world to find someone, yet here we are without any result.'

I pull the trigger, and Cheung Wu falls to the floor.

'Listen now. This is the last time I will be talking to you about this. Find me Huan Li! The first person to bring her to me will get twenty million dollars and a house in your chosen area. Chyou, you will take over from Cheung Wu, but don't get excited. Look at what happened to him. This will be you, if don't find Huan Li, dead or alive.

'She is too intelligent to be free; she could destroy us easily.'

Chapter Thirty: London

Jude

'What is going on, Jude?' says Sarah. 'You call me, tell me to meet you, then say that it's not safe. You bring me here and then tell me that my father was killed by some powerful organisation.'

'Sit down, and I'll answer all your questions. Your life is in danger; you can't go back home,' I say. 'I was forced to work for an organisation called "Red Gama" which operates the European hub. Their mission is to take over the world and remove any hindrances. Your father was a hindrance, one of the biggest distributors in Europe. He was set-up, killed and rendered bankrupt.'

'What? How do you know all this?'

'I told you, I was forced to do what they told me. They took over my restaurant and sold an illegal drug called Demalon from it. They've just killed my mother; the only person who could help me was murdered. I was supposed to be incarcerated today, but someone helped me escape by pure luck. I have lost everything; I'm sure you saw my face in the news, the malicious lies being told about me; I wasn't sure you would come.'

'Why would they want to kill me? My dad is dead; they've already taken everything away from me?'

I watch her struggle to keep her composure. 'These people are pure evil. I was sent to watch you, but you kept trying to revive your father's company. That doesn't sit well with the big boss.'

'Oh, right! So the way we met was a lie, what a fool I am! How do I know you are not lying to me now?'

'What am I going to gain by lying to you? I'm as good as dead.'

'That is the problem; you've nothing to lose but everything to gain.'

'What am I going to gain? They have taken everything from me. I only have the clothes on my back and a few hundred pounds which won't last a week. If you don't believe me, you're free to leave but, I am warning you, you will be killed.'

'Why tell me all this? Why not just let them kill me?'

'I need your help; I'm just a chef. I read your intel, and I know you are good at programming. We need to find a way to destroy this Gamaplug; billions of people worldwide are using it. This high-speed technology has enslaved the world; you need to find the secret code being used. That is the only hope we have to tear down their stronghold. They operate on different continents. We know they operate all over the world; I'm sure there are people across the globe as frustrated as we are.'

'OK. Let's say I believe you; we can't live here.' She looks around the dirty room.

My skin is itchy and I feel unclean.

'I have no money; I might end up on the street. I got this place so that we can talk privately. They accept cash without asking questions.'

'My grandfather has a place he gave to me just before he died; it's a small two-bedroom in Covent Garden; I couldn't bring myself to sell it.'

'I would advise against going there; they know everything.'

'I don't think they will know about this place; none of my workers knew. He didn't write it in the will; he gave it to me in person.'

'If your name is on it, they know!'

'It was bought through my grandfather's company; it's not linked to my dad. The company now has a new name that is not linked to me; it's untraceable.'

'They are the most dangerous people in the world; they have the power and the resources to find out everything about you. I bet they already know and are waiting for us there.'

'So what do we do? We can't stay here!'

'Jesus! I don't know. They mustn't link us together. OK, let's go to your place in Covent Garden. If we die, we die!'

Chapter Thirty-one: New York

Martin

Hiding in an abandoned train station has its advantages, but it is taking longer than expected and we need to make headway. Watching my family being humiliated in front of the world by people who have been our neighbours for years, and listening to them speak ill of us, shows the kind of world we now live in. I place my head on the desk. Edward has switched off the television, but my mind is still not at rest. Where are my family?

'Martin!' I hear my name being called. Lifting my head, I turn to see Edward looking at me with great concern.

'I've been calling you for some time. Where did you go?'

'Sorry, lost in thought; I didn't hear you. With everything happening around me, I'm getting more frustrated by the day.'

'I have good news; I've made contact with someone in Lagos. He is handling the African hub. We have all the continents, apart from Europe, and I know they will reach out soon. We have agreed to work together; that is the only way to bring down the Gamaplug network. Each continent will create an electromagnetic format, a secret code that we will combine. It's using advanced technology, but it can be done as I told you before. I have been working all day and coding with the others to find a way forward.'

'Edward, thank you, but I can't rest. You saved my life, but I couldn't save my family from these callous men. Look at the situation. Things have become so bad that five dollars can't buy anything, and we are grateful that we can eat at all, even if it is so little.'

'Don't worry about food; I am a hacker. Remember, I have money; we're going to be OK. Bobby will not kill your family; they are baiting you to lure you out of hiding. If you don't show up after a while, I'm sure they will assume you are dead. That is the only way you would abandon your family.'

'Can't you trace them? You promised me you would.'

'I will, but we need to be careful. They have the world's best hackers working for them; we can't just go into the network. I have to build layers of code to snoop into the network without them noticing.'

'Edward! They have milked the world dry, and they need to be stopped!'

He nods. 'I agree. We're working on it, but we need money to develop more advanced fibre optics to stop access to Gamaplug. We have formulated a plan; Ana from Rio de Janeiro handles the finances for the continent and knows how the finances are distributed across the world. She will assist us in writing a code to rob the organisation without them noticing. We will bring them down. Don't worry, Martin, we will!'

***

Leah holds her two daughters closely.

'Where are we?' she yells. The room has three single beds with a toilet and no window. Her daughters are sitting on one of the beds, crying. She has no idea how to comfort them.

'Why are we here, Mum?' asked Leila.

'I don't know; it has something to do with your dad. He is a wanted criminal.'

'Where is Dad? Why isn't he helping us?'

'I don't have an answer to that.'

'Are they going to kill us?' she asks, shaking.

'They would have done so ages ago if that's what they intended. We're going to be OK!' she says. 'Please don't cry anymore.'

Bobby

Staring at the screen and watching those children cry gives me so much joy. If only Martin could see his children now. His pride and joy are rotting in a secret jail.

'You still haven't found that fool?' I ask.

'I think he must be dead; no one can remain underground for that long. We have been monitoring everyone he knows. He would surely reach out to someone, but we've heard nothing. We shouldn't spend our time and resources looking for a man that is most likely dead. He doesn't have any money; how can he survive?'

***

President Dan is in his office in the White House. One of his advisors knocks and enters.

'Sir, there is a large protest outside. We have never seen this number of people before.' He switches on the television. 'These scenes are being repeated in all of the states.'

He watches the news and sees people holding placards protesting against the deteriorating economy. An average family can no longer afford to eat properly. He lets out a huge belly laugh.

'Call the National Guard to disperse the protesters. I don't want to see them here tomorrow. If they refuse to leave, I authorise the police and national guards to use live ammunition. Let that be a lesson to them.'

He turns to his advisor and shrugs. 'Why do you worry about these people? They mean nothing to us.

'We are making money; by the time we leave here, we will be billionaires. Someone has to pay the price. They have not seen anything yet; it is going to get worse. We have taken away medical insurance; you get treated and pay in full. We have been too lenient with these people, they have grown lazy, and now everyone must work hard. The government is no longer responsible for its citizens. Taxes will increase, and they will pay, if they're over eighteen, whether working or not.

'I don't care how many people we have to eliminate in the process. They must comply.'

Chapter Thirty-two: Lagos

Segun

I knew Lola would come back here, and she would not be coming alone. She doesn't understand what she is involved with. You cannot dine with the devil and expect everything to work out.

As soon as she left, I carried everything that would fit into my backpack and moved to the place where I actually live. Unfortunately, I had to watch while she was taken away in a car in the thick of the night. I knew something terrible was about to happen to her and her family.

I've had multiple missed calls and texts from her. I know what is happening; they are trying to find me through her. I have finally been able to get help from other countries. I responded to the coded SOS, and we have found a way to bring down these oppressors.

Lola needs to feel the pain and become desperate. She has been protected for too long by her father and me. She will understand her situation when she loses everything the way I have.

Lola

Why is he not picking up his phone? He got me into this mess. I have accepted my fate. I will no longer go against these people. I have less than twelve hours to locate Segun.

I go back to the house in Oshodi. I knock on doors but everyone looks at me strangely. I am getting desperate. I stand outside the unpainted house and start screaming, 'Segun! Segun! Where are you?' People come out of their homes.

I have been wearing the same clothes for three days, the same clothes I wore when I last saw Segun. I have not slept or showered. I have no money, and I am homeless. The only thing I have now is my car, and I can't afford to leave this place as my petrol tank is almost empty.

A woman approaches me, angrily. 'Are you crazy? You have been shouting for hours. There is no Segun here; go back to where you came from.'

'He is here,' I scream. 'I know it.'

I shudder as I think about what was going to happen to my father. Time is ticking.

'I met him here three days ago, and he told me this is where he lives.'

'Well, as you can see, there is no one living there now. It is empty; you need to stop shouting. This is not the right house. If you don't leave in the next five minutes, do you see those young men?' She points and I see five angry-looking men staring at me. 'They will be forced to beat you. Is that what you want? I came to warn you. Now leave!'

I'm finished! Segun has killed me! I sit down on the dusty ground sobbing uncontrollably. The men approach me, lift me forcefully and throw me into my car.

'For God's sake, just leave!' they say. 'Go and cry somewhere else. We don't want any trouble.'

I shake myself, realising I am in a dangerous situation, and I drive for a short distance, but I can't leave until I have found Segun. I call his number and text him again, waiting, but there is no response. The next thing I know, everything goes dark.

***

'Where is Segun?' someone asks, as I open my eyes, groggily. 'We have been watching you for thirty-four hours and there is no sign of him. We have searched several houses close to the place you saw him. No one has heard of him or seen him before, even the family he said took him in. He lied to you, made a fool of you, and you fell for it. Now, you will have to pay the ultimate price.'

'Please! You can see that I have been deceived, and I honestly don't know where he is.'

'I spared your life all these months because of your loyal father. I have reached my limit; your family is of no use to me, dead or alive.'

'Please spare my father's life. I have two hours left; I can still find him.'

'You are so stupid. You never had a chance of finding him, he knew what would happen, and he used you as bait.'

My father is dragged out of his cell and thrown in front of me. He is emaciated, having lost so much weight. He is wearing only trousers so I can see the bruises all over his body.

'I'm sorry! I did this to you. Please forgive me,' I beg, before completely breaking down.

My father lifts his head slightly, but before he can speak the big boss nods. My father is shot three times. Before I can react, his body is dragged away as if his life was worth nothing.

I fall to the floor where he had lain. 'Kill me now,' I say. 'There is nothing to live for.'

The big boss starts to laugh. 'Kill you! That would be easy; I want you to suffer. You killed your father. He died because of you; everything you've done led to your father's death. You cannot come back from that.

'To make this more enjoyable, your father's business partner, Bankole Gerald, is at your family home at Abuja telling your mother and brothers that you sent an assassin to kill your father because you want to take over his wealth, showing them all the evidence they need.

'You have no home, no money, or family to turn to. Where will you go? Pampered child, there is no daddy anymore to help you. Your only hope is to find Segun; you are the only one that can. If you find him and hand him over, I will not kill your remaining family.

'Segun is a very dangerous man; his father told me of his intelligence. He can't be left to roam the streets. He needs to be contained.'

'I can't help you. I don't know where he is,' I say. 'He is not picking up the phone or answering text messages. Kill me and leave my family alone; they are innocent. I've lost everything; I can't survive this.'

'I don't care how you survive; but you will,' he says menacingly. 'You can live under a bridge for all I care. Time is running out. I will grant your wish and dispose of you, but before I do that, I'll kill your remaining family in front of you. Now, get out of here and look for Segun. You are embarrassing yourself!'

I drag myself up from the ground. I killed my father! Where do I go from here? If I see Segun, I'll kill him myself!

Chapter Thirty-three: Kabul

Ahmed

I need to get out of here. I have gone through the pictures I took; I know he has a secret room behind the bookcase. I think I can identify the book that holds the key to entering. What is Mohammed doing with a textbook on quantum physics? That seems strange; the other books are all on history and philosophy. I need to find answers before leaving here because I can never come back if I go. Mohammed will be looking for me, and I know what is waiting for me outside.

I need to get into his office tomorrow night, but how can I enter without the cameras seeing me? I can't find Jabar. I walked to the surveillance room again to look for him, and he was not in his seat.

I asked one of his colleagues, 'Where is Jabar?'

'We haven't seen him in days. We sent some men to his room, but the space was empty. We have reported this to Mohammed. Some of the men went to the city to look for him, but no one can find him.'

'Thank you.'

This situation is getting worse. Mohammed is becoming more unstable; I fear he will wake up one day and kill us all.

Yusuf

'Mohammed is becoming even more paranoid,' I say. 'Jabar's disappearance will cost him some sleepless nights. What is the next step, boss?'

'Have you put Ahmed's family to work?'

'Yes, sir, they are in the outskirts of Kabul. No one knows the location apart from us.'

Chapter Thirty-four: Sydney

Henry

'Mr Graham, I'm sorry to inform you that, after testing your urine, we found residue of Rodroxtone. It's part of a group known as "club drugs".' The doctor is staring at his notes. He raises his head. 'Can you remember anything that happened to you in the last twenty-four hours? This is a severe offence, and I think you need to report it to the police.'

'Thank you, doctor. Unfortunately, I can't remember or guess who would put Rodroxtone into my drink, but I'll file it with the police to be safe.'

I just wanted to confirm what I already knew. My mother drugged me; the person I trusted the most set me up with Cynthia. *I'll make them pay*, I murmur to myself.

I get into my car and drive to the location in Guildford. I receive a text from Tom on my new phone telling me to meet him. Honestly, I hate my life. Going to the office is getting more difficult and my son is still in Moreland Mental Hospital. I got to spend some time with him recently, and I'm grateful he's improving. My greatest fear is bringing him home to these horrible people to be kidnapped or worse. Carl is due to be discharged next week. How will I answer when he asks after his mother?

I park the car cautiously, cars are being vandalised all the time out of anger; Sydney is becoming more dangerous every day. This organisation is making things intolerable. People are getting desperate and the crime rate has gone up; no one is safe anymore.

***

'I'm making headway,' Tom explains. 'I've contacted people from various parts of the world facing similar problems to us who want to find a way to destroy this organisation. So far, we have New York, Lagos, Rio de Janeiro and Hong Kong on board. They represent the various continents being controlled by Gama. The only reason for the delay is that we still need someone from the European hub. We are developing a coded platform.'

He shows me encrypted numbers.

'We need to build a more sophisticated network that can bring down Gamaplug. We don't have the money because we have all lost so much to this organisation, but Ana from Rio de Janeiro has devised a way to fund this operation without the organisation knowing.

'The big bosses are given a benchmark for the amount of money they must bring in every month. The more problems they cause, the more money they will make. Everything is already privatised, homes are being possessed, and interest rates are beyond measure.

'You need to change your persona; your caution must be hidden. They are always watching you. Your mother called me yesterday troubled about you; this is not good. You are a politician, and lying should be your forte. If they should suspect you, we are in trouble. How many times do you need me to reiterate this to you?'

'I know! I am just disappointed in my mother, that's all. I can't believe she drugged me. The funny thing is that I shouldn't be surprised by her actions, but she always manages to shock me.'

'We need to move forward; I can't do that if you keep moving us backwards. This isn't about you or your mother; this is about breaking free from the shackles of the oppressors.'

I nod. 'Don't worry; I'll get as much information as I can. Anything you need, I'm at your disposal; just make sure you keep my wife safe.'

***

I enter the sitting room. My mother is sitting beside Cynthia, holding her hands, trying to comfort her.

'Henry, honey! We have been waiting for you for some time, I called your mobile, but you didn't pick up.'

'I placed it on silent, Mum. I'm a very busy man.'

'Why aren't you using your Gamaplug; that would make your life easier?'

I ignore her last statement. 'What is going on?' I ask, looking from one woman to the other.

'Cynthia came to me in tears and distraught; she thinks she is pregnant.'

I start to laugh. 'Let me guess; I'm the father! I supposedly slept with you three days ago, and you can confirm that you're pregnant. Wow! Congratulations.' I walk up to her and hold out my hand.

'Henry, what is wrong with you? Her intuition cannot be wrong.'

'I am not arguing with you, Mother. That is why I said congratulations. You are going to be a grandmother again. Let me know when you give birth.' With that, I walk out of the room.

'Wait! Where are you going, Henry? We need to discuss this,' my mother's voice trails after me.

Chapter Thirty-five: Rio de Janeiro

Ana

I have been working non-stop for days; I distribute their money globally and know what goes to whom. I have to be able to take some money without them noticing. They have independent people who don't know each other and cross-check my work to ensure nothing is amiss. They usually send me a spreadsheet showing the total amount they have generated for the month from the suffering and pain of others. The funds are then broken down to each hub. When that is done, the hub breaks it down further for each individual, not counting the head, whoever that is. I need to take the money from the bank days before receiving the spreadsheet.

We need billions of dollars to build a robust platform sophisticated enough to destroy Gamaplug and not be noticed. It is tricky; we are working underground. I'm excited to be working with intelligent people; Edward, who lives in New York; Huan in Hong Kong, Segun from Lagos and Tom from Sydney. They are a formidable force but, in order to completely sabotage their technology, we need someone from the European hub. We have sent many SOS messages; I hope they communicate soon. We need to identify the fibre 4.0 in each continent that Gamaplug uses to communicate with other technologies and corrupt it, which will bring it down. We have been working together for weeks now, developing the N60 postnanometer. It is faster and better than the N24 developed by Gamaplug. We will place it in the capital city of each hub that will allow the program code to bring down Gamaplug. But first things first; we need money!

My heart is beating fast. Encouraged by my team (the people working with me to bring down Gama), I've been monitoring the money going in and out of the primary account managed by Brazilian City Bank. The money is kept there until the end of the month. The big boss has access to the account and regularly monitors it a day before the bank manager Fernanda presents the expense report with the breakdowns for that month.

I have to grant Huan Li from Hong Kong access to steal one-and-a-half billion dollars into her secret account that no one has been able to find. We have been writing the code that will overwrite the bank's security. I have two days.

We will have an eight-minute window. God! I hope it works. We will steal the money without leaving any trail behind. The big boss will be livid because he will see the money has disappeared, and the bank will not be able to account for its whereabouts. Most importantly, we can't afford to make any mistakes, or our cover will be blown, and we're all dead.

Ana, you need to remain calm; I keep repeating to myself. *I'm in the office and being monitored.*

'Ana!' My name is being called; I was miles away. I shake my head, open my eyes and see Carlos. 'I have been calling you,' he says.

'Sorry! How can I help?'

'The big boss is in a good mood; we have surpassed last month's income. You will have to distribute the money evenly. It is a vast amount, and a large bonus will be given to us all for our excellent performance. I just wanted to come and tell you the good news; you will be more prosperous than ever. It's a good day!' He turns and leaves my office.

Thank God! They won't know what has hit them in two days; then they will be singing a different song.

Chapter Thirty-six: Hong Kong

Ping Wu

'I want her face plastered across all media platforms, to be repeated every five minutes. I want them to state her height and the possibility of disguise. I want her found, no matter where she is hiding.

I just received confirmation from my best cyber gurus that she infiltrated the bank system, took out all her money and created a mirage that the system still thinks the money is there. The worst part was that it took my people two weeks to find this out, a team of the best ten! She did this by herself, using her computer.'

'Ma'am, she left her computer. She didn't take anything from the house, it was there when we searched,' says Chyou.

'Did you find anything on her office or home computer?'

'No, ma'am, the minute we logged in, a virus uploaded itself into the system, and the computer crashed.'

'I have a terrible feeling that she is up to something. Is her husband still alive?'

'The chances are slim; you ordered his death.'

'Find out if he is still alive. If he is, I want him on the six o'clock news pleading for his wife to surrender, or he will be killed.'

'Yes, ma'am, but if he is already dead, what do we do?'

'Find someone who looks exactly like him. His face will be beaten anyway. With the right camera angle, it will be difficult for her to tell the difference; find his replica ASAP!'

Huan

Living like a hermit is getting harder; I need to move away from this apartment and find a house with a yard. I keep bumping into people who live in this building, and they want to be friends with me. The problem is that they think I am a man. I dress, walk, and act like a man to draw less attention to myself.

I am living in a slum, and the amount of noise pollution can drive you insane. I have work to do; I need to concentrate. Working closely with the team across the continents gives me great joy. I am privileged to be working with such intelligent people; Edward, Segun, Tom and Ana. I know we are experiencing a delay because we haven't been able to find anyone in Europe to help us, but we are hopeful. The task in front of us is enormous and frightening.

We are planning to take down the most powerful organisation in the world. The next two days will determine whether we move forward with our plan or if we are all dead. We are attempting to break into one of the world's most secure banks, Brazilian City Bank. I have cross-checked and double-checked the program we have written for two weeks now. The money will be moved to a small bank in Barbados, where I'm keeping my money. I wrote a powerful code that disguises the money; nobody in the bank knows that my money is there – the power of technology.

Brazilian City Bank has eight security layers that protect its clients' money; each layer has a team of people monitoring and protecting it. The code needs to be filtered through the layers without being noticed. Moving a considerable sum of money is difficult, especially billions of dollars, without anyone noticing. I've just finished writing the final part of the program that will show the stolen money is still in the account even though it has been moved. The money will disappear but they will not be able to trace it.

I stretch. I have been working for hours. My back is aching. I switch on the television only to see my husband. This must be a joke? My husband would never plead for me to give myself up. He would rather be killed. This cannot be my husband. The man on screen looks like him, although he has bruises over his face and a swollen eye. They are saying that the authorities have agreed to reduce his sentence, and I'll not be arrested if I give myself up. That is the joke of the century! These people are getting desperate. It is good to know that I am giving them sleepless nights.

The prison my husband was sent to is the deadliest of all jails. He can't be alive. He couldn't have lasted that long. I stare at the man closely. Apart from his bruised face, he looks fresh. Those bruises have been inflicted on him today. My husband went to prison previously and was beaten; those scars were still on his face, below his eyebrow and chin. The scars on this man are not the same. This stranger has been brought in to pretend to be my husband. He looks healthy, and no one can be in that prison for that long and not look skeletal. This confirms what I already know;

my husband is dead. These heartless people have murdered him, and I will have my revenge.

Ping Wu

'I told you to get me a replica that will appear on the news, not an imbecile! I don't think he will convince her to show her face.'

'He looks exactly like her husband. The commissioner for correctional services had her husband killed immediately after you gave the order. When this man was brought to us, we had to beat him, punch his face and even use knives to make him look authentic.'

'Time will tell if she is convinced. I want fresh eyes; I need to find her. Maybe we missed something; no one can be that intelligent to outsmart all of us. She must have made a mistake somewhere. She has an aunty, where is she?'

'In the United States.'

'That's good. I'll contact my colleague there and they will find her. Why didn't I think of that before? That is the only relative she cares about? This will bring her to me!'

Chapter Thirty-seven: London

Jude

I look around the house; it is a typical Victorian home, small but cosy. I don't know how long we can stay here before we are found out. The clock is ticking to find a way out of this situation.
We need help.
'Do you have a first-aid kit in the house?' I ask, flopping down on one of the sofas in the living room.
'Yes, let me get it from the bathroom, we need to look at your leg.'
I try to pull up my trousers, but it is impossible. Sarah returns quickly carrying a first-aid box.
'Please can I have the scissors.'
She hands them to me and I cut my trousers to inspect my badly swollen leg, it looks nasty. I elevate it using cushions.
'I will help you to bandage your leg, you are lucky it is not broken, but first let's apply ice to take down the swelling. I will show you round the house when you have rested your leg.'

***

I turn to Sarah. 'We can't do this alone; I asked Roger for help, but he is dead.'
'What is happening here is happening worldwide. I stopped watching the news because it is so sad to watch. There must be people who want a change as much as we do. Follow me!'
We enter one of the rooms, used as a study.
'I thought you didn't use this place that often.'
'I do sometimes. I told my dad and his staff that I was travelling abroad. I come here to relax and get away from everyone, that's why my laptop is here. I also love to code, hence the desktop computer and monitors, but I ran my family business and couldn't pay much attention to it. The time has come to put those skills to good use. First, we need help; I'm sure there are people out there, and I'll find them.'

'Fantastic; but how are we going to survive? We don't have any money.'

'I know. How do you think I survived after discovering they had taken all my father's millions? Nobody knows about my inheritance from my grandfather.'

'You can't touch that money; they will find us if you do. They emptied my account.'

'I keep some cash in this house; I didn't want to use an ATM after lying that I was out of the country. It's in a safe in my room; I should have about twenty-four thousand pounds. I know that's not much money in the present economy, but if we manage what we have and eat once a day, it should last for months. Hopefully, we will have found a way out of this by then.'

'Or we'll both be dead.' We look at each other in silence for a moment. 'I'll head out and see where we can buy food while you look for help online, but be very careful. They are monitoring everything, and you can't afford to slip up.'

I put on my cap, pull my hoodie over it and add sunglasses. I shaved my hair and moustache in the dingy motel just before going out to meet Sarah. I pray no one recognises me. I am a disgraced chef, my face is still all over the news and now a ransom is being offered by the Metropolitan Police for any information about me. I open the main door; my head bent as I head out to look for any supermarkets that may have supplies. I have been through hell, but a bandaged leg and pain when I walk will not stop me from doing what is necessary to survive.

Why are people still outside? I look at the time. We didn't get a chance to sleep, and it is 4.00 am. I'm standing in front of a 24-hour supermarket yet I can't get in because of the long queue. People are getting agitated. A woman screams, 'I've been waiting for over two hours to feed my children.'

I know chaos will follow if people are not allowed in. One of the men in the queue marches up to the security men standing outside the supermarket, and insists on being let in. They try to push him back when others join him. The crowd proves too much for the security men, and they force their way inside the supermarket. We push forward, grabbing what we can find. I have never before seen this kind of craziness, but my life made a turn for the worse when the big boss came into my life. I fill the only shopping basket I can find, with the little available food.

As I leave, I wipe way my sweat. That was crazy; I had to fight my way out of the supermarket with people trying to steal the little I had. I paid for what I bought but, once outside, people try to steal it from you. This is what this country has turned into. People are carrying knives to defend themselves, nowhere is safe.

I need to get off the streets. I'm exhausted. I've not mourned my mother; I haven't had a moment to myself to even think about her. I secure everything I've bought in my backpack and jog back to the house, hiding behind cars, constantly looking behind me. I don't know who might be following.

I open the door to the house. Everywhere is in darkness. Why are the lights not on? I lock the door behind me, trying to find my way in the dark. *Where is Sarah?* I bump my leg on a chair and cry out. *Shit!* My injured leg is throbbing; I think I might have finally broken it. I am powering through the pain. *This is not my house; I don't know the layout.*

I finally locate the study and gently open the door. Sarah is working at her computers; her screens are on, and they are full of computer programs, a language I don't understand.

'What's happening? Why is everywhere dark?'

'I've located some people online. You've been gone for hours. What happened?'

'The queues were ridiculously long; we had to force our way into the supermarket. And my leg slows me down. You must be exhausted by now; we haven't had the chance to sleep.'

'We will sleep, but I need help. I was careful when I found a coded SOS from the dark web; they were looking for someone in Europe. A lot has been done on their side, but they are experiencing delays. The work cannot be completed without everyone from each continent being involved. I'm excited. I'll tell you more about it tomorrow. You're right, we need to rest to be refreshed to tackle the task ahead of us.'

Chapter Thirty-eight: New York

Edward

We have to do the impossible, write the coded programs in conjunction with our allies from various parts of the world. I've never been in such high spirits and terrified simultaneously. The task of bringing down the most powerful technology in the world requires the best minds, working in unison. We seem capable, but first, we need the code to break into Brazilian City Bank. We have been testing it for the past twenty-four hours on our test site that we developed to replicate the bank programs, and tomorrow is the day of judgement.

Where is Martin? He has been sulking for days now since his family were taken away to God knows where. Now is not the time to fall apart.

Martin

I feel so useless. I am a police officer; I have not been helpful to Edward apart from going to the stores to buy groceries using the money he provides. I need to do something. I'm losing my mind; as the saying goes, an idle mind is a devil's workshop.

I go to find Edward. 'I need to do something,' I say to him. 'I can't just sit around doing nothing.'

'Oh! You are helping.'

'I do nothing; I sit around while you do all the work. Give me a task. Something to take my mind off my family.'

'OK! We should have discussed this weeks ago before I got distracted with the work in hand.

'So, from information gathered from Ana Santos in Rio de Janeiro, the big boss answers to someone higher than him. It would help if you could find out who that person is. I suspect Fred Demson.

'There is no trace of him on social media. I went online to look for information on him, but there is nothing apart from a page stating he is the owner of Overland Investments. He had a vision and invested billions of dollars in Gama Lab, which became the

"

most significant breakthrough in the neural sensor. He created the best technology the world has ever seen; Gamaplug. This man's company is in the double digits of trillion dollars. How sadistic can you be, having all that money and still wanting to destroy the world? All networks are wiped clean; absolutely nothing can be found on him apart from that page. How is that possible?'

'What can we do?' I ask.

'I don't know. In the world of the internet, there is nothing we can find. He has a family nobody knows anything about. He has the best team working to prevent people from talking about him. We need to go back to our old methods of investigation. We need to confirm whether he is the leader; he must know that his technology is being used for such evil intentions.

'If he is keeping his life a secret, the most powerful man in the world, all leaders consult with him. That should raise an eyebrow. What is he hiding? You need to find out where he lives; I suspect he is based in New York because his Overland Investments office is here.

'I was at a secret meeting they held near Central Park; the only person there in authority was someone they referred to as the "big boss". The strange thing was, I didn't recognise him; he is not a notable man, but he commands attention from the present president to the wealthiest people in North America. Let's think about it, the richest man in the world without question is Fred Demson, and he was not at that meeting. If they want the most powerful and successful, he should be number one on their list because they are using his technology to oppress the world.'

'So, we can only get to the leader through this "big boss"?'

I nod and bring out a sketchbook. 'Let me see if I can draw his face. I doubt we will find anything about him. I'll also go to Fred's head office and see what I can find about him. He's a ghost.'

'You need to be careful; you know they are looking for you. It is very dangerous, even with the disguise.'

I turn and look in the mirror. 'I don't recognise myself, man.' I grew a beard, I have gone blonde, and changed my eye colour from green to brown. 'I'll be careful; I'm glad I can be helpful with something.'

'Martin...' Edward reaches out and touches my arm. 'Don't go looking for your family. That is a suicide mission; I know you are frustrated but you can't be useful when you are dead.'

I walk out of the deserted underground station with my hoodie in place. Edward doesn't understand the guilt; I put my family in harm's way. As soon as I am able, I'll find out where Bobby is, and kill him. Fuck justice!

Andrew Hughes

I have just received a report from the Asia division; they need my help to find the aunty of a woman called Huan Li who lives in Hong Kong. I recognise her; she has won many awards for her genius mind and revolutionising telecommunications.

I turn to my men. 'I need you to find this woman's aunty. We need to send her to Hong Kong; where they will be waiting to receive her.'

I turn to the issue at hand. 'I am very disappointed in you, Bobby. If I knew you were an incompetent fool, I would have disposed of you long ago. I made you director of the FBI and instantly changed your life. I chose you over your partner, Martin. I have come to realise I made a big mistake. You told me Martin would be a big threat to us if we don't find him. Here we are; you are still looking for him. You arrested his family; he still didn't surface. Where is he?'

'I'll find him, sir. He will not give up. If he's alive, he will try to save his family. That is the kind of person he is; we will use his weakness against him.'

'I need you to understand; I made you, and I can destroy you. Don't waste my time. You have one week to find him, or I'll replace you. The safety of this organisation is of utmost importance; I'll not allow anyone to jeopardise it. Don't show your face here until you get the result. I want. Now, get out!'

Chapter Thirty-nine: Lagos

Lola

I'm roaming the streets of Lagos, and I can't even call my friends to help me. The shame and humiliation that the daughter of the former senate governor is homeless. Where can I go? I don't have any money; I'm starving. I slept on the side road, praying I was not killed or raped. What kind of life is this?

It's a jungle out there. Soldiers are everywhere. I keep my head down, careful not to draw any attention. I can see people being flogged by the soldiers. Lola! Look at your life; I was born into wealth, now I've nothing! I need to get to the only property I have, the burned-down house in Gbagada. Sleeping in a burnt house is better than sleeping on the road. I'm determined! I'll blend into the environment and hope I am not harassed in the next six hours.

I feel a sharp pain in my back. I turn around, screaming, tears pouring down my face, and face a soldier with a whip in his hand.

'Where are you going, young lady? A strict curfew is enforced today; no one roams the streets between 6.00 pm and 6.00 am. Look at the time? It's 4.00 am. What are you doing outside?'

Shaking in fear, the pain of the whip still on my back, I fall to my knees. 'Sir! I was robbed; I'm trying to get to my house on foot. I don't have money for transport. I've been walking for hours.'

'Where are you going?'

'Gbagada, sir!'

'I'm supposed to lock you up, but I can see your pain and frustration. I'll let you go, but you can't stay on the street. If the others find you, you will be locked up. Look for a place to stay out of sight for the next two hours.' He points in the direction of a bus station. 'Go and hide there.'

I run to the bus station. There are already people hiding inside, hoping the soldiers won't see them. I lie down on the floor and join them. I hope I can survive this day. It is inevitable I will die soon, either out on the streets or at the hands of the big boss.

***

I enter the condemned house. There are no doors or windows, and the walls are black. It smells of smoke and ruin. It doesn't matter, it has a fence around it, and I will be safe, temporarily.

I'm mentally exhausted. I sit on the dirty floor when the events of the past couple of days hit me, and I start to cry uncontrollably. My father is dead; I was my father's daughter. He loved me without measure, but I am the reason he was killed. I don't know whether my mother will want to see me; I don't know the kind of false evidence they have shown her. I close my eyes; a brief nap is all I need. Then I need to find a way out of my predicament.

Am I dreaming? Someone taps me. I lift my head from the destroyed desk I used as a pillow and rub my eyes. No! It can't be! I rush towards Segun hitting his chest. 'You've ruined my life with your morality. I should have stayed away from you. Then maybe my father would be alive today.'

'Calm down! Your father's death was inevitable. There was nothing you could have done to change his fate. Your father had a solid moral compass. Everything he believed in was contradictory to the principle of Green Gama. Why do you think it was easy for them to kill him?'

'I hate you! I should hand you over to them.'

'They are watching you, so decide now. You have ten minutes before I disappear. Are you coming with me or would you prefer to take your chances with them?'

'How can we escape without them noticing?'

'I came over the back fence. Follow me!'

When we reach the fence, he lifts me so I can try to pull myself over. 'You need to stretch yourself; we don't have much time,' he says urgently.

I finally climb to the top and jump down. I wait for him then run behind him, getting into his car. He gives me a cap. 'Wear this,' he instructs.

'Where are we going?'

'You don't need to worry about that; just know you are safe. Keep your head down. I know they told you to find me or they will harm your family. But, if you present me to them, they will kill me, you, your mother and your brothers.'

What do I do? I'm stuck between two evils. What I do know is that my family must not die. I have caused them so much pain. I wish I could turn back time; I wouldn't chase after those who killed Chioma; I would keep my head buried in the sand.

'I have contacted people from different parts of the world who face the same problems as us; I told you about them. We've found a way to bring down this organisation. The oppressors will be dealt with soon, and they will feel the pain they have brought upon us.'

'How long will this take? My family will be dead by then.'

'Do you even know whether they are still alive?'

We arrive at a bungalow in an isolated place. I can see land for miles around.

'Are we still in Lagos?' I ask.

'Get out of the car. You have a lot to learn. I need you to be determined. We need to take them apart piece by piece. They took everything away from you. You didn't kill your father, they did. Hold on to that!'

Lekan Glada

'Where the hell did she disappear to? I gave you simple instructions, and you couldn't deliver. Get rid of them all. Then find her. I know if you find her, you will find her accomplice.'

Chapter Forty: Kabul

Ahmed

I receive an encrypted text stating that I must leave the premises before sunrise or I'll be killed. I came here with the only clothes I was wearing. I need to go the same way. I mustn't raise suspicion.

I race out of the room, avoiding the cameras. We are not allowed out of the compound, but patrolmen leave the compound daily, going around the city to ensure everything is in order. The next shift will be leaving in twenty minutes. I need to get into the boot of the bulletproof car.

I look around to make sure it is safe. The patrolmen are already dressed and ready to leave. *How do I get into the boot without being seen?* Then I see one of the young men forced to work for Mohammed carrying water and food to the car. I follow him to the vehicle, making sure no one sees me. I hide beside the car until the boot opens. The man places the stuff inside, and I put a stick in the way to prevent the boot lid from fully closing. When I am sure that the man has gone, I climb into the boot. I only hope that they don't open the boot before they leave the premises. I hold on tight to the two pistols entrusted to me; they are loaded. This is the only way I can hope to survive this.

I don't know how long I am in the boot. I know from the movement of the vehicle that they have driven for some time after leaving the compound. I can hear them chattering about the number of people they have murdered and the pleasure they derived from seeing them suffer before they died.

I hold my pistols in both hands when the car stops. I know they are going to open the boot lid. The boot opens. I shoot the first man I see; and leap out of the boot. He falls and the others race out of the car.

I join the scattering and screeching crowd, running for cover. Bullets are flying everywhere. Breathing heavily, I drop down behind one of the fallen bodies on the ground, using him as cover, and shoot the man hiding on the left side of the vehicle, while trying to avoid gunshots from the other two men.

The commotion quietens down, and I know I have seconds

before they come for me. I crawl along the ground, inching forward, keeping my head down, and look under the car. I can see their legs and, without stopping to think, I shoot at them both. They drop on the spot and start screaming, not so brave now. I run to where they are lying, begging for their lives, and shoot them point-blank in the head. I then pick up their ammunition, get into their car and drive off.

I need to get to Hussain and Yusuf, who have to explain what is going on. A text pings on my phone. It reads: 'Don't go to the base, or you'll die. Everything is not what it seems.' I press the link attached to the text that shows the location of a house, located at the top of the mountain, and head in that direction.

I drive for a few miles and abandon the car. I'll have to walk the rest of the way. They will trace the vehicle here. There is a huge bag containing semi-automatic guns and I place the other firearms inside. This will be a long journey carrying such a heavy load, not forgetting food and water.

I quickly become exhausted, dragging the ammunition bag on the floor, the food and drink on my back. There is no road; I can't even find a path. It is a rocky slope with no firm ground. *How do I navigate this with everything I am carrying?*

I drop my load to test every path. I need to get to my destination. It is still dark, and I have to get to the house before morning. After accessing the route ahead, I go back to retrieve my load.

Eventually, I arrive at the mud-brown house. I watch the house for a few minutes. I need to be careful, as the instructions came from an unknown destination. I don't know who to trust anymore.

I knock on the door, and Jabar open it. 'Come inside quickly,' he says.

I enter, dragging my loaded bags with me. I peep outside to ensure I wasn't followed before locking the door. 'What are you doing here?' I say. 'This is one of the worst parts of the city. I've been looking for you for days.'

'Sit down! We have a lot to talk about,' Jabar replies.

There are two couches; I sit on one of them.

'I know you have many questions, but I'm delighted you decided to come here instead of going to the base.'

'What is going on?'

'Hussain and Yusuf are not who you think they are. They are

the worst human beings you can think of. They are wolves in sheep's clothing. You think Mohammed is evil; they are a million times worse. Unfortunately, they promise to care for your family while sending you on false assignments.

'Hussain tried to kill me. My job was to assist you when you arrived on the premises. After tampering with the surveillance camera, I received a text to return to the base, stating that I needed to make Mohammed paranoid by disappearing. I discovered it was an assassination plan. I was falling into a trap. I'll not get into the full details now, but I managed to escape. Now, I can't locate my family. They are no longer in that house, and I don't know where they are.'

'Why should I believe you?'

He hands me a phone. 'Look through the texts I received from Yusuf and their plans for you.'

I scroll through the texts. 'What does Hussain hope to gain by doing all this? He is not with Mohammed or us. Whose side is he on?'

He shrugs. 'I know he is the one funding Mohammed. We need to find a way to stop him. He is too rich, but I have no idea who his benefactors are.

'During my time there, I was able to steal some of the systems from the base. I worked for Hussain for five years before being sent to investigate Mohammed. I was always fascinated with the advanced technology used in the base. I set up mine using their IP signalling. I have been in this pit for days looking for a way out of our predicament. I finally got a response today; I found help from other continents. Even though our situation is unique, they believe Gama's organisation still controls us. They will assist in any way to help bring down Hussain Atta.'

Chapter Forty-one: Sydney

Tom

Finally, we are complete; Sarah Philips has joined the group from London and will oversee the European hub, after screening. We cannot be too careful; the organisation we are against is powerful. We have spent weeks developing a different security level because Gama monitors every system. The great heist is happening this afternoon, which will be 1.00 am in Brazil. This will determine the next step of action. We have worked tirelessly to prevent hiccups, but you never know what might happen on a live network.

This organisation's headquarters will reside in New York because Gama Lab's headquarters is also in New York. We have called the system that will bring down Gamaplug POWERA, and each letter corresponds to the six continents in which Gama resides.

P-generation for the European hub (PG)
O-generation for the North American hub (OG)
W-generation for the African hub (WG)
E-generation for the Australian hub (EG)
R-generation for the South American hub (RG)
A-generation for the Asian hub (AG)

Everyone is responsible for their hubs. The components needed to develop one POWERA will cost roughly fifty million dollars.

The tricky part is that fibre 4.0 was installed underground across the globe, which allowed Gamaplug to have the fastest transmission. That transmission needs to be stopped. The only way it can be done is if we find the source point, which we believe is in New York.

We have all synced our time for the operation at 1.00 am Brazilian time. I am responsible for level one and two security bridge. We have to break into eight security levels without hiccups. All this needs to be done in eight minutes. I start to panic. I don't think it can be done.

Henry

I have to be at the bungalow in Guildford for 2.00 pm, without fail. Tom has been working non-stop, writing code, testing, and rewriting. I have seen the final program code. I don't understand it, but it is supposed to penetrate a network and steal a large sum of money. Everything needs to be done fast, before the situation becomes even worse.

If I hadn't promised Tom to play along with this charade, I would tell my mother where to stuff it and move to my own house.

Yesterday, I was summoned by the big boss. She told me I had to plan for my future. I will be the new prime minister by next year. I need a suitable wife, whom the world must see with me, and they have chosen Cynthia Coleman.

I would rather die than marry that idiot, Cynthia. I could see her smiling when she was brought forward and introduced to the other members, telling everyone she was expecting a baby with me. I don't doubt that she could be pregnant. She is crazy enough to have raped me or stolen my sperm. My mother stood beside me proudly. She congratulated me on my great success.

But I can't be thinking about this now. It's too depressing; I need to help Tom ensure that everything they do is working smoothly. He took sick leave from his job as head of security for my mother by faking a doctor's letter saying he had stage 3 lung cancer and required urgent treatment. He was given indefinite leave, but knowing my mother he will be fired soon. She believes he will die quickly and doesn't want that responsibility.

I tidy up my desk and instruct Rob that I would be out for a while. First, I need to visit my son.

***

I rush into the bungalow. I see Tom busy at work and look at the time. It is 2:15 pm.

'Sorry I am late.'

'Shush! I need to concentrate. This operation will start soon; the code is ready, and we are counting down the clock. Today will be the start of POWERA. The work has just begun if we can successfully steal this money. Are you ready, Henry?'

I nod miserably. 'I dread going home. I'm supposed to get married to the most horrible person God has ever created in two weeks. She is worse than Satan itself. I cannot marry her; I'll end up in jail because I will be forced to kill her.'

'What you are doing is for the greater good,' says Tom. 'You know every member of White Gama that handles the Australian continent. Hopefully, we will be able to expose them all, but you have to befriend them and play their games. That's the only way we can beat them.

'Now, let's concentrate. It's time!'

Chapter Forty-two: Rio de Janeiro

Ana

It is precisely 1.00 am. This is the maintenance period between 1.00 and 6.00 am. I wipe away the sweat on my forehead with my sleeve. I manipulate the several surveillance cameras installed in my place, it shows I am sleeping. They think they are wise, but I am wiser.

This must go well, or we are all finished. The program is uploaded. The system should be brought down without setting off any alarm; this gives us access to all bank accounts. We are watching the system, looking at the time anxiously, it should be down in 5,4,3,2,1...

'Dear God, what is wrong? Why is the system not down?' I shout to the others connected via video conference. We don't have time.

'I'm checking; I am responsible for security level 8,' replies Edward in New York. He is typing frantically to find out where the program got stuck.

'Level 8 is clear.'

Wait! What! How did I miss this? My heart is racing. There is another security level; this was added yesterday at 2.00 pm by the bank. We need to decode it now! This is our only chance; this is the first time Purple Gama has accumulated 3.4 billion dollars in a month.

'We have six minutes and counting,' shouts Sarah in London.

The team is looking at security level 9. I hope it doesn't need voice activation.

'I got it!' yells Segun in Lagos. 'I am adding the required program now. They have set a secret alert that completely shuts down the system internally and prevents you from accessing the network.'

'We have five minutes,' says Sarah.

'Stop telling us; we all have our timers set,' responds Huan in Hong Kong.

We watch anxiously as Segun presses 'enter'. Dear God, please, this must work; we don't have time to test it. Wow! We all shout as the network opens up. We have four minutes to grab the money.

I enter the Purple Gama account. They are responsible for the Asian hub. We are not greedy. We are just taking a percentage of the three-and-a-half billion dollars they have accumulated. One-and-a-half billion to be precise.

'Huan, are you ready? I will be granting you access now to move the money to the secret bank in Barbados.'

'I'm ready,' Huan replies.

The money is moved, but the account is still showing 3.5 billion dollars. If checked, they will not notice until they try to access the total cash. We have two minutes now! We need to put the system back the way it was, or the alarm will go off.

'Is the money in Barbados?'

'It's transferring!'

'We're almost out of time,' says Tom urgently. 'The transfer needs to be complete before we can put the system back up.'

'Done!' Huan screams.

We have sixty seconds and counting with everyone working frantically as a team to bring the system up before the alarm goes off. Just in time, every layer is put in place.

'Thank God! Thank you!' I repeat over and over.

'Edward, you will be given primary access to the account because we believe everything we are going through stems from New York,' Huan says.

Edward addresses the team. 'Everyone who needs to rest should do that since we are all in different time zones. The shit is about to hit the fan tomorrow, so we need to be ready. The money is hot right now; we will start distributing funds in a day or two and let the dust settle. They will look for it. We must begin developing POWERA and acquiring components without raising alarm. We will set up another meeting shortly, taking into account the time zones. Thank you, everyone, for a job well done. Good night.'

I need to rest; I have to be in the office at precisely 7.00 am. I have been getting to the office at that time for weeks now. That mustn't change. Today will be an interesting day; for the first time, the big boss will be sweating. I laughed hard. He will feel what I've been feeling for months now – despair!

Adriano Cardoso

'What the hell happened?'

How can one-and-a-half billion dollars disappear into thin air? And the bank not even notice until this afternoon when we came to do the monthly money distribution.

'Someone must pay for this!' I shout. 'Heads will roll! Get me the managing director of the bank. He is the only one who can grant access to such a large sum of money.'

How can someone break into a bank and steal that kind of money without being caught? We change the password and codes weekly. What the hell is going on?

'I want to see the cyber security personnel for the bank.'

I have to resolve this problem today. I just spoke to the master. He has summoned an emergency meeting, and I have to fly out tonight. If I don't resolve this mishap before I go, I am finished.

The bank is on lockdown. Every person must be checked and double-checked. I want my team to go into the system to determine how this was done. They must have left a trace; I want whoever is responsible found. This cannot be allowed to happen. It is a shame on the organisation.

The managing director is brought before me, shaking uncontrollably.

'How can I lose one-and-a-half billion dollars from your bank? You will have to find a way to pay it back, but I know you don't have that kind of money, and the bank will be forced to file for bankruptcy. If you don't want me to destroy your whole family, I am not just talking about your wife and kids; I'm talking about anyone related to you, either by marriage or blood, get my money back!'

'Sir, they hacked into the system and stole the money.'

'Then find those who dared to steal my money. I need answers and fast.' I look at my wristwatch. I have five hours before I board my private jet to take me to JFK airport in New York City. I don't know the last time I experienced such anxiety and fear.

One of my men tells me that the cyber security team did not know the system had been hacked.

'They are useless! Kill them all, not just them; their families as well. This should be a lesson to everyone that I take no prisoners.'

Now, to face the big boss!

Chapter Forty-three: Hong Kong

Huan

After working non-stop to ensure the heist was successful, I can finally rest for a couple hours. The money will be broken down based on our various tasks.

I look at the draft picture of POWERA sent by Edward; what we want is to stop the processor from communicating with the neural sensor. This processor will intercept the N24 postnanometer developed by Gama Lab. It will be the fastest ever produced, and the interference will be strong enough to disrupt communication, but it needs to be strategically placed for this to be achieved. Can this be done by just six people? How do we source the components without alerting anyone from their organisation? These are not components you can buy off the web; they need to be developed and tested.

We have just been informed by Ana in Rio de Janeiro that her boss has called an emergency meeting. Every member of the organisation's homes is being searched and laptops confiscated. They believe this was an internal job. She has informed us that she will not use her computer until everything has calmed down.

They are checking every bank in the world to find that money; it is an enormous amount to disappear suddenly. The money will never be found. I assured everyone that even the bank didn't know they had the money. But danger is lurking and ever present. The big boss is screaming that heads must roll and the culprits must be found. No one is safe, and we must keep our heads down. Ana has warned us that all the organisations are working together.

We are working frantically to wipe any trace we might have on the web. We have created a separate communicating channel. We have had to shut down twice now; they almost broke into the channel. Dear God, who are these people? The encryption they are developing will prevent us from accessing their network, making our job more difficult. They monitor all activities on the web; limited access is presently being given to people.

I'm exhausted, and I need to rest. It's been a long week. We will regroup when we know the outcome of this investigation. No one is safe; our enemies have the best people working for them, and they have access to unlimited technology.

Ping Wu

How can one-and-a-half billion dollars be stolen without anyone knowing? The investigation is now being done as a unit to find the culprits that dared to steal from the organisation. All the best people from around the world have been working round the clock to find out what happened.

We know that a group hacked the system because no single person could decode 9th-level security. The master insists we find these people because the only reason someone would be bold enough to steal that much money from the organisation is to bring it down. We need to stop them before they stop us.

They made one cardinal mistake. We found a trace in the code used for 9th-level security; someone in Lagos hacked into the system to prevent it from shutting down. We just need to find the IP address and that will lead us to the others. The big boss in Lagos is working on getting information. He has a list of suspects and is sending out his men to check their various accounts. There are not many people with enough skills to pull this off. His number one suspect has been missing for a long time; his name is Segun. His face is pasted all over the media, and a huge ransom of ten million naira will be paid to whoever discovers his whereabouts. The big boss has instructed that the whole of Segun's family by blood be wiped out.

The organisation is now on high alert. This incident is forcing us to reassess and reprioritise. Every member's account has been checked, all calls and texts inspected, and everyone is a suspect. I'm confident we will find them all, but this incident has given the organisation a bad name, and more people will feel bold enough to come after us.

An emergency meeting has been called, and I'm on my private jet on the way to New York, feeling unusually nervous about what is about to happen.

Huan

I wake to discover that they have identified Segun as being one of those behind the heist. I understand this is because the final level security program was written at the last minute. We had a limited time; mistakes were bound to be made. His face is now plastered all over global media. The president of Nigeria has called him a terrorist and is asking for international assistance.

We can't afford anyone to be distracted; developing a system that can bring down Gamaplug needs everyone's full attention.

Chapter Forty-four: Emergency Meeting

Fred Demson

It was a sight to behold as several of the most expensive private aeroplanes ever produced, Boeing 767s, landed at John F. Kennedy International Airport, seven in total. The seven deputies alighted from their private jets with their security teams, and each had a gold Bentley Continental GT waiting to pick them up and take them to headquarters. It would have been a joyous journey, but they all knew they were here to be crucified by their master.

I am sitting on my antique gold chair, my throne, seething with anger. How can this happen on my watch? We have all the technologies known to man at our disposal, yet twenty-four hours have passed, and they haven't been able to catch the culprit they identified. We have to change our strategies; we have become complacent.

I look around at the assembled deputies.

'I never believed a day like this would come. I chose you all for a reason, and now I'm beginning to regret my decision. I gave you power and wealth. You had one assignment; to help me take over the world, and here we are, some miscreants have robbed us, we have the best team in the world yet you can't find them.

'All I have been hearing are excuses. If one hub fails, you all fail. Why would a group steal such a large sum of money? The person you identified vowed to bring down this organisation which means he is working with others like him. How can someone living in the African hub know about the dealings in the South American hub? This means his accomplice lives in Rio de Janeiro. Who knows where the others reside?

'I am disappointed in you, Adriano Cardoso. I picked you from the gutter and made you head of Purple Gama. You had the whole of South America in the palm of your hands, and your revenue was impressive. I need you to explain to me how this could happen?'

He hesitates to answer, and I can see the cold fear spiralling through him. 'Sir, I don't know how it happened. It is the most secure bank in the world.'

'This is all the more reason we must bring them down now!'

'Lekan Gbada, you have responsibility for the African hub. How can that man abscond for months? You said he must be him because you recognise his expertise, yet you look at me like a moron and do nothing.

'So, we are changing our strategy. What we discuss here stays within these four walls. We have a leak somewhere; they know our plans and use them against us. We need to use an element of surprise in order to catch them.

'Starting from today, all resources will work together. This simply means we generate money the usual way, but our teams will work together to catch these people. I need you to find my money and those responsible in seven days. Use everything at your disposal from Gamaplug, satellite, telecommunications, anything to find them. Their lives must be miserable for daring to come against me. It is a vast amount of money to disappear into thin air. I'm surprised I haven't received any information on the money's whereabouts. Does it mean I have incompetent fools surrounding me? How can you have let these people outsmart you?

'I want you all to listen to me. I chose you all; I can dispose of you too! I think you have become too comfortable in your world and have forgotten your responsibilities. Millions of people can do what you do if given the same opportunities I gave you all. The next time such a thing happens, you are all dead!'

Just look at them. They live in the most expensive houses, drive the most expensive cars, and fly everywhere in private jets that cost multimillion dollars. They have forgotten they had nothing when I found them.

'Now, I want you all out of here and back to your respective countries. I don't care if you have to turn the world upside down. Work together! Find them! They are hiding somewhere, working together, plotting against us, and we must prevent this from happening again. Can you imagine what our opponents are thinking now? They will become bolder and believe they can challenge us. After all, a group of people just managed to humiliate us.

'I called this meeting not to wine and dine you but to reprimand you. Go back home and re-strategise. The definition of insanity is doing the same thing and expecting a different result. This is the last warning; I have worked too hard and invested heavily in each of you for you all to fail me. Eliminate as many people as necessary but get me results. Now get out of here!'

I watch them leave my presence, looking sullen. I call my PA to bring me a certain file and he rushes back with it almost immediately. I open the file and bring out the pictures of seven people I have chosen to replace the seven deputies if they fail me. They have a similar background and hunger for success. This is what pushes them, and they are willing to sacrifice their whole family to achieve their goals. The world is mine; no one will take it away from me!

Chapter Forty-five: London

Jude

Sarah turns away from her computer and monitors. She has been in front of her laptop and desktop computer for days. 'I see that your leg has improved tremendously.'

'Yes.' I shake my leg vigorously. 'I still experience slight pain but it is much better, I'm sure it will have healed completely in a couple of days.'

She removes her glasses and places them on her desk. A lot has happened, both good and bad and she is about to update me.

'Two days ago, we were able to steal one-and-a-half billion dollars from Brazilian City Bank, which I told you about. That is fantastic news; the plan is to develop technology so advanced that it will ultimately bring down Gamaplug. We will need to source the respective components, and each member will be responsible for developing part of the technology. Edward in New York has taken the reigns on this. Putting our heads together, we have sketched out what this advanced technology should be. It will comprise a postnanometer, fibre optic, and advanced programs. We have decided to call it POWERA.'

She shows me a sketch and I stare at her open-mouthed. 'Jesus! How can this be done without anyone noticing? Can a team of six or seven people develop all that from what I'm looking at?'

Sarah smiles. 'It can be done; I'll need your help where necessary. The problem we are facing now is that this organisation has stepped up their game after the robbery. Every transaction over twenty thousand dollars from any bank is currently being monitored and traced; an alert is sent to the head of the hub. This is a major setback; sourcing and developing these components costs millions.

'All systems are being closely monitored. They check people's phone calls, text messages, computers, emails, and local mail. Our security layers are encrypted to prevent illegal access, but a couple of hours ago, they penetrated the sixth layer before the system locked, preventing them from moving further. This is our online forum; if they discover it, we are finished.'

'This is dangerous, Sarah; I warned you before, we are dealing with extremely powerful and ruthless people.'

She smiles at me again, but I can see the fear in her tired eyes.

Sarah

Ana in Rio de Janeiro has been offline for hours now. She could only send us a warning about the online checks because she is being closely monitored. As a result of the robbery, every home in Rio is being combed. Luckily, a heavily paid handyman has helped Ana to build a secret compartment in the closet where she displays her shoes, to hide her equipment. It was not easy, Ana made sure the money transfer to the handyman's account was made to look like it was sent from his boss's account. This is a warning to him that if he decides to spill the information he will be arrested for stealing ten thousand Brazilian real.

Somehow, she passed the initial camera sweep, but it was a narrow escape. We must move forward slowly but surely; that is the only way to achieve anything. We need to buy these components little by little with the money we can access at that time.

James Cooper

I have been in a meeting with the other hub bosses; we are all afraid. We need to find Segun. Hopefully, he will lead us to the others. I have sent some of my men to Lagos to assist in finding that annoying individual. The whole of Nigeria will be turned upside down. Every home will be searched.

It is difficult because he is not using any technology. If we are wrong, then he knows how to cover his tracks. We have to do this the old-fashioned way, go from home to home, but we don't have time; the clock is ticking. We are distributing money on the streets; the good thing is that people are desperate. His face is placed on flyers, billboards, and media. Anyone that finds him will receive a ten million naira reward.

Jude

Sarah wipes away a tear.

'What's wrong?' I ask.

'They are looking for Segun,' she says. 'The one who ensured the success of the heist. His face is everywhere; and they are taking fingerprints of occupants when they knock on their door.'

'Jesus! Is there anything we can do?'

'We have to create false fingerprints for him. He is now bald and has shaved his moustache and beard. But there is nowhere for him to go; they will find him, so he will have to hide in plain sight.

'We are creating a new identity for him and his partner in crime; a lady called Lola. She will pretend to be pregnant and wear a fake pregnancy bump. I hope it works, and they don't look too closely. They need to be the best actors anyone has ever seen for this work, because if they are caught, we are finished.'

Chapter Forty-six: New York

Martin

It feels wonderful to see New York again; I have been underground for too long. I look around in awe, it is not the same New York I used to know and love. People everywhere have a dejected look on their faces, and the homeless line the streets. I find it difficult to walk on the sidewalk. I heard on the news that the country's economy is at its lowest since the Great Depression.

A male pedestrian bumps my shoulder as I walk. 'Watch where you are going, man,' he yells at me angrily.

'Sorry!' That's all I can say. He stumbles away, murmuring to himself.

What is happening? I could see frustration everywhere. The rich are getting richer, and there is no more middle class; you are either rich or poor.

Concentrate, Martin, on why you left the safety of the underground in the first place.

A lot has happened in the past couple of days that delayed my venturing outside. Edward wanted to ensure that it was safe and that the heist, two days ago, was successful. Now more than ever, an immense responsibility has been placed on us.

We need to find Gama Lab's headquarters and steal their system configuration. We initially thought I needed to learn more about Fred Demson, but presently we need to find data junctions of Gamaplug in each continent. I have been walking the streets now for an hour. How can a massive company like Gama Lab not have an address? They have small technical stores everywhere if you have problems or want to purchase their products.

I couldn't ask people, but based on our findings, we narrowed our search to Park Avenue. I've looked at every building. The company's logo is not displayed on the building. So, what are they hiding?

I am watching the comings and goings of the two massive buildings I suspect are owned by Fred Demson. I watch as a man comes out laughing with some of his colleagues. I take some pictures, making sure not to be seen. I need to prove that my suspicion is correct. The man wanders off towards the underground to catch a train, and I follow him closely. I need to steal his wallet; I am sure that is where I'll find his company ID.

I move closer to him, as he waits for the next train to arrive. I slip my hand into his pocket as I bump into him. 'Sorry!' I utter. He straightens up, and I place his wallet into my pocket without anyone noticing.

It's time to head back to my prison. I am tempted to go and find my former partner, whom I have named 'Bastard Bobby'. But Edward has convinced me that the new FBI director would reside in Washington DC and it would be much too dangerous to attempt to travel there. We will bring the organisation down first, then I'll find my family. Bastard Bobby is not stupid enough to kill them. He wants me, not them.

I enter my prison; I know I should be grateful to have somewhere to hide and rest my head when millions are homeless on the streets. The problem is that when you have stayed underground for too long, you begin to long for freedom.

I remove the wallet from my pocket, and call out to Edward. 'I stole a wallet, and I hope I'm right...' I begin to say, entering the computer room.

He is engrossed with whatever he is doing with the computer. I take out all the cards in the in the wallet; bank cards, a gym membership card and a plain transparent card with nothing written on it.

'What's this?' I nudge Edward and show it to him.

He looks at the card intently, turning it around carefully. 'We need to use ultraviolet light, they have used invisible ink. It is not visible to the naked eye.' He opens one of his drawers and pulls out an ultraviolet light which he moves over the card. We can see the man's name is Jacob White, and he works at Gama Lab as a technical specialist.

'This is good, Martin. Now you know the address of Gama Lab, we need to find a way to get into one of the most secure places in the world.'

'I took pictures,' I say, removing the SD card and put it into one of the laptops. 'I watched the buildings; they had nine security men from what I could see from the outside. Their workers don't display their ID; they enter and swipe the ID that allows them into the building. Why such secrecy? What are they hiding?'

'We need to be very careful. This organisation has upped their game, making things more difficult by the day, and we need to start building POWERA if we are to achieve our target within a few months.

'They are trying to monitor and trace the web. We are protected, but we can't be too careful. They almost penetrated our encryption. We must find a way to hack into their system and find their configuration. The only way we can gain access is in their company system. They have a secret hiring system, a long and vigorous method. The employees are scrutinised carefully; believe me, that card you stole will have been deactivated; we can't use it,' Edward explains.

'There is a meeting scheduled with the other members from around the world. We need to help Segun. We are creating fake fingerprints to help prevent him from being caught. I'm keeping my fingers crossed that these people don't use biometrics, but if they do, we hack that system. We can make two sets of fingerprints, one for him and the other for Lola. Once their fingerprints are scanned, this false information will show up.' He points to the screen.

'We have given them different identities; they have new names, he is an electrician, and she is a hairstylist. We want jobs that will not raise suspicion that they live in a rundown place and must look the part.'

I turn to face Edward. 'You know I have not given up on my family, but I trust you when you say they are safe for now. The guilt kills me every day, not knowing whether they are dead or alive. What is the point of living when the most important people in your life have been taken away?

'Whatever we are doing, we need to do it fast; I'm losing my patience daily, and I'll be forced to surrender if things don't change soon. I know that won't guarantee their safety, but it will give me peace of mind that I did what was right for them.'

Chapter Forty-seven: Lagos

Segun

My life is in danger; how do I prevent this impending doom. It's been announced in the news that no one in the country should leave their house. Travelling within and outside the country has been banned for the foreseeable future.

Lola is shaking uncontrollably in the corner of the room.

'Control yourself,' I hiss at her. 'They will be looking for any sign of fear; we must show confidence.'

'Do you think they will not recognise me? My face is everywhere, even with the braids and pretend pregnancy?'

'We have rehearsed this. You will tie a scarf on your head and darken your complexion; I bought everything we need. They will be here today, and we must be ready. You will have to change the way you speak; you are supposed to be an uneducated hairstylist; you need to speak poor English or in our native language, Yoruba. We need to convince them; we are both dead if they should find us.'

Lola

We live in a one-bedroom house surrounded by land. It is shabbily decorated; all the electronic gadgets from laptops and monitors are hidden in a fake wall we had to build and paint quickly. The living room contains an old, worn sofa and the most ancient television I have ever seen; it's like a flashback to the 1980s.

It was not easy hiding the gadgets without being seen, but we got lucky. We live in one of the worst areas in the state where most of the wiring and insulations are outdated. We often experience short-circuiting which leads to blackout. Most security camera have stopped working. We watched as people frantically tried to fix the problem.

I stare at my reflection in the mirror. I am unrecognisable. I have painted my face and body with body paint to make myself look darker and I am wearing the baby bump, silicone prosthetic tummy. I look like I'm eight months pregnant.

I start practising poor English. It's difficult as I speak English very well! Dear God, spare me from death! I've managed to escape many times before, please reunite me with my family.

I turn around and see Segun staring at me. 'You're fidgeting! You also need to practise your walk. You are pregnant, and your pregnancy weight will slow you down.' He walks up to me and places a small device on my belly, telling me to pull down my skirt slightly.

'What is that?' I ask.

'It gives the fake baby a heartbeat and movement if they check. I hope they don't tell you to strip to verify your pregnancy. The team was able to falsify your medical records, but we cannot be too careful.'

I reach out and touch his arm. 'Segun, I'm afraid. The videos we have watched show just how vicious these people are. They enter people's homes, and interrogate and torture them for hours if they think they are at all suspicious. They even burn down their houses.'

'We will be fine,' he says reassuringly. 'We have changed the way we look, so we are unrecognisable. I'm wearing a dirty shirt and trousers that I intentionally rubbed with animal dung, and I reek. I'm surprised you are not holding your nose and vomiting at the same time.'

I laugh in spite of my anxiety. 'I'm so nervous; my sense of smell has shut down. Look at where we are living? We are not exactly in a five-star hotel; the whole place smells.'

Someone bangs hard on the door. 'It's time,' Segun whispers as he rushes to open it.

I rub my hands together quickly. *Lola, try to breathe. You can do this!*

It's like a stampede. About thirty people enter our little living room. It is so jam-packed we are ordered outside. I move slowly; I couldn't move fast even if I tried; this fake pregnancy bump is heavy.

The men set about searching the house; it is small but they are thorough. Segun has made sure the place looks dirty. He has refused to flush away a stool for hours and, when he finally did, the house still smelled. I can hear the men whispering and looking at us with disgust. That is the point we don't want them to be too comfortable.

They take our fingerprints. Thank God for our incredible team for helping us create fake identities to match our fake fingerprints.

We are asked a round of questions, told not to think and to answer immediately. I'm glad that Segun insisted I practise. I have been doing that for hours.

'Where do you work?' one man asks me.

'I walk into my shop in the Ojuelegba area.' My English is deliberately bad. I demonstrate with my fingers.

I hear the man whisper, 'This will be a long day; I'm interviewing an imbecile.'

The men who have been searching the house come out. I can see them taking off their masks and trying to breathe fresh air.

The superior walks up to Segun and punches him in the face. 'You and your wife are the dirtiest humans I've ever seen.' He looks at me in disgust. 'Woman, I would have hit you, but I can see you are pregnant. Who lives in such filth?'

I have disposed of all our old pictures. I remember how I looked before, with all my glamorous things; very different to now.

They have searched the whole house and found nothing. Still they don't leave. We have been standing up for hours, and the weight of the prosthetic tummy is agony. I stumble backwards, and Segun rushes to help me. 'Are you OK?' he asks. 'Is it the baby?'

'I go sit down, leg kill me, and I go pee,' I say in broken English.

'You will keep standing, and you can pee on yourself,' the man in charge says. 'We are not done with you yet. We are searching the whole area to ensure you are not hiding something, but looking at you, I think we will be unlikely to find anything. I still need to do my job.'

Segun squeezes my hand to encourage me; it is going to be a difficult time while we wait.

Chapter Forty-eight: Kabul

Yusuf

I can still feel the sting on my cheek.

'How could you fail me? It was a simple assassination plan, and you weren't up to the job. How hard is it to kill Jabar? Now he is nowhere to be found.'

I rub my cheek, and bow my head in front of Hussain. 'I don't know what happened; he arrived at the base as instructed but wouldn't enter. He kept asking for his family. He was acting strangely. He pulled out his gun and shot two of my men before running away. We pursued him straightaway, but he managed to escape.'

'Yusuf, you're one of the few in my inner circle, you have never failed me before, but this incident cannot go unpunished.'

'Please, sir! I'll find him.'

'How can you possibly "find him"? Do you have any idea where he is hiding? He knows everything and that puts us in danger.'

'There is nothing he can do, sir; we own everything from the media houses to the banks. He doesn't have any money, he doesn't have any friends, where can he go?'

'Stop talking! Or I will be forced to kill you myself. Apparently, Ahmed has also disappeared. He killed some of Mohammed's men in order to escape. How did he know not to come to the base?

'I've just got back from a meeting with the master; things are not running smoothly the way they should. We will lose everything if we don't fix the problems around us. Everything has been placed in our hands. We control half of Asia.

'You are no longer my right-hand man. This new development has been passed on to all my men to humiliate you further. You will now work with the security men until you locate Jabar and Ahmed. Do not take any chances; search everywhere. I don't think they have left Afghanistan, but we can't be sure. If you don't find them in the next forty-eight hours, your pain will be more acute. Now get out of my sight!'

Ahmed

I stretch; my back is stiff and painful me as a result of sleeping on a mud floor. There is no proper sewer system and you have to do your business outside. I can't complain, I'm alive, but where is my family?

Jabar has explained that Hussain has help from the outside; they are a part of the same organisation. Our goal is to bring down Hussain; as he controls everything, and Mohammed answers to him. I have to find a way of bringing Mohammed over to our side. That is the only way we can hope to succeed against Hussain.

But how do we get Mohammed's ear? He is looking for us everywhere; I don't know how long we will be safe in the mountains.

Jabar

'Hussain is no longer comfortable with Mohammed; he is becoming more rebellious. He wants Mohammed to be made to look bad, and for his people to love him instead. Hussain wants them to think he will be the one to save them, not knowing he is behind their ruin.

'He will kill Mohammed. He wanted you to do the job, now he will send someone else to eliminate him. Half of the men in Mohammed's compound work for Hussain. A note was left on his bed this morning. Do you remember Ghani, the head of security whom you fought the first time you entered the compound?' I say.

'Yes, he hates me,' says Ahmed. 'He never spoke to me after that day; how can he help?'

'He works for Hussain as well, he has been working there for a while now, and he is getting restless and wants to leave. Hopefully, Mohammed will read the note I arranged and believe he is the only one with enough resources to go against Hussain.

'We have found ourselves in a precarious situation. I have given the team from other parts of the world all the information on Hussain. They will identify the big bosses in their continents, but we all know they all answer to one man. Edward in New York believes the leader who is responsible for destroying the entire world is Fred Demson; since it is his technology that is being used. Fortunately, Gamaplug is not used much in Afghanistan; Mohammed, Hussain, and his inner circle are the only people using them. We still have to help them bring it down since it is used in other countries in Asia.

'How can we help Yusuf? We don't have the technology or infrastructure to do anything. You only have this laptop; Hussain has just disconnected your access to their data. We need Mohammed; we will get him on our side; better the devil you know than the devil you don't.'

Mohammed

I'm no longer safe in my haven; the number of men I eliminate on a daily basis is ridiculous. Very soon, I'll have no one guarding me. To make matters worse, the most dangerous man I have ever met, Ahmed Nazar, is working for Hussain and was sent to kill me. He managed to escape after attacking some of my men. When the patrol car did not come to the compound, I sent some men to look for them only to find their corpses on the ground and the car a few kilometres away. We have searched every home in the six-mile range where the vehicle was abandoned and came up empty.

I have a headache; I don't know who to trust anymore. My secret sponsor is acting erratically; in his last conversation, he said I'm slowly going insane and refused to transfer the millions of dollars he promised.

I enter my house; I'm the only one with three bedrooms on the upper floor and a living room and kitchen on the ground floor. I massage my head, I don't want any painkillers; I don't know who wants to kill me.

I take the stairs to my room. There is a note on my bed. No one is allowed into my room without my permission, even the cleaning lady who has been working for me for five years. I pick up the note and read it. What is this? The note drops from my hand and I look around my room in fear. Hussain Atta is the man helping me. He gave me this life I'm living? How is this possible? I think I'm going mad!

Chapter Forty-nine: Sydney

Henry

I am picking up Carl from Moreland Mental Hospital today; he is being discharged. He will have questions. Where is his mother? And why is his dad marrying another woman weeks after her disappearance. Even worse, that stupid organisation, White Gama, is insisting on a society wedding, televised for the world to see. So, the country's citizens can barely eat, the cost of food is astronomical, and the government is not supporting people with subsidies, and I will showcase an elaborate wedding, sparing no expense. I don't want to marry this woman, but the team is saying I have to play along. The only way to beat them at their game is if they don't suspect us.

I can see the happy smile on my son's face; and tears fall down my cheeks as he hugs me. I can't remember the last time my son hugged me. 'Thank you,' I mouth to the nurse who brought him to me.

'Where is my mum?' he asks, looking around, searching for her.

'Carl, you've just been discharged. Can we talk about this when we get to your grandmother's house?'

'I don't want to stay at Grandma's house; I don't think she likes me.'

'Don't say that; she loves you with all her heart.'

'Can't we just go home. I want to see Mum?'

'Of course, whatever you want. We will go home.'

Right now, I hate my mother, and all this pretence is too much for me.

Tom

The work is becoming more complex. I am tasked with building POWERA with the team while Henry stays close to the organisation and provides updates on what is going on. The next task is breaking into the most secure company in the world, Gama Lab, to steal the system blueprint. That place is like a fortress.

We are faced with the problem of the number of security men guarding the doors, not to mention the many cameras mounted at every point. The central system can only be accessed by face detection and voice recognition.

Martin in New York has been taking photos of everyone who goes in and out of the building. There is no information on the company and its employees. Developing an ultraviolet card similar to the one Martin stole, making it undetectable by the system when scanned, is difficult; every employee is scrutinised by the security team daily. We need to get this done in a week. That is the only way we can find out the configuration of their system.

The money needed to build POWERA is distributed in small amounts, so as not to raise suspicion. We are sourcing the components gradually. I am developing the 'E-generation' part of POWERA. A few components have arrived already, processors and post nanometers, the little I can buy at a time. The organisation monitors everything. I have had to open several PO boxes under different names, and I pick up my deliveries at night. I'm exhausted.

Tom, how did you find yourself in this position? You were just the head of security for Mrs Graham? I keep asking myself.

I walk downstairs to the isolated room where Mia, Henry's wife, is staying. I switch off the light and drop off her food. 'Please let me go! Please! I'm begging you!' she pleads.

I lock the door behind me without saying a word, switching the light back on as I leave. She doesn't understand that this is the only way to stay alive.

Henry

'Where is Mum?' Carl asks as soon as we arrive at my house. I haven't been here since Mia's disappearance. My housekeeper is doing a good job cleaning and keeping the fridge stocked in my absence.

I take a deep breath. 'Carl, your mum left me!'

'I don't understand; she can leave you, but how could she leave me?'

'I know she is coming back; she just needs some space. She loves you very much, and would never abandon you.'

'What's going on, Dad? Did you fight? Are you getting a

divorce?'

'Carl, you just got back. Too many questions! Let me prepare some food for you, and after eating and resting we can talk. I have taken time off work to be with you. I want you to know you are the most important thing to me.'

I can see the despair written over his face. 'Carl, look at me! Everything is going to be OK, I promise you.'

My son disappears into his room and I rush to the kitchen. I called my housekeeper from the car on our way back from the hospital to help prepare some meals.

My phone rings. I pick it up and sigh heavily. It's my mother.

'Hello, Mother.'

'I was worried. You should be back by now; we are waiting for you; your dad, Cynthia and myself.'

'We are not coming to the house; Carl doesn't want to stay there. He's just got out of hospital; I don't want him to see Cynthia.'

'She will be your wife in less than two weeks; he needs to get used to her. Why doesn't he want to see us?'

'Mum, I'm not having this conversation with you today; I need to care for my son. When the time is right, he can meet her. If you come here, do not bring her or I will be forced to make her leave.'

'Henry, you have to understand this is bigger than what you want or Carl wants. The most important is what White Gama wants.'

Chapter Fifty: Rio de Janeiro

Ana

The past couple of days, since the heist, the environment in the office has been hostile. The boss is angry, and the big boss is under pressure to find the culprits.

Unfortunately, I've not been able to communicate with the team in days. I'm being cautious; we are watched more closely than ever, and they have seized every laptop and computer we own. I know people have been in my apartment while I was at the office. Everything was placed back the way I left it, but I have a touch of obsessive compulsory disorder (OCD), and no one can arrange my things the way I would. My books were not angled in the correct position.

What they came to do, I do not know. I have checked for hidden cameras, mics and other listening devices. I bought one of the most advanced detectors to help sniff out semiconductor electronics, and I detected ten cameras and listening devices in my bedroom, bathroom, living room, and kitchen. Trying to check for these bugs took days because I needed to be careful as I am being closely monitored. These people are perverts. Why would they mount a camera in my bathroom?

My secretary's voice comes over the intercom. 'The boss wants to see you now!'

I have never been more frightened in my life. Have they found something? Am I going to be killed today? I rush out of my office; the boss doesn't like to be kept waiting. My heart is racing as I take the elevator to the fifth floor, where I am directed to go straight into the office. Never a good sign!

'Sir, you want to see me?' I am relieved not to see the big boss, only Carlos and his personal assistant standing waiting for me.

'Take a seat, Ana.' I sit down nervously, looking from Mr Montes to Carlos, wondering what they want.

'Ana, I am sure you know that one-and-a-half billion dollars was stolen from the organisation's Purple Gama account a few days ago. We are under tremendous pressure to find the people behind it.

'I know you studied accountancy in school, and you're very good at it, but after further investigation, we found out that you're also gifted; getting a fully-funded scholarship in Brazil is very rare.

'We have spent days combing through your laptop, Gamaplug, phone calls, and text messages. We found nothing, and we realised you don't have any friends. Now, the reason I called you here…'

A laptop is placed in front of me; I can see encrypted codes on the screen. They bring out another computer and show me my sister and her children with guns pointing at their heads.

'I need you to decode this encryption in five minutes, or your only family will die.'

I feel the colour leaving my face. 'Please don't hurt them.'

I look at the codes; I can easily decode them, but if I do, they will know I was involved in the heist. They have their suspicions, but they are not sure. But what about my sister and kids? What am I going to do now?

I wipe away sweat with the sleeve of my shirt. I start typing the most absurd codes I can imagine to prove that I know nothing about programming.

Carlos looks at his timer. I hit my head with my palm, and look up from the laptop. 'I don't know what I am doing.'

No one answers. I hope I have made the right judgement call. If not, my only family are about to die. I continue typing rubbish, and it keeps bringing up errors.

'One more minute,' Carlos says.

I start typing faster. I have doubts about my decision, but what else can I do? I have nothing to lose. They would kill my family anyway if I decoded the encryption. These people are animals.

'Time's up!' The laptop is turned towards my boss, and some men walk into the office and carry the laptop to the corner. I know they are checking to see whether I have any skills in programming. Not one single command I entered was correct; this is the definition of gibberish. My boss keeps looking at me without uttering a word. One of the men walks over to my boss and whispers in his ear.

The laptop with the live feed of my family is placed directly in front of me. 'Ana, you have made the decision today to end your loved one's lives.'

'Please, sir! I don't know anything about programming. I'm an accountant; you have been watching me.'

My boss nods, and the laptop is taken away. I can hear my family begging for their lives.

Everyone leaves the room apart from myself, my boss and Carlos.

'Ana, you can go as well!'

'Please, what has happened to my family?'

'You will never know. You decided their fate; live with it,' responds Carlos.

Carlos Ribeiro

The boss is anxious, and that means trouble. We need to find the person who helped that guy from Lagos to steal the money. This is an inside job; he cannot have acted alone. Someone gave him the information, and Ana is one of the few people privy to the details.

'Find out what the other two know, today, or we are all dead. Go now, get it done! And keep a close eye on Ana; I still don't trust her.'

Chapter Fifty-one: Hong Kong

Gama Lab Invasion

Huan

Time is ticking; we need to build POWERA fast. I'm responsible for the A-generation aspect of the development. I have ordered a few components that I need, but my attention is divided. We have been working closely with Edward in New York, looking at all possible access to Gama Lab. Martin, the partner who works with Edward has been following an employee, who works in Gama Lab. We know that his stolen ID has being deactivated, and it will set off an alarm if someone attempts to use it. The only way to get access is to steal an ID the very day we are going to use it, and the person we steal if from must not be aware of this theft. We need to put everything in place by tomorrow; we will break into Gama Lab before 3.00 am (GMT-4) in the morning.

Martin has been watching the building round the clock. He has informed the team that at 3.00 am there is a shift change, and a new security team takes over. Four minutes before the changeover, they have downtime.

They have a cleaning crew; the same people have been working there for four years. We can only have a thorough knowledge of what is happening through external workers; they come in the evening and clean the place, monitored closely by security. They have twenty-six cleaning crews because the building has fifty-four floors. Martin followed one of the cleaners, Charlie Harper, and noticed that he sees an out of job waitress daily before going to work. She was happy when we gave her two thousand dollars to administer sleeping pills to him.

When he didn't show up for work, we placed Martin Hills as Charlie Harper into the Borough Cleaning Agency system as a backup. We knew the boss would call the backup crew to help bail him out.

***

Martin must be on the 15th floor and access the system at precisely 2.57 am when the changeover happens. We found out that Jacob White lives in Manhattan and jogs in Central Park at 7.00 pm every evening after work without fail. That is the time to strike; it has to be done tonight.

We have developed similar features that the face detection system uses to identify an individual and created a facial prosthetic identical to Jacob White that Martin must wear. The curve of the cheek and his nose makes him a little older; after all, Jacob is slightly balding and in his fifties.

I am glad that Martin is an ex-cop; he is so shrewd. I was concerned about him being able to get Jacob's voice correct but he intentionally struck up a conversation with him on the train and recorded his conversation. We are looking for the way he pronounces his words 'Ayyyy! I am Jacob White, the code for today is...' The code is given to you after you have swiped your ID, carried out facial recognition and have been inspected by the security men. Only then will the head of security provide you with the code. The good thing is that Jacob is a lonely man and was glad to have someone to talk to.

It will happen tomorrow evening after work, when the operation is go. We have all synced our time. We need to get the code of the day from Jacob, and Martin needs to race back to the underground to do his facial prosthetic make-up, which will take about three hours.

We hope everything will go as planned. We have to be in and out without being noticed. Martin comes in as part of the cleaning crew, accesses the 15th floor as Jacob White, and must leave with the cleaning crew. We have to access the system for three minutes; immediately after the new shift starts. They monitor all the floors, and two men watch over the cleaning crew on each floor. He will be going alone, but once he can log into the system using Jacob White's access code encrypted into his ID, we can access the system to get the information needed.

Unfortunately, Ana will not be joining us from Rio; this is a significant setback for us, as we might need her expertise, but we don't have time. I hope she is OK; we have not heard anything from her in days. Segun and Lola are still not free from danger. Nigeria is on lockdown, and many more people have lost their lives. Unfortunately, some men were mistaken for Segun, being similar in looks, and were killed. At least they are still alive but living in constant fear. We knew this would happen, the organisation was not just going to fold their arms and do nothing after one-a-half billion dollars was stolen, but we never anticipated this many problems.

Ping Wu

I look at my security team, and think, *We have just a few days left before the master sends for us, and I doubt we will come back alive.*

I have sent men over to Lagos to assist Lekan Gbada. The big boss for Africa is looking for a man called Segun. He arrested five men who looked and spoke like him, but to be absolutely sure they were brought in front of his father to be identified. His father informed us that none of those men were Segun. The only reason he is still alive is to help us find his son, after that, he's of no use.

He had help from others; my gut feelings tell me Huan Li is involved, but I'm not sure. I don't have time to look for her now, but I'm ready for her; they have found her aunty and brought her back to Hong Kong. The one thing she treasures the most is the woman who raised her. She spent a fortune providing her with a beautiful life in New Jersey where she resides. I took great pleasure in her kidnap; a seventy-year-old woman, on her way to the supermarket.

When the time is right, after resolving this particular problem and securing my position with the master, I'll be coming for you, Huan Li. I never lose! I always get what I want, and I want you dead.

Chapter Fifty-two: London

Jude

I need to help the team in whatever way possible. I return from a trip to the various P.O. boxes we have opened to pick up some of the components required by Sarah, and find her pacing.

She checks her wristwatch again. It is set to 6.00 am, 1.00 am in the eastern time zone.

Today is D-day. Honestly, we have had to live in fear of the unknown for the past two days. The task we are about to embark on will be the hardest, we need to be tactical, and this operation needs to be carried out with military precision.

'Calm down,' I tell her.

She is waiting for feedback from Edward in New York. Martin is supposed to meet up with Jacob White from Gama Lab. He needs to steal his company identity card without being noticing and replace it with the previous one we stole.

'I went past your family home and noticed that it has been taken over by some strange people,' I say to distract her. 'I watched for about ten minutes; people went in and came out carrying boxes. Something weird is happening, and we need to find out their plans.'

'Right, but you are no longer in the organisation, Jude. You need to be careful; they take over everything you own and declare you bankrupt, exactly as you said. We know this. We have to bring them down and expose them to the world, it's the only way. That is what we are doing.'

Sarah

I am waiting for a response from Edward on whether we can execute our plans today. I keep looking at my wristwatch, and Jude is trying to keep me calm. It is 2.45 am; we should have heard something by now. Martin was supposed to meet up with Jacob White at 8.00 pm EST and it's already 9.45 their time. If he fails to swap those company IDs, we are finished.

'Sarah, you need to breathe,' says Jude. 'You told me Martin was a police officer and was good at his job. I'm sure he knows what he is doing.'

I can't relax. We have had to go from one Herculean task to another for the past weeks. We are about to break into Gama Lab, the most secure building in the world. Unfortunately, three minutes is all the time we have. One mistake, Martin is dead, and everything we have been working for will be destroyed.

A coded response pop's up on the team's screen; we are good to go. Relief washes over me. Now, the real work needs to begin. In less than three hours, Martin will be in the building with the cleaning crew, and he must find a way to distance himself from them and make his way to the 15th floor.

'It will help if you rest, Sarah. That is the only way to be mentally prepared; you have been working non-stop, checking and double-checking every detail. You will be useless to the team if you don't take care of yourself. We are lucky that we have not been found; I honestly didn't think we would last this long, living in this house.'

'I logged into the HM Land Registry and changed the property ownership. It is buried so deep that it is registered to an Indian lady if they manage to find it. They have the best team working for them, but they can't monitor every system; the only thing they can do is set notifications if anything is triggered. I was smart enough to go through the back door.

'I went through the system. All your properties have been possessed, even your mother's house in Scotland, and all your accounts have been closed. Jude, you have nothing!'

'I knew this would happen the minute it was in the news that I was a criminal; that is what they did to your father. I'm surprised they could take over your house, not knowing where you are.'

'They own the whole of Europe. They can do whatever they want; even the government answers to them. That is why we need that system blueprint to know the system configurations and specific places to place POWERA to intercept. I've been given the P-generation (PG) aspect of the development.

'Jude, I'm going to try and close my eyes for an hour. Please wake me up when it's time; today's success will determine this project's future. Martin must do all this without being noticed; no one must know that the system was logged into.'

Jude

I watch as Sarah goes to her room. I have not been helpful; the only thing I've been doing is cooking with the limited food supply, while she sits in front of her laptop for hours on end, writing programs and chatting with teams worldwide. I want to do more; I may not know programming or how to build equipment, but I can still be useful.

I stretch out my left leg; thankfully, it's finally healed completely. I am relieved it wasn't broken, I can't take the risk of gong to a hospital. I must have strained it when I jumped down, trying to escape from those men. Luckily, I'm made of thick skin. That was the only way I could survive my heinous father. I will go out there and try and find as much information as possible on the European organisation, Red Gama. I already know who the big boss is; it's time to flip the script on him.

James Cooper

We have two more days, or we are all dead. The master, Fred Demson, was not joking when he said we would all be replaced if we don't find those who stole the money. A solution has been agreed on with all the other big bosses on the daily video conference we have set up. We need to pull our money together and replace the one-and-a-half billion dollars and find someone that looks like Segun and pass him off as the man we are looking for. Hopefully, that will buy some time before we find the real culprits. No one must hear of our discussion. This is a matter of life and death.

Chapter Fifty-three: New York

Martin

We have been working on the facial prosthetic make-up for over an hour to make me look as close as possible to Jacob White. The picture sent to the backup cleaning crew is Jacob White. The good news is that nobody pays too much attention to the cleaners. The job of the security team is to make sure they don't enter an unauthorised room.

Edward looks at me and nods in approval.

'Martin, you need to be careful; this is very dangerous. This is the flash drive; insert it into the desktop computer you will find on the 15th floor. This will give us access to their network and, hopefully, we will be able to download the system blueprint before anyone notices. Keep your head down, and try to be invisible as much as possible.'

'Don't worry so much, man; I was in the police force for eighteen years and sometimes worked as an undercover cop.'

I look at myself in the mirror; my nose is slightly crooked. Jacob White told me when I was chatting to him that he broke his nose when he was a teenager. I don't recognise myself with the receding hairline, thin brown hair and brown eyes.

I put on the cleaning uniform and wave at Edward as I rush outside to take the train to meet up with the other cleaners. I have worked as an undercover cop but never on this scale, with such a limited amount of time to prepare for anything that could go wrong.

I enter the Gama Lab building with other cleaners, and am instructed to clean the thirteenth floor with one of them. I don't even remember his name. Is it Jeff? There are twelve rooms on that floor that need to be cleaned. I put my head down; and the security men allow us to take the staircase to our various floors, following closely behind. Bastards! Taking the stairs, most cleaners were panting when they got to their floors. I found out that they do this daily and are treated like scum.

I speak to Jeff. 'I'll clean six rooms while you clean the other six.'

I glance at my synchronised wristwatch. I have an hour, but I need to be on the 15th floor at exactly 2.45 am, and I then back downstairs with other cleaners at 3.05 am when the new shift takes over. I don't understand a company that cleans their building at odd hours during the night, especially a building with fifty-four floors!

I enter one of the assigned offices, and a security guard stands by the door. How can I leave without him noticing? I can see that he is bored; he keeps playing with his mobile. I have to leave each office I clean, and I can't be there for more than twenty minutes.

I speed-clean, finishing in forty-five minutes. I run over to the security guard telling him that I've finished cleaning, but I need to use the bathroom assigned to the cleaners which is on the ground floor. Holding my stomach and bending over, I break wind. The security holds his nose and looks at me with disgust. 'Get out of here,' he says. 'And make sure you go to the right floor.'

I race to the stairs; I can't take the lift, due to the security cameras installed inside. We didn't have enough time to decode them. I reach the 15th floor, use the Jacob White ID card, and hear a voice that tells me to place my face in the scanner in front of me before reciting the code of the day. *Don't sweat, Martin, you can do this*, I tell myself.

I was able to get the 'code of the day' from Jacob White by paying a stripper called Ginger to help extract the information from him. He was excited when I took him to a strip joint and offered to pay for his private dance. The fool gave up everything easily when he saw some skin, even where we can find his desk.

I place my face and play Jacob White's voice recorder, 'Ayyy! I am Jacob White the code for today is 91-45-38.' The door is supposed to open now. What is the delay? I have to be at the technical office in five minutes.

The door opens. There are security cameras everywhere, so I drop to the ground and start to crawl with my head facing the floor. The room is the third on the right. I hope I was not given the wrong information.

I push the door open. No one is allowed on this floor, not even the security men. If any cleaning needs to be done here, it is done by a particular lady who has been working for the company for five years. She is the only person employed by Gama Lab allowed to clean the technical rooms and directors' offices. I am still crawling; I know that Jacob White's desk is the first one I see when I enter the room. I make sure my face can't be seen above the computer, insert the flash drive, and set my timer for three minutes. I hope the team can do this in the stipulated time. I need to get out of here before they look for me in the toilet.

Edward

The unity team, that is what we are now calling ourselves, can see that Martin has been able to get into the system. We have come together, united in a common purpose, to bring down the organisation.

The program is downloading. This will break through the firewall; we have two minutes to get the blueprint and shut down the system before the secret alert goes off. We all know what to do. Combing through the system looking for the blueprint, we start downloading it onto the flash drive; we have one minute, it is huge, 74%…

We watch with bated breath, from our hiding places around the world, praying that it reaches 100% before the one minute is up, because we have instructed Martin to remove the flash drive at precisely three minutes.

We know it is impossible for Martin to avoid being picked up by the security cameras when he enters the 15th floor, the only thing we can do is alter the video to remove him from the feed. Hopefully, by the time they notice he will be long gone and the surveillance team, knowing their fate, are not stupid enough to tell their superior.

Martin

I disconnect the flash drive, drop silently to the floor and start crawling forward, fast. I can hear voices, the changeover is happening, and all the cleaners will be assembled and counted. I crawl to the door, then follow the same procedure as before: the ID, face detection, and voice recognition with the day's code. I run down the stairs, avoiding the cameras. I can see some security men ahead of me. What floor am I on? I put my head down, looking at the ground, trying not to be noticed. Thank God it's the fifth floor; cleaners are allowed on that floor. Now to reach the ground floor before they notice my absence.

Chapter Fifty-four: Fred Demson

I've been planning world domination for twenty years, after years of enduring bullying at a young age. Everything I have done has been strategically planned. Now the seven-day deadline is up, and the idiots I placed in powerful positions have not found the culprits responsible for stealing one-and-a-half billion dollars. I have several inside men watching these big bosses and reporting to me directly. I know they held a secret meeting last night, not allowing anyone apart from themselves inside their conference room. The security team was told not to guard the door but leave the premises altogether. This now raises the question, what are they up to? They think they can outsmart me; I got to this position through my own determination and hard work.

I call my trusted PA. 'Carlton! The seven new replacements that we have been secretly training, are they ready to take over?'

'Yes, sir, they are very much aware of all undertakings in all continents, and they have exhibited outstanding leadership skills.'

I look at my wristwatch. 'Are all the big bosses here?'

'Yes, sir! They arrived this morning; the meeting will take place in an hour.'

'Bring the new recruitments to the meeting. I want those idiots rattled. The truth will come out; I'll make sure they turn on themselves.'

***

All seven big bosses are taken to a much larger conference room. They look at one another questioningly; they had met for hours yesterday to try and find a way out of this predicament. They knew today's meeting would not be easy, but they have vowed to stick to what they had discussed.

They enter the room and see six men and two women seated with the names and continents displayed exactly as they are seated. What is going on?

Fred Demson is seated at the head of the table. 'Take a seat according to the continent displayed!' he says. 'I'm sure you will be surprised to see some new faces at this meeting. These men and women are your potential replacements.

'Today, the truth must come out. I gave you an assignment a week ago and provided you with all the resources required, and I have not yet received an update on the investigation.'

'Sir! Lekan Gbada stands up. 'I am responsible for finding the perpetrator since the connection was traced to Lagos, the African hub. We have been working tirelessly to find this man called Segun.' He lifts his hand and five slides show up on the boardroom display.

'This is the picture of the main suspect; you can see he has been badly beaten in an attempt to force him to reveal his accomplices. He has identified a particular individual who helped him in Rio de Janeiro. Her name is Fernanda.' Her face is displayed on the board. 'She is the bank manager of Brazilian City Bank. She holds all information about the bank's security; after all, she has been working for that bank for fifteen years and as a manager for four years. We would have given you this information before, but we were only able to piece everything together at the last minute and wanted to share this excellent news face to face.'

All eyes turn to the head of the organisation. The seven original bosses hardly dare breathe. Will he believe this lie? They need to buy more time to find the real culprits. If he realises that they have failed, they will be killed for sure.

They look at their replacements; sitting with a smug look on their faces. Everyone thirsts for these positions but they do not realise that the head that wears the crown does not rest easy. But they will not be promoted today. The original seven will make sure of that.

Fred Demson is quiet for a long time.

'Where is my money?' he asks eventually.

'As of this morning, it is in your Swiss bank account,' says Adriano Cardoso of the South America hub.

A laptop is placed in front of Fred Demson. One of his men shows him something on the screen and whispers.

Fred continues. 'I have checked your bank accounts to see whether you replaced this money yourselves. There don't appear to be any disparities, but my team will continue to investigate.

'You are trying to tell me that two people alone pulled off this heist? It was too elaborate and masterfully planned to have been *carried out by so few, because, from what I can see, the bank manager doesn't have the skills to break into an encrypted firewall. She may know when it's the best time to steal the money, but she can't actually take it – unless she was also working alongside someone from the bank's cybersecurity team?'*

'Everyone working for cybersecurity in the bank has been killed; as per your instruction, sir,' says Andrew Hughes.

Fred Demson looks at the assembled men and women in disbelief. 'I don't believe what you are telling me. From now on, you're all on probation, and no meetings must take place between you all without your men present. You will be watched closely, and your progress measured. Any more mistakes, It won't be a meeting I'm holding but your funerals. I need you to find everyone involved in trying to bring this organisation down, no more surprises, do you understand me?'

'Yes, sir!' the seven responded in unison.

They would live to fight another day!

Chapter Fifty-five: Lagos

Lola

Tears flow down my face; how long can we continue like this? We were able to deceive the men who came to interrogate us, but they spent hours combing through the house and the surrounding area. I'm glad all the electronics we possessed were switched off, as they brought electronic testing equipment to search for signals. The amount of weight I was carrying, pretending to be eight months pregnant, did not help the situation. My back was hurting me, and, at one point, I had to plead to be allowed to sit on the dirty ground. I was immensely relieved when they left, but the situation has not improved. The whole of Nigeria and Africa is still in lockdown, and we are not allowed to travel within the country. The desperation to catch us is so high that I'm reaching breaking point. The uncertainty of the situation is driving me crazy.

'Martin Hills managed to steal the blueprint without a hitch,' Segun points out. 'There were a few hiccups here and there, but overall it was a successful operation.'

'Yes, but handling the W-generation side (Wg) of the development will be more difficult than we anticipated. All borders have been closed till further notice. The components we need are supposed to be coming through Namibia in Africa. What are we going to do? So much needs to be done, and we have such a limited time. We can't afford to let down the others on the team. We have to find a way,' I remind Segun.

'We know that the money stolen has shaken their organisation, and they are finding ways to frustrate our operation. They are winning! Looking at the blueprint, we need to erect P-O-W-E-R-A simultaneously at specific location points in seven different countries on seven continents, to disrupt the communication of Gamaplug.'

'Lola, I understand your frustration, but we can't afford to lose hope. And we can't break our role. After you went to bed, I saw some men in the surrounding area. They were up to something; knowing Green Gama, they have installed some form of additional monitoring equipment.'

'I'm carrying about 3.1 kilograms of prosthetic belly every day; the only time I can remove it is when I'm taking a bath, this is hell, and you know it.'

'You have been through worse,' say Segun. 'The most important thing now is getting those components. My contact in Namibia who is helping to source them is terrified. He said homes are being raided in the middle of the night by military men, and people are dragged from their homes and killed if they suspect they are working against the government. The problem now is getting those components to the port. He has strategically dismantled the components into smaller bits and placed them in different sacks of wheat. He is transporting fifty sacks of wheat; some contain just wheat, others have the components in with the wheat. The border is closed, but they allow perishables. I hope those sacks are not searched even though I bribed one of the superior officers, or the only two people willing to risk their lives will die, and there is no hope for building W-generation.'

Lekan Gbada

Fred knows we are lying about finding those responsible for the heist. We need to up our game if we hope to retain our positions as big bosses within this organisation.

My bedroom is constantly locked with a premium security door, yet I constantly use my bug detectors to check for bugs. I know my men answer to the master; I am only a figurehead.

I enter my bedroom; the only place we can hold our private telephone conference meeting without prying eyes 'We are in big trouble,' I tell the other bosses. 'We have limited time to find that asshole, before we are replaced. He is the only one who can lead us to the other perpetrators. I have searched everywhere in Nigeria; he hasn't been found. Where the hell can he be hiding?'

'We need to up our game; they are making us look like fools,' says Sophia Richardson of the Australian hub. 'I was watching my replacement carefully at the meeting; she even has my gestures; they are being trained to be us.'

I hear Hussain Atta's voice. 'Lekan Gbada and Adriano Cardoso. The pressure is on you to find these people from Lagos and Rio de Janeiro. We must work out and understand why they need this huge amount of money.'

'To bring down the organisation, obviously,' says James Cooper from the European hub. 'We have to find out their plans.'

'They can only communicate with each other through an encrypted format; we will assign the best team we can find to break down the web and find them. This needs to be done immediately,' says Ping Wu from Asia_2.

'I agree. The boss wants us replaced; he thinks we are incompetent. If we allow these people to continue to play us for a fool, not only will we be replaced but killed too,' says Andrew Hughes.

'Let us allow them to think they have fooled us; adding more restrictions makes them more careful, and we need to set a bait. Let's remove all restrictions and pretend we are no longer searching for them. We choose some scapegoats and show them to the world, then let's see what they do,' says Adriano Cardoso.

'That's a good idea!' I say. 'Let the game begin.'

Chapter Fifty-six: Kabul

Mohammed

I sit in my office, feeling unsettled. I have not slept well in days. How can the man I hate the most be the one pulling my strings and dictating to me? I have spent days analysing and thinking back to the day I was recruited for this job.

I was an orphan, life was not pretty, and I had many unpleasant jobs like carrying and spreading manure on the farm. An older man walked up to me and said he would change my life, but I had to be prepared to be ruthless. I would be given 1000AFN if I could murder an entire family. I had never seen this kind of money before. I didn't even think about it when I entered their home and murdered the man, his wife and three teenage boys.

Look at me now? I'm the most feared man in the country, yet I have no power. The millions of dollars deposited into the Union Bank of Afghanistan for me to control have been frozen. I own the bank, yet I have no control over the finances. I'm forced to believe that Jabar is correct. His name was signed at the end of the note. If Hussain Atta has set me up, I'll find him and kill him myself.

I have to change tactics. He is powerful and wealthy, I'll play the ignorant dictator, but I'll do everything I can to bring him down. First, I have to find Jabar.

Ahmed

'The steps you are taking are dangerous, Jabar. How can you say you are going back to the Ahedan compound? They are mercenaries. Mohammed will kill you without even blinking an eye,' I say.

'What are we supposed to do? We have been sitting here for days, not doing much. We need to expose Hussain and all his puppets, and stop them. The only person capable of doing that with the right technology is Mohammed. If I die in the process, so be it!'

'You must be very careful; strange people have been lurking around this area. I suspect they work for Hussain. We will be discovered; we should leave this house.'

'This is what I am saying, Ahmed. We are not safe here; the only safe place is the Ahedan compound with Mohammed. I know all the men working for Hussain who have turned against him and those devoted to him. This will give us leverage. I explained that in the note, he will be terrified. He won't know who to trust.'

'Mohammed is the most paranoid person I have ever met; I worked closely with him as his bodyguard. He will use you to his advantage and eliminate you when he's done.'

'I know the kind of man he is. He is heartless and conceited. But what choice do we have? We have to play him at his own game.'

'I understand what you are saying, but we must be wary of him.'

'You don't go into the lion's den and not be prepared. We will use him to our advantage, never letting our guard down. We will recruit men on our side, never giving him all the information. He is cunning, but we need to be smarter than him. Eat or be eaten!'

Jabar

Ahmed has decided to stay back and watch me enter the Ahedan compound. If I don't signal to him in an hour, he will know something has gone wrong, and I'm likely to be dead.

This is the last resort, I keep telling myself.

I drag myself reluctantly to the side gate. I know the camera is watching, and the door will be opened in 3,2,1…

The door is pulled open, and I am dragged into the compound with so much force that I fall forwards.

'Jabar! What are you doing here? We have been looking for you for weeks.'

'I need to see Mohammed; he is expecting me, and it's urgent.'

I hear laughter. 'Mohammed is expecting you. He gave an order for you to be killed.'

'Just tell him I'm here.'

'Your funeral,' laughs one of the security men.

One of the men runs to inform Mohammed that I am here.

My heart is pounding, and I suppress a shiver. *This is a stupid idea, Jabar! Why did you come back here?*

The man hurries back and looks at me with surprise. 'Mohammed wants to see you in his office.'

I get up and dust myself down, smiling. 'I told you he wants to see me,' I say, walking towards his building.

'Don't be too smug,' one of the men yells after me. 'You could still be about to die.'

I knock on Mohammed's office door. 'Come in!' I hear.

I open the door, and see the shocked faces of his right-hand men. No one utters a word as he asks to speak to me privately. I watch them leave reluctantly.

'Jabar! Why am I not surprised to see you? I could have you shot right now. You confessed to being a spy sent to destroy me.'

'You won't kill me because you need me. I'm the only one who can help you bring down Hussain and make you the most powerful man in the country.'

'What makes you think I want Hussain dead? I could just hand you over to him and be done with it.'

'You're a leader, not a follower. You don't want to answer anyone. I can give you the power you crave.'

***

Yusuf hurries into Hussain's office. 'We have a problem! Jabar is having a private meeting with Mohammed as we speak.'

'This is not good! He can provide information about our whereabouts. We have to move to location B now. I'm not taking any chances; find a way to stop them, and fast.'

'Yes, sir!' replies Yusuf, rushing out of the office, shouting for everyone to pack up and start moving to the underground passage.

Chapter Fifty-seven: Sydney

Henry

'Dad! How could you do this to Mum? You said she disappeared without telling anybody; now you say you want to marry another woman?'

'You don't understand. I don't want to marry her, but I have no choice.'

'What is that supposed to mean? I know you and Mum had problems and separated, but I never thought you would marry someone else.'

I look at my son with teary eyes, and I feel like punching something.

'Please, I can't explain it to you now, but believe me, everything I do is for you and your mother, to protect you.'

'Will that woman live in this house with us?'

'Not if I can help it, I don't want her around you. She is a slow poison that destroys everything around her.'

'If you don't love her, then why are you marrying her?'

'One day, I hope to explain everything to you and your mother, for now try to trust me and remain calm.'

Tom

I raise my hands in the air in triumph. We did it! Yes! We got the blueprint without a hitch. I am so proud of Martin. Now the real work starts; the shocking report we just got from Huan Li in Hong Kong is that they have lifted the restriction on money transfers. Everyone in the team is excited, but I'm wary. Why would they lift the ban? They would never give up that kind of money.

I have seen those arrested in connection to the heist trending on all media platforms. They were sentenced to death in Rio de Janeiro and Lagos for stealing one-and-a-half billion dollars. The team believes we were able to deceive the organisation into arresting the wrong people, but I'm not so sure. I know we are restrained by limited time and workforce to develop POWERA, but we can't just relax and stupidly seize the opportunity without thinking. Unfortunately, no one is listening to me. Edward in New York will transfer a massive amount of money to everyone in the team, so we can work faster. We will be given access to withdraw the money we need in an encrypted network.

Henry

I have left my housekeeper at home with Carl. I don't want him to stay at home by himself. I warned her not to allow anyone, especially Cynthia Coleman, into the house. She turned up at the house twice this week and made a scene about how horrible I am for not asking after my pregnant fiancée. God, I hate that woman so much! I have booked an appointment to see the big boss to plead for a replacement 'wife'. I don't want to kill anyone, but I'll be tempted with this woman.

'Let me get this straight,' she says. 'You want any other woman from the organisation but not Cynthia.' The big boss looks at me pityingly and starts to laugh. 'Do you know why I'm laughing? Do you honestly think you can bargain with me when I give an order? I chose Cynthia because she is the best to bring our goals to fruition. I didn't choose her to be a good wife to you, but she will make a fantastic prime minister's wife. She is a manipulator, a goal-getter. She will push you to do what is right for the organisation. You will be married in three days. You have not introduced her to your son yet, do the needful, or I will be forced to intervene, and you will not like the outcome.'

I scream at the top of my lungs as I drive to see Tom. I'm going crazy! Marry Cynthia. I have to find a way out of this; I'm tired of playing their game. I have a list of all the members in the Australian continent and their net worth. I have been a member of this organisation for months, and my wealth has grown exponentially. I am worth one hundred million AUD against my humble five million when I joined the horrible organisation. They have taken over everything. They have finished building the nuclear plants, and the weapons developed are being sold to several unscrupulous nations worldwide.

I enter Tom's private home. 'You look frustrated,' says Tom.

'I *am* frustrated! I'm getting married to Satan in three days' time.' I look around the room and see Tom's new equipment. 'What's all this?'

'This is some of the equipment and components needed to develop the E-generation (Eg) section of POWERA. We have our work cut out for us. Getting some of the components is tricky, and testing to ensure they work is even trickier. I'm constantly faced with one problem or another. We are developing something that has never been done before.'

'This is the list you asked me for; it comprises of all the members, their position in the organisation and their net worth. I don't have access to the big boss's net worth, but it will be more than all of us combined.'

'Whatever you do, you mustn't touch that money, Henry. I can see you are worth a great deal, but that money must be returned to the people.'

'I don't need it. The primary issue for me right now is how to get out of this forced marriage.'

'You don't have a choice, unfortunately. You have to marry her. Make sure you have separate rooms. Under no circumstance must you sleep with her.'

I hate my life! This is hell.

Chapter Fifty-eight: Rio de Janeiro

Ana

I've been extremely cautious after the fiasco in my boss's office. What surprises me is that everything seems to be back to normal. My boss is no longer looking stressed, and I have been informed by the team that they are no longer looking for the culprits. The organisation has arrested innocent people, it's all over the news.

I have access to the funds I need to build the R-generation of POWERA. I can understand Tom's reservations about the debacle of the Gama organisation, he constantly tells us it is a set-up, and we need to be careful. The problem is that we need the funds now, not the small transfers we have been doing. It is causing a delay in developing POWERA; we have no choice but to take the risk if we are to finish in a month.

We have had to work incessantly. I have rented a warehouse. I have just taken a month's leave; I'm surprised my boss approved it. I'll be living in the warehouse; all the pieces of equipment and components will be kept there.

***

The big bosses connect to the conference meeting set up by the best cyberteams employed by the organisation; their sole purpose to find the people who stole the money. The cybersecurity leader says the trap is working…

'Vast amounts of money is being transferred from Barbados to different countries. The transfers are encrypted to look like a file and are ping-ponged from one continent to another. We are trying to find the countries that have access to that money. We know from our investigation that a bank in Barbados is being used to hold the stolen money. We have not investigated further because the instruction is to find the people behind the heist, not necessarily the money. They are getting too comfortable in their dealings. I know they will make a mistake soon, and we will catch them.'

'Do you know how much has been taken out of the account in

Barbados?' asks James Copper from Red Gama.

'Yes, sir, two hundred million dollars was taken out yesterday. It was distributed, but we don't know where and we're breaking down the security, bit by bit, so as not to draw attention. We are now at 46% and will get full access soon.'

'The minute you get full access, let us know immediately,' Adriano Cardoso instructs the team leader for security. 'We need to find those responsible and eliminate them immediately. Do you understand?'

'By tomorrow, we will be able to identify the IP routing that will allow us to know the countries that received part of this money.'

Adriano Cardoso

The conference call disconnects, and I call my head of security. 'What happened to the three suspects with the expertise to pull this off?'

'Two of the suspects were killed, sir. They have the skills and are best positioned to pull a heist. The only person still alive is Ana Santos. She doesn't seem to have the necessary skills in programming. We have been monitoring her for days but haven't seen or heard anything. She's taken a month's leave starting tomorrow; we will watch her whereabouts.'

'Don't spend too much time with her; by tomorrow, we will know the people that stole from us. If an IP address shows Rio de Janeiro, I want her taken out of the picture.'

'Yes, sir.'

It is bad enough that other bosses look at me like an incompetent fool who allowed one-and-a-half billion dollars to be stolen, putting others in this predicament. We need to tie up loose ends. We have given her too many grace periods. That ends tomorrow.

Ana

There are cameras all over the house. I have to sit in a particular position and not move if I don't want to be sighted with my laptop. It is getting uncomfortable; the worst is the one in the bathroom. I'm forced to use the guest bathroom because I know it doesn't have a camera; I only use the main bathroom to brush my teeth.

I'm planning to leave tonight. I know the man at the reception desk informs my boss whenever I go out of the apartment. The building has a large swimming pool and gym on the ground floor with an outdoor shower. That is the only way to escape this building without being seen. Everything I need, I have smuggled into my office bag. I have been doing this for the past week and keeping it in the boot of my car. I have also been making regular trips to the pool, so as not to arouse suspicion when I go.

I take the lift to the ground floor wearing a swimming suit, with a towel tied around my waist. I wave at the receptionist as I head towards the pool. He waves back and gets up from his seat to watch me. I know he will come to check on me before leaving for the day and inform the boss.

The pool is deserted. The apartments were given to the directors working in the company. I make sure he has left the building and handed over to the man who works the night shift. The timing is perfect.

I hurry to my old car parked on the street further from the building. I change into a black top and leggings; with black scarf wrapped around my head and neck, covering my hair. I am going to stay in the warehouse I have rented under a false name. I will need to hide there until we bring this organisation down. I can't do the accounting work and POWERA simultaneously; something has to give. I am taking a considerable risk; they will look for me, wondering where I have disappeared to. What choice do I have if I hope to build R-generation? It requires my undivided attention and can't be accomplished under the present circumstances.

Chapter Fifty-nine: Hong Kong

Ping Wu

I glance at my alarm clock. It is 1.14 am. Who could be calling at this ungodly hour? It must be important. The call connects. 'Madam! There is an urgent request for you to connect with the other bosses now.'

I jump out of bed, and dress hurriedly. This must be the breakthrough we have been looking for. 'Gama, connect the conference call.'

'I have good news,' says the head of cybersecurity. 'We have traced the origin of the transaction. It's from New York. We can't identify the precise location and the person responsible for distributing the money.'

'Where did they distribute the money?' asks James Cooper. 'This information is essential to finding solutions to our problems.'

'We know that the person had help from Rio de Janeiro. They knew about the security, account details and the best time to steal that money, which means they knew that account had that money,' replies the cyber head.

'Thank you for much,' says Andrew Hughes from Blue Gama, obviously seething with anger. 'You have done a good job, but continue your search; we need to know where the money was distributed.'

'Do you have any idea who it could be, Andrew?' asks Hussain Atta from Asia_1.

'We know for a fact that the money was stolen by people in New York, Lagos and Rio de Janeiro. We already know who is responsible in Lagos. We need to find out who was involved in New York and Rio de Janeiro.'

'Three people have the expertise and information to carry out this heist. Two are already dead, but the last one claimed she doesn't know how to do programming,' Adriano Cardoso says. 'To be safe, I'll order her death. The major problem now is identifying the person from New York; that is where Andrew needs to help us.'

'The only person I can think of has been a thorn in my flesh for months, but he is just a police officer; he doesn't have the skill to pull this off, unless someone is helping him. His family is in detention, yet he still hasn't shown his face. We thought he might be dead, but now I've come to realise he is alive and planning a major coup.'

'These people have eluded us for too long; we need to find them. The only way to stop them is to work as one unit, all our resources become one, and our sole purpose is to bring them down.'

'We are just buying time; we all know what the master is capable of. If we don't get this done in the next couple of days, we will lose everything we have worked for all these years.' says Sophia Richardson from White Gama.

'We will send our best agents to New York; that idiot must be found. Do you think he is still in New York?' asks Lekan Gbada. 'Every satellite and every network will be used since he no longer uses Gamaplug. We will find him if he is still alive.'

'We must do what we have never done before; every home and underground will be searched. All must be done simultaneously at night when everyone is resting for the day. The manpower will be made available to do this. In two days, many more agents will arrive in New York. The order is to shoot to kill!'

I smile as the call disconnects. We are getting closer.

***

After disconnecting the call, Adriano Cardoso calls for his head of security to go to Ana Santos's apartment.

'Kill her. I don't want any excuses. I want her dead now! All her accounts must be frozen. She has played me for a fool for too long. I believed her when I watched the live video of her shaking, crying and pleading for the lives of her family, insisting she doesn't know how to do programming. She may be one of the best accountants, but she is not the only accountant who can do the job. We need people we can trust around us.'

Edward

Everything is going as planned; I have been able to source the right equipment since the restriction has been lifted. It's all progressing smoothly, and I'm afraid something might go wrong suddenly. The news trending is the death penalty for the offenders who stole one-and-a-half billion dollars. Their execution is happening tonight and will be televised to the world. I feel so guilty to see the innocent take the blame for our crime, but what can we do? We must remember the reason we are here; to finish building POWERA.

After meeting with the team, I'm glad we are all moving forward in the different aspects of POWERA we are handling. I was thrilled that Ana Santos could join us at the meeting. She informed us that she took a month's leave from work and lives in a rented warehouse where she is free to build R-generation without any obstruction.

Every operation we have done has been successful. No one is looking for us anymore; they have other problems to concentrate on. I know we have to be careful, this organisation never gives up, but we have a reason to celebrate for now. We are winning, and we will continue to win!

Chapter Sixty: London

The Organisation's Attack

Sarah

'You look more relaxed, Sarah,' says Jude.

'Yes, the successful operation by Martin Hills in getting the blueprint of Gamaplug has moved things forward. Everything seems to be working as planned; Jude, we have managed to outsmart the organisation. They don't even know what is going on.

'There is still much to do. I need to finish the (Pg) of POWERA in six weeks. We found out that each continent has its access point, which is the only way we can disrupt the Gamaplug operations. POWERA will have six access points.

'The good news is that all the components, processors and equipment I need have been ordered and, as you can see, some of them have arrived. I have been working hard to build and test; this type of work usually requires a team of people to build, but we don't have that luxury. We will now put it together and test it to see if it works.

'I haven't seen any deliveries to the house; how were you getting this equipment without raising suspicion?'

'I have a storage unit not far from here; everything is delivered to that address. I was going to tell you today but you beat me to it. I have been so engrossed with all the operations, we took on lately.'

'I'm glad everything is going well. Let's hope it continues like this.'

New York

Airport workers are astonished at the number of private aeroplanes landing at John F. Kennedy International Airport, in New York. Everything is secretive. They are directed to a different section of the airport. No passports are checked. The passengers look like secret agents.

There can't be less than a hundred thousand arriving from different parts of the world. A directive has been announced that the airport will be closed at 8.00 pm due to technicalities, and everyone should be in their homes by 10.00 pm.

How can one of the busiest airports in the world be closed?

Andrew Hughes

Andrew Hughes smiles as he watches as planes land. This operation is happening tonight and will catch people unawares; it is being carried out in secrecy. We have planned what needs to be done. This operation is happening at 2.00 am when everyone should be safely in bed. Every home, every patch of land, everywhere will be searched at the same time. We will leave no stone unturned; wherever Martin Hills is hiding in New York we will find him. These people are the very best. A face recognition detector and a fingerprint scanner will be used. I know he might have changed his appearance, but he will not be able to hide from us, and whoever is helping him will regret siding with that fool.

***

I look up as Bobby walks into the conference room, where a large computer screen shows the layout of New York City and the position each agent will be stationed in by 1.30 am. Also in the conference room, seated are fifty-six of the best agents and the head of every force in the world from the FBI, KGB, MI6, Mossad and so on.

I continue addressing the agents. 'This is the most critical operation you have ever done. This man…' the picture of Martin Hills shown on the screen, 'is a terrorist, and he wants to bring down this operation. Don't be fooled by his innocent look; he is intelligent and dangerous. We will not be using the police force for this operation because he was loved by many, and we don't want anyone helping him to escape.

'Bobby, you will take a leading position in this operation because you worked with him for eleven years and know him best. You have disappointed me for months, trying to find him and failing. Do not disappoint me today; I want his head. Where are his family?'

'Still in detention, sir. What do you want us to do to them?'

'Leave them there for now; let's see how this operation goes. You told me he loves his family; I'm surprised he hasn't come looking for them after all these months.'

'I'm sure he has been looking for them, sir. But he knows if he shows his face, he will be killed. I'll not fail you this time; I have been waiting for this opportunity for years, and I long to see him suffer.'

'Bobby, this is not a personal vendetta; telling me that you want to see him suffer means you want to torture him before he dies. Listen to me; I want him killed immediately he's sighted. If you fail me on this, you will take his place.'

'Yes, sir, of course, I'll do as you say.'

Bobby

The big boss doesn't understand how long I have waited in the shadows while Martin has received all the accolades and recognition from our peers. Now, it is now my turn. I am the director of the FBI unit, and he is a fugitive. I intend to rub his nose in it before ending his life. No one will take this opportunity from me.

I look at the plan once again to ensure I have everything right. Everywhere is being covered. Martin will have nowhere to run. The big boss doesn't understand this is the best news I have heard in months.

I have passed folders with all the information they need on Martin Hills to the head agents; everything from his age and height to his favourite drink. I'm beginning to wonder if I knew him at all. He is very cunning; we have not been able to find him in months which tells us he has had help. We need to find that person. Tonight we will bring them both down!

Chapter Sixty-one: New York

It is dark and silent in New York City, but the whole city is surrounded. The routes leading out of the city are blocked, and there is no going in or coming out. Helicopters hover in the sky, and agents are stationed on the ground, equipped with a picture of Martin Hills and possible transformations he could have made. They also have biometric devices to identify finger mapping, face recognition and retina scan. The directive is that he should be killed on the spot when identified. The time for the operation is set for 2.00 am. Every homeless person has already been checked and identified and taken to an isolated building where they were instructed not to leave or be shot.

Anyone seen roaming the streets at that time will be eliminated without mercy.

Martin

I turn to Edward. 'What's wrong? You seem restless. You have been watching that screen for the past hour.'

'Look at this. I am connected to the satellite overlooking the city. Can you see the amount of dots? Those are people. Have you ever seen this number of people in the city at this time of the night? Something is going on.'

'What do you think could be happening?'

'Whatever it is, it's not good. We need to go to the safe room now. I have opened it already. All the monitors and computers have been shut down with a code – anything that tries to access them will be infected them with a computer virus and a little surprise.'

'Don't you think you are overreacting?' I say.

'No, now hurry!' shouts Edward.

We rush towards the safe room, a dark, smelly room separate from where we have been staying. As we retreat, I can hear footsteps; they start to run…

We rush through the abandoned train tunnels into the dark path, careful not to disturb the cobwebs, or they will notice that someone has been through here. We fall to the dirty, smelly ground, crawling along on our hands and knees.

The safe room is 12x18 feet with a titanium steel door that looks like part of the building which cannot be opened from the outside when locked from the inside. We hurry inside.

'I developed a biometric scanner inside the safe room that verifies my identity and approves access,' says Edward. The door closes behind us.

We watch the secret cameras installed in most underground areas for safety. About fifty people flood into the underground. Some enter the computer room with the monitors, computers, and other equipment; the leader must have communicated with the Gamaplug. In the next four minutes, an additional ten join the five in the computer room; others search the whole area.

Bobby

I enter the room. *Why would someone be living in an abandoned underground with the latest technology?*

'Where are they?' I shout.

'We didn't find anyone; the whole place has been abandoned. We are trying to log into their system to see what we can find.'

'I need people here to dust for fingerprints, and I want the whole underground searched. I believe they are still hiding,' I say as I leave the room.

One of the cybersecurity men connects to the system and a timer comes up on the screen counting down; 3,2,1... 'Everyone get out!' he screams as the room explodes.

The bang lifts me of my feet and slams me to the floor. I am coughing, trying to get off the ground, with smoke everywhere.

What the hell just occurred? This shouldn't be happening.

I pull myself up shakily and enter the smoky room. The agents' lifeless bodies are lying on the ground. Other agents pour into the room, choking and covering their faces against the smoke.

'We need to leave; it is no longer safe. Get out of here, but search everywhere in this underground. They are trying to stall us.'

I look around the room one last time, my sleeve over my mouth, before walking out. Everything has been destroyed, the technology room, the supposed bedroom and the toilet. I am certain this is the work of Martin Hills. No one else could have done this.

I join the agents searching the underground.

'It all looks abandoned, sir; look at the cobwebs.'

'I don't care. Search the place.'

We continue through the cobwebs until we reach a dead-end; a massive steel wall.

'No one could get through this wall; it has no handle and there's no door,' says one of the agents.

'I need to be sure; bring someone here to see whether they can bring it down.'

'Yes, sir, someone will be here shortly.'

'Stay here!' I say. 'Do not leave under any circumstances, OK? Report back to me when the team arrives to take it down. Meanwhile, let's continue the search.'

I'll not give up; Martin Hills, your life is in my hands.

Chapter Sixty-two: Lagos

Segun

I connect to the encrypted team's group video call scheduled every two weeks. It's been challenging to have these meetings because of the heavy surveillance from the organisation. I know something is wrong! Edward and Martin have not connected to the call, and it's been two hours now. We have all tried to get hold of them individually, but we have all failed to contact them.

Tom was right; it was too good to be true. Why would the organisation relax all orders on money transfers, importations etc, if not to set a trap? We all need to keep a low profile until we hear from Edward or Martin in New York.

I disconnect the video call and sigh heavily. I have a terrible feeling that something is happening to them, and there is nothing we can do to help.

'You worry too much,' says Lola. 'These men are resilient. Do you know how many near-death experiences they had? They always manage to escape.'

I shake my head, I'm not so sure. Things are going from bad to worse; they are coming after us with everything. We don't have the workforce or the resources to fight them. All we have are our wits. I'm beginning to think that will not be enough. I know how difficult it was to get those components and equipment. We had to pay people to risk their lives to send it to us. When it comes down to it, we don't have anyone apart from people in the team. They are the only ones passionate enough to risk everything because we have all lost so much.

New York

Back in New York, three men are standing in front of the steel wall.

'The easiest way to break steel is through the hinges,' one of them says. 'But we can't find any.'

'No excuses! I need to know what is behind this wall,' yells Bobby.

'Sir,' one of the men, responds, 'the alternative is to use explosives, and that is not a good idea. The explosion has affected the structure; believe me when I tell you, this will all cave in soon. We shouldn't be down here. It can be monitored away from here. If anyone is behind this wall, I doubt they will survive when everything comes tumbling down.'

'We have searched every nook and cranny in New York City; this is the only place we didn't find anyone, yet we know someone was living here and they had enough computer expertise to set a bomb for us; that person needs to be found and fast.'

Bobby

About sixty agents have searched the whole underground and found nothing. How do I face my boss? He will kill me. This plan is not without flaws; we had limited time to execute it, but how did he know we were coming?

I turn to the three engineers. 'I don't care; set the explosion.'

'Then everyone must leave the underground before it detonates.'

'I know this will affect the buildings above ground,' I say to the engineers, 'but we've never cared before, so it doesn't matter.'

I hurry out of the underground. I need to give an update to the big bosses soon. At least I can tell them I did everything possible to find Martin Hills.

When the explosion goes off, we feel the ground shake. All the agents are now stationed around the entrances and exits of the underground. The engineers have informed me there is no way anyone could have survived the explosion. If they managed to keep safe, they can't get out of the underground.

I'm not taking any chances; I have instructed the engineers to seal all the entrances and exits after an hour if no comes out. Then I can tell the big bosses that Martin Hills is dead and the operation was successful. I would have loved to see his face, slowly watching as the life left his body, and the pain he would feel if I murdered his family in front of him. I know that Martin is in NYC; he has lived here all his life, and his family is from Long Island. He would not leave his wife and children to hide in another state.

I signal to one of the men. 'I want cameras in every area watching the underground; if anyone comes through here, I need to know.'

Martin

We watch everything from the screen streaming from the hidden camera.

'Are we safe?' I whisper to Edward.

'I don't know,' he answers. 'I built this safe room, as a place to hide if something like this should happen, but if they use explosives, even if the steel wall resists it, the whole underground will cave in, and we will be trapped.'

While we are trying to think of a way out of this predicament, there is a loud explosion. All the screens go dead.

'Shit! Shit! What do we do now?' I turn to Edward.

'The door is still shut, but we have no idea what is happening around us. We are not safe here. We can only remain for seventy-two hours. And there is no food and water.'

'Then we have to find a way out.'

Edward nods. 'I'll open the door in the next twelve hours, but I don't know what we will see outside. But we have to leave the underground before the whole place caves in.'

Chapter Sixty-three: Kabul

Jabar

I can see the uncertainty in Mohammed, but the greed in his eyes at the possibility of being the most powerful man in Afghanistan is taking over.

I look at my watch. I have twenty minutes left, or Ahmed will return to the temporary house thinking I have been executed.

'Jabar, I need all your information on Hussain, or I'll kill you myself.'

I smile at him, resorting to mind games. 'If you kill me, you will have nothing, and you will still be a puppet controlled by Hussain.'

'Where can I find him?'

'He has a house in the city centre with several underground floors. It houses over one hundred people, including technical, military and financial experts. He has men all over and outside the country who answer to him. You can't just go to that house, which I suspect will be empty now. You need to plan wisely, or you will die.'

'Why should I believe you? If he is so powerful, why does he need me?'

'Hussain is being hailed as the hero who will deliver the Afghan people from a dictator; you. He will raise the people against you. The plan was for you to be eliminated eventually.

'It would help if you shared your plans, because you don't have the workforce to bring him down. He has people working here that answer to him. We can use a few of them to our advantage because Hussain will not know they are double agents. But, right now, I need to bring in Ahmed; you need him on your side. He is one of the best military people I know.'

'What! No! He murdered my people; he needs to die to teach the others.'

'You need him. You need all the people you can get, and not just anybody; intelligent people. He hates Hussain because he was the one who murdered his family, not the war. He wants revenge, and we need to give him a chance. After that, you can do whatever you want with him.'

'What will my people think? They will see me as weak.'

'You need to be wise and unpredictable. You do not answer to them. They answer to you.'

He hesitates. 'Go and get him,' he says eventually. 'But I don't want to see him. I deal only with you. If I discover that you are deceiving me at any point, I'll kill you slowly. Do you understand me?'

***

I rest in the new room assigned to me two days ago. Mohammed will not know what hit him when I'm done with him. The two most powerful people will kill themselves then I, Jabar, will rule Afghanistan.

Hussain

I lean back in my seat. I have a lot to deal with right now, and the last thing I want to worry about is that lunatic Mohammed. The head will replace all the big bosses if we don't find the people responsible for infiltrating the bank system. He didn't believe us when we sold him the false story that we have captured and killed those responsible. The scary thing about the head is that you never know what he is up to. Every day we get to breathe is borrowed time.

The instruction given to Yusuf is to eliminate everyone in the Ahedan compound; that is happening tonight. We had to delay the attack because some of my best men were sent to New York to help capture another lunatic, Martin Hills. I'm getting reports that he has been killed in an underground explosion. But I have learnt not to believe anything until I see it with my own eyes.

The time has come for me to take over Asia_1; no more hiding in the shadows. The people love me and see me as their saviour. I'll use them to fight for me, I'll give them guns and food. The goal is to eliminate Mohammed Pir.

New York

Edward

I open the titanium door by entering the code on the inside door lock. All we can see is concrete blocking the door. How do we get out of this? The whole underground is filled with debris.

'We will need to use all our strength to get out of here,' says Martin.

'We can't continue to stay. We will die from starvation or the underground caving in; we know this will happen soon. It will take hours to find a way out of the underground. And where do we go, if we manage to escape alive?'

'The only option is to use my late sister's house in Brooklyn; I went underground when the FBI wanted me for hacking; what choice do we have?'

I trying to push the concrete out of the way, sweating profusely.

'Help me with this one,' shouts Martin.

I joined him in pushing the heavy concrete. It shifts a little; we just need to apply more strength.

'We will get out of this,' Martin tries to assure me, but my faith is dwindling. 'I will have to start all over again with the work I have done on OG.'

'Let's not think about that now; we can rebuild. The most important thing is getting out of here alive; we don't know what awaits us outside. We have the money, and you have the expertise.'

'What about the people in the team? They must be worried by now, not knowing what has happened to us. Do we still have a team supporting us if we leave here, or are we on our own?'

'Everything will be fine,' he says. 'Now, push with all your strength at the count of three, OK?' We push the concrete, and it moves a little. There is a small space; we have to squeeze through.

'Keep moving! We'll get through this; we have been through worse.'

I wish I could be so certain.

Chapter Sixty-four: Sydney

Henry

I study my reflection in the mirror. This is the saddest day of my life. I have been forced to put on a black suit that my mother brought to the house yesterday. She was talking endlessly about the preparation that had gone into my wedding. I wish I could escape with my son, run away into the sun and never have to face Cynthia Coleman again. I insisted that I didn't want to see her, so I have not set my eyes on her in three days. If only she would disappear, if wishes were horses.

My son enters the room in his matching black suit. He is supposed to be my best man. I hold him tightly and whisper, 'I'm sorry, this is never what I wanted.'

He stares at me. 'I don't understand. You hate her, but you're marrying her anyway, and we don't know where my mum is?'

'Carl! I need you to listen to me carefully.' I lower my voice. I am aware that, very soon, my mother will barge into the room. 'Immediately after this wedding, you are going to boarding school. I don't want you in this house; it is not safe, do you understand me?'

'Dad, please just tell me, what's going on?'

'Nothing that you need to worry about. This is between you and me, OK? During the school breaks, I've made arrangements for where you will go; I'll come and see you all the time. No matter what happens, don't come into this house until I tell you it is OK. Everything will be fine.'

I hold on to my son and quickly wipe away a tear before he can see. 'We will be fine. I promise.'

***

In this spectacle of marriage, which my mother has arranged, I'm a man whose wife disappeared just a couple of months ago who is now marrying his childhood sweetheart. The horror of it all is that over two hundred and fifty people are present, including prime ministers, presidents, and heads of industry. In a nutshell, all the White Gama members are here.

I stand on the right side of the altar erected in the grounds of my mother's house for this wedding, my son at my side, waiting for my nightmare to appear. I force out a smile and tell Carl to do the same. These people are not here for a joyous wedding; they just want to ensure I follow the big boss's instructions.

I watch as my bride walks down the aisle in a white embroidered gown, her face covered with a veil. I turn my face away; I didn't want to watch her. My life will be even more of a nightmare from today onwards.

She stands by my side, and I reluctantly lift her veil. I am on autopilot, saying, 'I do' when necessary. I don't listen to the priest, until I feel Cynthia pinching my arm. I shake my head, and the priest repeats, 'You may kiss the bride.' I lean over and give her a peck on the lips, trying and failing to prevent myself from gagging.

My mother jumps up from her seat, clapping happily, while my dad watches me warily. He doesn't understand what is going on. I look at Carl and smile sadly. I nod and he understands; a car is waiting at the front of the house to take him directly to school.

This organisation has ruined my life. They suck you dry; they take and take, thinking everyone is governed by money and power. I hope Tom and the team have moved forward in this operation because I can't keep up this charade for long.

Tom

Having had another meeting without Edward and Martin, I think something terrible has happened to them. I hope they are still alive. They are paramount to this operation. Hopefully, we will hear from them soon, but, while we wait for news, we need to concentrate on our assignment. We count down the days, six more weeks before combining our work and testing POWERA.

Right now, Henry is getting married. God! I feel so sorry for him; he is the only one still working for the organisation. We need someone on the inside but at what cost? I have researched Cynthia, the woman he is being forced to marry, and gathered information on her; she is heartless and callous. I've records of her destroying lives to serve her purpose. The organisation sure knows how to pick them. They have given one of the nicest men I know, one of the worst humans on earth as a partner. It will slowly kill him.

I have to help. I'll involve the team. Henry doesn't fully comprehend his situation. That woman intends to murder Carl and make herself the only important person in Henry's life. She has waited a long time to have him, and now is her time.

New York

Martin

Everywhere in the underground is dark and dusty. My eyes are stinging, and we can't see clearly. After what seems like hours, we have managed to squeeze out of the blocked titanium steel door. Edward is panting and coughing at my side, his hands on his knees, trying to breathe. I tap his back, 'We don't have time; we need to move this debris. They are everywhere; we still have a lot to do.'

'I'm not a trained cop; I don't have your fitness. I sit behind my computer day in, day out. That is my strength; I need a minute, Martin.'

I smile. I know Edward is irritated, and so am I, but we don't have time to wait or complain. Looking at the damaged structure, it is not strong enough to support the load and will collapse soon.

'Edward, we need to move!' The only way to get out of this underground is by pushing more debris out of the way.

He sighs heavily and stands upright. 'I'm coming!'

There is a loud noise behind us and more dust and debris falls.

'We have to go now. Everything is about to collapse!' I yell, desperately trying to push a way through. 'If this is the end of us,' I cry out to Edward, 'remember, I love you, man. Thanks for everything.'

Then the ground begins to shake as everything around us begins to break apart and fall.

Chapter Sixty-five: Rio de Janeiro

Ana

With everything happening in New York with Edward and Martin, I don't want to disturb the team with my problems. We have not heard from them in ages. How can I tell them that the organisation is looking for me too?

I tap into all the cameras in my apartment building to see what has been happening there. The organisation can be sneaky. I know that eight people broke into my apartment in the middle of the night, dividing themselves into groups of two to search the whole place. Everything was turned upside down. About thirty minutes later, my boss entered my apartment. Then more people came, and the entire building was searched. The security guard was questioned for hours, badly beaten and taken away in a car.

One of the best things about being a great hacker is being able to give yourself a false identity; that is how I was able to rent this warehouse. I am fully paid up for a year.

My old car is parked inside the warehouse to be safe. I have removed the plate numbers and buried them. I was able to redirect their tracing to another vehicle and disable the car tracking device in my car. All the details linking me to the car and warehouse have been changed. I'm safe – for now!

***

I attend a unity team meeting.

'We need to find out what is going on. We can't just sit here, not knowing anything,' says Huan Li. 'Hours have turned to days. I suggest we connect to the street cameras closest to the underground location where they were hiding; that is the only way we stand a chance of finding out what is happening and help.'

That is a good idea, we concur.

'There are twenty cameras in total, I'm sending everyone the layout and schematic diagram now,' I say. 'Let's take four each to be fast. I will take the four from the buildings opposite. Tom takes the four on the left side of the underground. Huan takes four from the right, Segun, the four behind the underground and Sarah the four in the underground.'

Everyone is typing on their keyboards; we need to connect to these cameras without anyone noticing. The world of technology makes the impossible possible.

I connect to the four cameras facing the underground. Dear God! I can see about ten people standing by the underground entrance; this can't be a coincidence.

'There are about ten people outside waiting for them,' I inform the team members.

'There are agents positioned everywhere. How can they escape without being noticed?' says Segun. 'We have to find a way to distract them but, wait, can you see everyone is running, the ground is moving, I think the underground just imploded.'

'The cameras are already down in the underground. What do we do now? How can they escape this?' shouts Sarah.

'No, wait! This is a good thing,' says Segun. 'Can you see them running to their cars. They are evacuating the area. Some of the surrounding buildings will feel the effect. I hope they don't collapse. We have to make sure they are not seen if they manage to escape.'

We watch as one of the street light poles falls to the ground, almost hitting the opposite building.

'We have to alter those cameras,' I say, 'but be careful. The best people from the organisation are connected and they will be watching.'

***

The big boss raises his voice in anger. 'I have given you everything; yet you continue to fail me.'

Mr Montes prostrates himself on the ground.

'Sir, I didn't know she was an expert in information technology. I sent you the video where we tested her; she was a good actress and has deceived us all.'

'Get up, now. I don't understand why you are begging. She lived in your building, yet she managed to escape into thin air. Things are going from bad to worse on all continents. We were robbed by a group of people we have identified as being from New York, Lagos and Rio de Janeiro. I know there are more. We must find

them, before they destroy us, but somehow they always manage to elude us.

'The head is breathing down our necks to find these people. Get Carlos!'

He is dragged in front of the big boss. He has been badly beaten and there are angry bruises and deep cuts on his body and face.

'Your job was to watch Ana. How did she escape?'

He bows his head, unable to answer.

'This is a disaster. I need to hear one piece of good news today, or heads will roll. If I go down, make no mistake, I am taking you two along.'

'She can't have gone far,' says Mr Montes. 'We hacked the cameras in her building to see where she went, but she seemed to know where they were and how to avoid them.'

'She has played us for a fool and continues to do so. You have less than twelve hours to turn Rio de Janeiro upside down and find her. I'm working on borrowed time. Fail me on this, and you will both get a bullet to the head. Get to work!'

Mr Montes and Carlos Ribeiro leave. Carlos struggles to breathe, due to the beating.

'We don't have time,' says Mr Montes. 'The boss is getting desperate, which means the head is desperate. We need to find Ana and fast. Gather all our men. Tell them not to take a break until they find Ana. She is hiding somewhere. Her old house is empty and trashed. You need to search every home.

'Carlos, this is our last chance, the boss is not joking, he will end us today if we don't find her, time is ticking, let's go!'

Chapter Sixty-six: Hong Kong

The Unity Team

Huan

I cover my mouth with my hand in shock as I watch the screen. The ground is vibrating. How can they hope to survive this disaster? What can we do to help them? They might be trapped under there. I know they are dead if they don't come out in the next thirty minutes.

I watch the two cameras still working my end. The exit from the underground is to the right. If something should happen to them, the plan and deadline will be halted.

We have connected to the cameras and made modifications without the organisation noticing. We made sure that what they see is delayed by five minutes. This will give us a chance to make quick changes if necessary. Please come out, Martin and Edward.

I bite my nails and my T-shirt is sticking to my clammy skin. From what we can see, the exit is blocked with a large stone; the organisation did a good job. How can they hope to get out?

The ground vibrates again.

Everywhere is dead silent, no one can speak, we watch our screens silently, hoping against hope that they will survive somehow.

The stone in the exit moves slightly. No, it can't be them!

I notice movement. 'I can see something,' I shout, staring at the camera with the team members.

'Is it possible they can have survived this?' asked Sarah. 'They must have nine lives.'

They are covered in dust, we can't make out their faces but from the height, it could be them.

'It's them, I'm sure of it. I will alter the video. That is all we can do. I think we should rest now and reconvene in the next twenty-four hours. If they are out and can reach safety, hopefully, they will find a way to contact us.'

The Organisation

Andrew Hughes

All the big bosses have connected to discover the outcome of the operation in New York. The best people have been assigned to this operation. It will be a disaster if we fail.

'Is someone watching any possible entrances and exits he could use to escape?' asks James Cooper.

Bobby addresses the bosses, feeling very proud of himself. 'I know for a fact that no one could escape that explosion. He is dead!'

'How can you be so sure? You incompetent idiot! You have been assigned to locate him and kill him for months, yet you continuously fail me. I elevated you to the position of FBI director solely for this reason,' I say. 'Looks like I chose the wrong cop.'

'Then we will assume he is still alive until we see his dead body. Why is no one physically on the ground watching?' asks Ping Wu from Asia_2.

'The ground was vibrating, and it was about to collapse. The best security team are watching the cameras all around the area. If he survives, we will know,' says Bobby. 'It's been over twenty-four hours since the operation began. They can't have survived. Our men are going there tomorrow to see whether we can enter the underground, but it is hazardous.'

I turn to Bobby, who is by my side. 'I want you with them. You will go there at the break of dawn. You will take all the equipment necessary; I don't care if those buildings do collapse on you. You will go into the underground and find the body of Martin. If you fail us, I have instructed the men to put a bullet to your head. I have realised you are a dead-weight pulling us down. I can't believe you ran out of the place because you are afraid to die. Trust me, death will come to you in other ways if you fail me. Now get out of our sight, imbecile!'

The six big bosses shake their heads as Bobby walks out of the conference room.

'We are in trouble,' says Lekan Gbada. 'The head will call for a meeting soon; he knows everything that is happening, and our asses are on the line.'

'I want to ask, Andrew, why did you assign Bobby to head up this operation, knowing he is incompetent?' Sophia Richardson demands.

'That was my mistake. He was Martin's partner for eleven years, and they were best friends. He knows him better than anyone.'

'I, for one, don't want to lose my position to the replacement the head is preparing to take my place,' says Adriano Cardoso. 'We have been lenient with the members failing us. No more!'

'I have spent much time thinking and analysing,' I say. 'We need to take back power. We need to prove to these people that they can't escape us. We must ask ourselves, what is it that they are using to bring us down?

'Gamaplug is the most powerful technology ever created. This is the technology we use on our opponents to bring them in line. These people are aware of this; they are not using Gamaplug, which is strange. I believe they are creating another technology to bring down Gamaplug. We know that they have the best people in information technology. We have a list of people using Gamaplug worldwide that will narrow down our search; those not on the list will become our main targets. They will need to source the right equipment and components worldwide, and it will not be cheap. We should monitor the ports. Let's start by impounding goods we suspect can be used against us. This is the way forward, and I hope you agree?'

Chapter Sixty-seven: London

Jude

I stroll into the house, feeling downcast.

'What's wrong?' asks Sarah. 'You were supposed to be back an hour ago; where are the goods?'

'I went to the PO Box address used for the orders. Luckily for me, I was being cautious. I saw two people in a car watching the place. I had an unsettling feeling that something was wrong. When I entered the building, there was a man and a woman talking and laughing, which was strange. Why hang out there?'

'We have three PO Box addresses registered in different names; 5947, 4658 and 5234. The orders we were expecting were delivered to number 5947. I decided to open number 4658, and I noticed the couple watching me closely, while pretending to laugh at each other's jokes. I ordered some books to that number just in case I might need to protect myself; the best thing I've ever done. I took the two bestsellers and left the place, followed by this couple. It's taken me ages to shake them off.

'I'm certain they are working for the organisation. We need to use another PO Box address; that place is compromised.'

'We need to get that equipment and components one way or the other, Jude. They are rare, and it took weeks before I could find them. I need to combine these components to build the PG and test it. They were costly; they run into millions of pounds.'

'They are watching the place. How can we pick up the order without them knowing?'

'You'll have to go at night, around 3.00 am. I will generate a power surge five minutes before you arrive, and everything will go down. You will have less than six minutes to get those components before the power returns.'

'Jesus! I'm not a policeman, Sarah. I don't have these skills. I'm terrified of these people.'

'What choice do we have? Without these components, everything we have laboured for, all our losses because of these people, will have been for nothing. We might as well give up.'

I can't stop trembling. We need to plan carefully. Without being sure everything is covered, I'll not place my life in danger again.

***

Sarah smiles warily, looking at the street view.

'There's a car parked across the road, so they can see people coming in and going out. They also have people stationed at the address. These components just arrived; in the previous deliveries, we had no problem, which means the organisation is aware of what we are doing, that is a problem.

'When the power goes down, I'll make sure no electronics work, which means I'll not be able to communicate with you. The good news is that no one will be able to use the torch on their phones, and most people don't carry battery torches. This also means they will not be able to communicate with each other. That is only temporary; it will come back up by itself. There are backups in place for such occurrences. That is why I said you have less than six minutes before everything returns to normal; you must disappear before that happens. You need to watch out for the one night guard inside of the building and the people outside watching who will not hesitate to eliminate you, if they should see you.'

I wear black clothes but pull on a balaclava, pulling my hoodie over it when I arrive at the destination. The car is still parked, in the same position, with about four people inside watching the place. I hope nobody is inside the address; it will be more difficult for me to get in and out.

I have my backpack to carry the components, and I have brought a torchlight that Sarah insists I must never use; I have to rely on my instincts. I look at my wristwatch. The lights will go down in the next minute or so. I need to move closer to the building without being seen.

The night is silent. Few people own cars now; the cost of fuel is astronomical. Only the elite few have the pleasure of owning and driving a car.

Darkness descends suddenly. I see only a little light from the building. The four people rush out of the car, trying to communicate with Gamaplug. One of them enters the building and is talking to the staff after instructing him to open the entrance door.

My heart is pounding so hard in my chest, I think I might have a heart attack.

I try to navigate my way to the door, in total darkness, to enter the building, making sure I am not followed. Thank goodness for the confusion! The unexpected has caught them unawares. I need to be very quiet.

An agent collects a torch from a member of staff and goes outside, I know he going to call his colleagues. I race to the location of the boxes. I am prepared; I studied the blueprint for hours closing my eyes picturing myself in the dark.

There are footsteps. *Jesus, I don't want to slam into anyone by accident.* I can't see a thing; I can't use the torch; this is the only way. I walk further inside, I hear voices, they are coming this way.

Now hurry, Jude, this is your chance. I run towards the storage containers to number 5947, the first locker, relying on my sense of touch to be sure. I open it with the key. I switch on the torch for a second to check that the components are there. They are coming! I quickly place them in my backpack, closing the box behind, and rush out of there, switching off the torch.

After bumping my head several times, I hide behind a pillar. I see the agents rushing towards the mailboxes.

I manage to navigate my way out of the building. I can hear panicked voices, people wondering what's happening. I get as far away as possible, before removing my balaclava.

The power comes back on, and my phone starts ringing immediately. I answer; the only person who could be calling me is Sarah. She speaks quickly. 'The parcel is being tracked; look for the tracking device and remove it immediately.'

I opened my backpack and search frantically, looking everywhere. They are coming after me. Where is the tracking device? Then I see the tiniest GPS chip on the left side of the parcel. I tear it off and throw it away, before running as fast as I can go in the opposite direction.

I don't know how long I run for, but you lose all sense of time when your life is in danger. I then jump on the connecting train, trying to steady my breathing as I look around. Finally, I arrive back at the house, satisfied that I'm not being followed.

I open the door and drop the parcel, panting heavily. I never want to do this again!

Chapter Sixty-eight: New York

Martin

If I was asked how we managed to escape death, I wouldn't have an answer. Everything was falling on us. We know the underground like the back of our hands, but with everything happening around us, we had to rely on our instincts. We ran fast; sometimes, we had to slow down and clear the debris from our path, hoping against hope that we wouldn't get trapped inside. Somehow we managed to escape the underground, without being seen. We were entirely covered with dust. We didn't have time to assess the damage done to the locality; we just needed to get away without being caught.

The biggest shock was that we didn't see anyone when we got out of the underground. We were so sure the organisation would be waiting for us. We walked for hours to reach Brooklyn. No one looked at us twice; everyone was too engrossed with their own problems.

What a joy to finally settle down in Edward's late sister's house. We have not moved from this position in hours, and our bodies are finally reacting to our ordeal. Edward kept the spare keys to his sister's house in a box in his backyard. I don't know how long we can stay here, but Edward has assured me not to worry. But, if this place is safe, why were we hiding in the underground?

'Edward!' I try to move, but I'm in too much pain. 'We need to contact the team; I know they will be worried about us.'

'I know, I have a computer and some old laptops in the house, they will have to do for the moment; I have not been to this house in five years.'

'Why did you leave your spacious house to live in the underground?'

'I was hiding from the FBI. I am one of the best hackers in the world. I discovered the abandoned underground; it gave me privacy from prying eyes.'

He struggles to get up from the sofa. 'I need to set up the computers. I hope they still work. We need to start all over again, and I need your help reordering those components for O-generation. We have less than three weeks to finish everything, and we're running out of time.'

'The organisation is after us. They will not give up; this is a minor setback for them. They be looking for us in full force.'

'Then let's hope they think we are dead, buried beneath the rubble. It may distract them long enough while we redo what we've lost. The only way to destroy them permanently is with POWERA, so I'll need your help to pick up that equipment and components.'

Bobby

My heart is beating fast as I instruct the men to clear the debris blocking the entrances and exits to the underground. Today will determine if I live or die. I wipe away the sweat on my head.

Please be dead, Martin! How did I get this wrong? This was my opportunity to prove to the organisation that I am the best and finally get the recognition I deserve. Instead, I stood before the big bosses while my boss berated me. I had to endure humiliation in front of them and my subordinates.

'Hurry up!' We need to make sure everyone is dead.

I enter the underground. I know it is not safe to be down here, but what choice do I have? The debris is cleared away as we check everywhere.

'Sir, there are no bodies here,' one of my men says eventually.

'I need you to be sure, we are not leaving here until I'm convinced otherwise. Check the cameras again as well.'

'Sir, we monitored the cameras, but no one has come out of the underground.'

Why am I shaking? It's carnage down here. How could they possibly have escaped?

This is my life we are talking about. The big bosses are waiting for my report, God! We need to find a body – anybody.

***

'Sir! The boss wants you to report in. We have been down here for four hours.'

'Did you tell him we haven't found anyone?' I shout angrily.

'Sir, we all report to the boss. We have to tell the truth; he is not just calling on you for information. He has several people reporting to him every second. You have to leave here, sir and go straight to the headquarters. Failure to do that means death with immediate effect. Please follow me!'

My life is over. There are three men behind me. 'Why are you standing there? Leave now!' I command, but they refuse to get out of the way, waiting for me to move. I have no authority anymore; the big boss must have instructed them.

I follow my former subordinate, who is trying to be respectful. 'Finish clearing and then report back to me immediately,' he instructs the men still working.

He turns to me. 'Sir, after you.'

I walk in front, followed by four men. Outside the underground, a black saloon car is waiting for me. The door opens, and I am told to get in. Two of them get in with me and I am sandwiched between them. Another sits in the front seat, and the driver pulls away.

'What did the boss tell you to do with me?' I ask the men. 'You have all worked for me for months. I have been fair to you all. You owe me this. This could be you at any time.'

None of them answer. I laugh bitterly. 'Oh, how things have changed. None of you would dare treat me like this an hour ago.'

I need to find a way out of this; then I'll teach them a lesson in respect.

Chapter Sixty-nine: Lagos

Segun

We need to be more cautious. We have listened to Martin and Edward's incredible tale of how they escaped from the New York underground by pure luck. I am glad they are still with us, but this is a significant setback.

The organisation is the biggest roadblock to accomplishing our plans. They are everywhere; they monitor everything. The situation is terrible; people are living in fear and impoverishment. They have lost the spirit to fight. We are the few people who still have the means and energy to fight our oppressors.

We have agreed not to communicate with each other for the next two weeks unless it is urgent, and then only through our encrypted chat box. We need to finish the different generations of POWERA. That is the goal now.

Lola and I have been working day and night developing W-generation. I am exhausted, but what choice do we have? We are staying away from the web, keeping indoors and only going out to buy a limited supply of exorbitant food.

The organisation went on a rampage looking for us. They have torn through the city of Lagos. They have appeared in my house, unannounced, on two occasions. Thank God for the monitoring device I set up that allows ample time to put everything away before they arrive.

Lola is still wearing her prosthetic tummy and it is now a permanent disguise. I fear that if they continue to come at some point, we will need to find a baby or pretend she lost it without the organisation knowing. One thing is for sure, she can't remain pregnant indefinitely.

Lekan Gbada

My men are monitoring everything happening in the continent of Africa. Nothing has been imported that is suspicious, and the dark web has gone silent. These people are always one step ahead of us. It's embarrassing.

My head security walks into my office. 'Tell me you have good news?'

'No, sir! We have searched every state in the country for this man. I believe he must be dead.'

'How can you stand in front of me and make such a ridiculous statement? Can a dead man aid in the heist of one-and-a-half billion dollars? What does that say about our organisation? We cannot find one person.'

'We have no leverage we can use against him. He hated his father, and now he is dead. The only person associated with him is the journalist; Lola. She lost her father, and she doesn't seem to care about her mother and brothers.'

'Has she at any point communicated with her family or friends?'

'She has not spoken to any of them, not once, which is why I believe something happened to them. We have been to the most remote places in the country, but they are not there.'

'I have fourteen days before I face the head again. Then I will lose my job or be killed. The definition of insanity is doing the same thing and expecting a different result. We need help from the people, and offer them large sums of money. They are desperate; let's turn them against themselves. Every vital piece of information will be rewarded.'

'The citizens hate us,' says the security man. 'Do you think they will help and not be afraid that we are setting them up?'

'The request will not come from us. We will use one of the friendliest faces in the world, an older woman, one of our members. She is willing to pay for any information on strange happenings in their area. We don't have much time. We can't rest until we find Segun. It's either his head or ours. Now, go and find him.'

This is a shame; we rely so much on Gamaplug, our greatest weapon for bringing down our opponent. Now that our opponents know about Gamaplug and all other technology we use, how do we hope to stop them?

Lola

Segun has been working so hard. I feel sorry for him because there is very little I can contribute. I assist him in holding a piece of equipment while he tries to connect another to it. I can see the progress he has made in days; I have a feeling of satisfaction that we are getting closer to our goal.

I turn on my only laptop, which we use to search for the latest news or developments. I see the image of an old woman crying on national television, offering thirty million naira for anyone who can provide vital information on suspicious activities. What do they mean by 'suspicious activities'?

'Segun! Come and see the news. Do you think the organisation is involved?'

'The government owns all the country's news stations; nothing can be broadcast without their approval. She is working for them.'

'They are getting desperate. Jesus Christ! Look at me; I need to give birth soon. I'm getting tired of carrying this fake tummy.'

'I've been thinking about that. We need to find a way to convince the organisation that you lost that baby; otherwise, they will try to trace the hospital you gave birth in. I have to falsify a death certificate and find a dead baby to bury in the backyard. The only way this will fly is to tell them we couldn't afford the cost of the hospital. We decided to have the baby at home, and it died.'

'But where can we get a dead newborn baby without raising suspicion?'

Segun turns to look me in the eye. 'Lola, have you not seen the news? People will do anything to get their hands on thirty million naira!'

Chapter Seventy: Kabul

Ahmed

The explosion brings down the block fence. There is much screaming and shouting, and a loud popping sound of guns being fired. I jump up from my bed, and run out of the room. People are running in all directions. I have to find Jabar. First, I need a weapon. Mohammed refused to give me one when he reluctantly allowed me back into the compound.

I keep low, with my back to the wall, creeping along, trying to determine what is going on. I see a few men I don't recognise barge into the main building shouting that everyone should get on the ground. This is a well-planned attack. It is 2.00 am when everyone is sleeping, and they have come in unannounced.

I hide behind a door. One of the men reaches the second floor where I am hiding. I sneak up behind him and punch him in the throat. He falls to the ground. I quickly pick up his submachine gun. I have to find my way out without being noticed. I don't know how many people are out there. The attackers all appear to be wearing black so I need to pretend to be one of them. I strip the unconscious man of his tunban and hurriedly put on his clothes. Maybe I can survive this.

I put my head down as I get out of the building. One of the attackers is coming my way, telling me to follow him and that the instruction is to kill Mohammed Pir. I follow him and about ten men searching the building that Mohammed resides in.

'He has to be here. Where is he?' he screams. He picks up his radio, and I can hear him talking to Yusuf, saying that he can't find Yusuf.

I back out, pretending to look for Ahedan soldiers. I must find Jabar and Mohammed.

I race to Mohammed's office. I know there is a secret passage. The door is wide open, and the office has been turned upside down. Looking outside, I can see Ahedan men kneeling in a group surrounded by men sent by Hussain Atta.

In the office, some books are disorganised, others lay on the floor, but I remember the quantum physics textbook still on the shelf. I pull the book out, and the shelf opens a little, revealing a space behind the bookcase. I rush inside before someone sees me, and the bookcase and shelf closes automatically.

I look around. It's a secret passage, as I suspected, but where does it lead to? The way is well lit and I walked along the narrow passageway for a long time only to reach a blocked wall. The only way out, that I can see, is to open the entrance above me. I push it open, strapping the gun to my side.

I climbed out to find several guns pointing at me. I lift my hands, and look up to see Mohammed, Latif, the head of bodyguard and Jabar watching me, refusing to lower their guns.

'It's me. I'm on your side,' I shout. 'Why are your guns still pointed at me?'

'How did you know about the secret passage?' asks Mohammed.

'Hussain instructed me to find out where you hid the nuclear weapons. I studied your office and reading habits. I know that you can't possibly read quantum physics, so the book stood out as being subspinous.'

'We need him,' says Jabar, lowering his weapon. 'He is the best; if you need someone on your side, you want Ahmed.'

'I don't know who to trust; today's events have destroyed everything I believed in for the past five years.'

'Hussain wants you dead. You are of no use to him anymore, he will not rest until he finds you, but I know you are a man of wisdom. You have a contingency plan. What is it?' I demand.

I can see Mohammed staring at us, doubt written all over his face.

Eventually, he says, 'I have a house just by the border between Kabul and Charikar. We need to get there without being seen. I have a truck hidden in this compound that we can use.'

'Hussain Atta has made himself into a national hero. He will be celebrated for bringing down the Ahedan Group. Everyone will be looking for you. We need your assistance to expose him to the people for who he truly is.'

To my relief, Mohammed nods and lifts his gun. 'I have everything set up in the new place, every electronics device and weapon you could need. I am very cautious. I never quite trusted the man controlling me. I'll do everything I can to take him out; I'm no one's puppet. But we need to leave immediately; they will discover us soon. Follow me.'

We follow behind Mohammed, weapons raised, checking left and right. He opens the door to one of the rooms with one of his keys. Inside the room, we discover more weapons, and he picks up the key to the truck. We pick up as many guns as we can amass quickly. We don't know what we will encounter on the way.

'The truck is bulletproof,' says Mohammed. He throws the key to Latif, who jumps into the driver's seat. I take the seat in front while Mohammed and Jabar sit in the back, guns in hand.

***

'I gave you a simple instruction, find Mohammed and kill him. How did he manage to escape?' yells Hussain.

Yusuf coughs and splutters out blood.

'You can't even find Ahmed and Jabar. The intel we received was that they were in this compound. So, where are they? I can't see them anywhere.'

Yusuf's whole body trembles as he lies in the dirt.

'The best soldier just walked out of here, and you are none the wiser on how he did it. He is now working with that psychotic man who is on the loose. I can't even imagine what he might do. He would blow up the whole world to prove his power, so I want him dead.

'I demoted you because of your failure, but I gave you this task because you knew Ahmed better than anyone else. My mistake! It won't happen again. Find them or just kill yourself and save me the trouble.'

Chapter Seventy-one: Sydney

Henry

Carl was driven to his new grammar school by my trusted chauffeur, accompanied by my loyal personal assistant, Rob. I didn't inform anyone that he would be leaving the house the same day as my sham marriage. My heart is breaking; I had just got my son back. Now I have to protect him from a self-serving, narcissistic woman.

The wedding, the reception, all of it was a blur; I just wanted to wake up from my nightmare. I needed the wedding to be over so I could lock myself in my room. I smiled for the cameras and shook hands with the elite guests that would report to the big boss. I watched Cynthia put on a show, smiling and waving. She even granted interviews, but I refused to answer any questions. The lies fell easily from her lips. She stated that we had known each other for over twenty-five years, lost contact when she left the country for work, reconnected months ago after my wife's demise, and the deep love we had for each other resurfaced.

We enter my house, and I turn to her and point towards the guest room downstairs. 'That is your room, Cynthia; I'll never share a bedroom with you.'

She bursts out laughing. 'Are you kidding me, Henry? We are married, I'm Cynthia Graham now, and I'm having a child with you.'

'That's very good! Have the child and name, but we will never share a bed, not in this life!'

'You will sleep with me, Henry, whether you like it or not. We work for the same organisation and the big boss will not be happy to hear this.'

'You are kidding me, right? Do you think the boss cares if have a good marriage? She just wants us to continue this charade in public. She believes you are evil enough to achieve everything she wants for the country. I'm surprised you settled for me. You are a goal-getter. I would think you would have gone for someone more like the boss.'

'Are you calling me a whore?'

'No! A whore is too respectable a word for you. You are

deranged, diabolical; your mother should have aborted you when she found out she was pregnant.'

I turn away, climbing the staircase. I need to get away from her; I want to strangle her so badly.

She follows me, shouting, 'How dare you insult me like this. Where is that stupid son of yours? I intend to make his life miserable. Carl!' she calls. 'Sweetheart, where are you?'

'When he doesn't reply, she looks up at me and asks, 'Where is Carl?'

I don't answer. I open the door to my room; but she follows me and tries to push inside. I resist with all my might and she falls backwards. I lock the door; I have installed a double-bolt lock for my door.

She bangs on the door. 'This is our wedding night. How dare you do this to me? I will make you suffer for this,' she yells. 'You think I'm deranged; you haven't seen anything yet.'

I hold my head in my hands; my head is pounding; I know Cynthia is not kidding. She will make my life a living hell. She can have the house; I need to move far away from her, only seeing her for public appearances.

How did it come to this? What did I do wrong? My beloved wife is being hidden in an isolated place, terrified for her life, not knowing she is in the safest place.

I have received a text on my phone from Rob telling me that Carl is safe and has settled into the boarding school. He has been warned not to tell anyone Carl's whereabouts. I know my mother will be here tomorrow asking questions.

I send a text to Tom informing him that I'll see him tomorrow. He said he has information that will help me with Cynthia, and I need all the help I can get. *Rest!* I tell myself. The battle continues tomorrow.

***

After taking a bath and getting dressed, I open the door to my room. I need to see Tom first thing this morning. I have not had an opportunity to find out his progress on E-generation; this is my ticket out of this horrible situation.

I lock the door behind me, putting the key in my pocket. I go downstairs to find my mother and Cynthia having breakfast. I ignore them and go to the entrance door. It is locked.

I walk over to Cynthia. 'Why did you lock the door? Where is the key?'

She doesn't answer me. I have never been so livid in my life; I can't take this anymore. I storm towards her. My mother gets up from her chair. 'Calm down, Henry!' This is your honeymoon; you should be at home.'

I point at Cynthia. 'If she doesn't open that door in the next minute, I'll kill her and then myself. Do you think I'm joking?'

I run to the kitchen and see the array of wine glasses on display. I remove one and smash it. I don't feel any pain as blood trickles down my hands. No! Broken glass will not be as effective as a knife. I open a drawer, and grab one before rushing to the dining room, knife in hand.

'Stop it, Henry!' my mother shouts. 'Stop it right now!'

'Then open the door. Now!'

Cynthia looks at me and smiles. 'You are weak; you can't do anything.'

I walk up to her and, with all my energy, I stab her left shoulder.

She starts screaming. 'Open the door or bleed to death, choose!' I say.

'What has come over you?' my mother yells.

Cynthia gives my mother the key and she rushes to the entrance and opens the door.

I walk out of the house without looking back. I can hear my mother calling my name as I get into my car and drive away. I hope she dies, but I'm not that lucky. I drive like a maniac. I'll not be coming home tonight; she brings out the worst in me.

Cynthia is working with my mother, but I know Mother; her greatest fear is to lose me. I will make her pick sides; she can't be my mother and Cynthia's best friend at the same time. My phone is ringing endlessly. I turn it off; let this be a warning to them, the Henry you used to know is no more!

I need to talk to Tom.

Chapter Seventy-two: Rio de Janeiro

Carlos

I wipe the sweat off my face; there are palpitations in my chest. The minutes continue to tick away. We have less than five hours to find Ana, or we are dead. We are searching everywhere using all available technology, but she seems to be one step ahead. Unfortunately, she left her mobile phone in the house. We could have used it to find her because of the tracking device we placed in it.

How did we miss this? We should have known, all that pretending. Coming to the office early in the morning, working without complaining and not asking after her family should have been a red flag. We were played for a fool while she planned with her cohort to steal from the organisation and put our lives in danger.

I hope I find you, Ana Santos, you will wish you had never been born. Death would be easy. I will slowly torture her but, before her demise, I'll kill her nephews and sell her nieces to sex traffickers while she watches.

Ana

I monitor the screen. I know I am not safe. The already-installed hidden cameras in the four corners of the warehouse show when someone attempts to enter the building. But something is wrong; the screen is static, and they are tampering with all the cameras in the city. When you enter the warehouse, it looks empty; a wall is dividing it. I use the other side. I cleared everything in the space I am using, packing it all into extra-large cardboard boxes which I then sealed. I have placed the boxes around the warehouse; some of the rooms have not been used in years. They look dirty and dusty; I poured sand and rubbed mud and dog faeces on them to make the boxes look old, worn, and smelly.

Segun had the idea, which he shared with everyone in the team. I had been in one of the dark rooms for hours when I noticed the cameras were not working. I got into one of the extra-large, worn cardboard boxes and I've been hiding in it for an hour. They will be here soon.

I hear movement. 'Search everywhere,' a voice commands. Fear clutches my heart. If they should search these dirty boxes, I will die for sure.

One of the men says, 'This place is abandoned; it smells so bad!'

'There is a car parked outside; it doesn't appear to be registered to anyone. The boss said to search everywhere, and we need to do that. Search everything!'

I hear two people talking as they enter the room I am hiding in.

'This place has no windows, and it is dark, there are cobwebs everywhere, there is no one here. I am not touching those disgusting old boxes. It's a waste of time.'

'We'll just tell the boss we checked the boxes.'

'That's a good idea. Let's get out of here before I die from the foul smell.'

I silently sigh in relief. *Thank God for incompetent people.* I can no longer feel any part of my body, but I must ensure the coast is clear before coming out.

This organisation will stop at nothing. It has destroyed the world economy. People can barely survive. They have taken everything away from me, including my peace of mind, but I have to live if I am to help.

Mr Montes and Carlos

The two men tremble in terror as they face the big boss.

'I gave you twelve hours to find Ana. I gave you all the resources you need, and you stand in front of me with a flimsy excuse that you can't find her. I knew this day would come when you would become useless to me.'

'Sir, we had limited time to search the whole city; she is not using any technology, and finding a needle in the middle of a haystack isn't easy. Please, we need more time,' begs Mr Montes.

'The thing I hate most is excuses. All I'm hearing are excuses.' The big boss clicks his fingers. 'Bring them in!'

His men enter with an older woman in her seventies, a young lady in her twenties with twin boys, about five months old. Mr Montes sees them and starts to whimper. 'Please, please, this is my family.'

Carlos tries to hold back a sob as they bring out his father and mother, both in their sixties, his sister, who is twenty-five and his twenty-seven-year-old brother.

'I told you I'd kill you if you failed me, but I felt that would be too easy. I want to inflict pain on you, the way you have caused me pain. You allowed a very dangerous woman to escape. She stole from us; she brought down our cybersecurity, a woman with nothing to lose. She doesn't care about anything, even her family. Now, you will feel the pain and the cost of failing me.' He looks at their families. 'Kill them!'

Mr Montes falls to his knees and covers his face as he hears gunshots being fired. His heart breaks. 'My sons!' he weeps. It took him twenty-seven years before he could finally have children, now he had lost his heirs, pride and joy, to a stupid mistake.

'There, there, don't cry,' the big boss laughs. 'Those children are not yours!'

'What!' He looks at the boss through teary eyes.

'Your wife knew your shortcomings and decided to get pregnant by somebody else. They are someone else's children.' Mr Montes looks at him doubtfully, as the boss shows him the records.

Carlos Ribeiro shows no emotion as he watches them execute his family. *The big boss thinks he can break me,* he thinks, *but I don't care about anyone. I lost my conscience a long time ago.*

The big boss looks at Carlos me and smiles. 'You are very strong, Carlos. It is a pity you answer to your idiot boss. End them!' he says, walking out of the building. 'The time has come for me to find this Ana myself.'

Ana

I climb out of the box and fall to the ground. My legs have fallen asleep and don't work properly. I have been in an uncomfortable position for hours. I strain my ears to hear any sound; everywhere is quiet.

I'm tired of this hide-and-seek game. It's time to end this and bring down this organisation. I have almost completed the R-generation. I hope just they have not destroyed any of those boxes lying around the warehouse.

Chapter Seventy-three: Hong Kong

Huan

I have made tremendous progress in the A-generation aspect of POWERA. We have two weeks left before the big reveal, and things have been relatively quiet on my side. We have decided as a team to concentrate on our various projects and then reconvene after the work is finished. I'm excited Gama organisation is going down.

I switch on the news and see 'breaking news' on the screen going round on a loop. The organisation owns every station worldwide; nothing is broadcast without their approval. I unmute the screen, and my heart skips a beat. Is that my aunty on the screen? She lives in the US. What is she doing in Hong Kong? She is as white as a sheet. The reporter states that she has been extradited to China to face the crime of selling young girls to sex traffickers.

What have I done? I cover my mouth with my hand in shock; I know this has happened because of me. They want to punish the most important person to me. She is a mother to me; she took me in when my birth mother died. How can I help her? I knew it was too good to be true, the organisation not reacting violently to the theft. They took my husband away. Now they want to take the only mother I have known away, too.

I sit behind my workstation in my house and hack into the station reporting the lies. I don't care if I get caught. They will not soil my family's name. I change the script on the teleprompter: 'It has come to our notice that she is innocent of the crime mitigated against her. She was kidnapped from her home in the United States and brought to China by an evil organisation...' As the female reporter reads the edited script, the broadcasting station goes down, and my television screen is blank.

Ping Wu

'What the hell just happened?' I yell. 'I want the reporter, and the station producers brought to me immediately. How dare they disobey me!'

I know Huan will not come out of hiding. It didn't work for her husband, and it definitely won't work for her aunty. I just wanted her to know I can inflict pain on everyone she holds dear. I haven't told the other bosses, my contemporaries, but I know she was somehow involved in the heist in Rio de Janeiro. We have a limited time left before we meet with the head, and we have failed to find these people at every turn. The question is, how are they outsmarting us? What are we doing wrong?

The producers and reporters came into my office, followed by my men. The broadcast crew have been beaten, and have swollen eyes and broken arms. I'm glad my boys have dealt with them appropriately.

'Why would you report such nonsense on live television?' I say. 'I gave this station the licence to report pre-approved news, and today I am disappointed.'

'That is not what we put on the teleprompter,' says one of the production team. 'I don't know what happened; please, this is our script.' He shows me words on a screen. 'We did everything you told us to do.'

'Even if the script was altered somehow, you were reading the wrong thing. You did not pause to say, I think there is a mistake, and the producers did not stop the news immediately, we had to do so on our side.

'I need good people in my team. I have little patience for fools.'

One of my men enters my office and signals to me. I can tell he has important information. I turn to my security men. 'Take care of them!' The crew is shoved out of my office.

'I have good news, sir, someone logged into the station system to alter the teleprompter, and we were able to trace the signal to a rooftop slum in Kowloon. I have sent some of our security people there. Chyou is leading the search.'

I nod in excitement. *Huan; you have made a grave mistake today. My men are coming for you.*

Chyou

The signal came from a particular area. There is a lot of illegal housing on the rooftop of an apartment building filled with people squatting together.

I instruct my team to divide into ten groups, four in each, to search the whole place and find the offender. This is good news. If I find the person responsible, I hope it is Huan Li. I know the boss will not hesitate to promote me. I was temporarily given Cheung Wu's position after the boss killed him for failing to find Huan Li; this is my chance to succeed where he failed.

I follow one of the groups, going to every building, searching everywhere. Some places have twenty people staying in a tiny shack. These people can't afford a laptop or have the expertise to operate it. I look at my wristwatch. We have been here for five-and-a-half hours; we have turned everywhere upside down and come up with nothing. What do I tell the boss now? He is waiting expectantly for this report.

Gama picks up a call; I knew it is the boss. 'Sir. It's a wild-goose chase. We found nothing. We searched everywhere. I think whoever is responsible did it intentionally to waste our time.'

This is not good, Chyou; expand your search. She could be anywhere, and make sure you check the identity of everyone there.'

'Yes, sir.' It's going to be a long day!

Huan

I know I made a mistake logging into the station without doing proper encryption to secure myself from being traced. I acted out of anger, but I'm not that stupid. They traced one of my false IP addresses, it will direct them to the wrong location, but I need to think before I act rashly. This organisation wants to take everything away from me, but the day of reckoning is coming, and you will pay for all the pain you have made me endure.

Chapter Seventy-four: London

Jude

I am a simple chef; how I became a fugitive and lost everything is still surprising to me. I'm glad it's coming to an end.

I have tallied the names of all the members of Red Gama while I was still a member of the European hub, and their leader is James Cooper. I have documented their goals, the people they have killed, made bankrupt, the corruption, and the destruction of the environment to serve their purpose. How they manipulated the government to allocate the best for themselves, privatised everything on the continent with the bulk of the money going into their pockets. They control the narratives; the organisation initiates everything happening in the world. They have ruined lives, and families have lost their loved ones. They have no sympathy, and everything they do is just for one purpose; to satisfy the head of the organisation who sits on his throne, controlling the world through his minions.

I'm delighted to watch Sarah work day and night to meet the deadline set by the team. Our challenge a few days ago made us more determined than ever. The organisation takes no prisoners in their approach to bring us down. The PG is coming together. I'm glad we have the equipment and every component needed; the cost of these products runs into millions of pounds. We will be able to do the test next week; this is a significant stepping stone towards destroying the organisation. I know it will not be easy, but I have lost everything. I don't care if it costs me my life to bring them down. I watched my mother die; I don't even know whether she is buried or has been dumped somewhere. They have taken over my restaurant, money, and properties.

I approach Sarah, who is still working hard. 'Sarah, you need to rest. I don't think you have had any proper sleep in weeks; you have bags under your eyes. It would help if you rested; we can't afford any mistakes.'

'I will sleep when I'm dead. I need to concentrate.'

She carefully puts the components together and ensures that they work.

I point at the food I made over two hours ago, lying untouched where I left it. 'Eat Sarah! The journey is still long. You need all your strength.'

'Why do you need me to eat so badly? The deadline is next week. I can't fail the team.'

'You need to eat; it will only take five minutes of your time. The eggs are already cold; let me reheat them. You can't live on coffee. We are lucky we can afford to eat, with the exorbitant food prices. We live like kings because we can eat twice a day, look outside, and see the number of homeless people begging for food.'

'The more reason, we need to fix this. I can't bear to watch the news anymore, it's being manipulated by the organisation painting the nation as great when we all know it is a lie. Look at the high rate of suicide legitimising mass genocide against civilians. I honestly can't continue like this. I will eat! Don't worry about me; think about the lives we want to save.'

James Cooper

I am furious.

'We have been tracking the components for days. We know these components are too expensive to come out of a person's pocket; we control the wealth of this continent. This makes me confident they are part of the people who stole one-and-a-half billion dollars in Rio de Janeiro. Now you tell me they disappeared without a trace with the components?'

'Sir, we have continued to monitor the PO Box, but no one came forward to claim it. The lights in the city went down before we knew what was happening.'

'How could you allow them to bring down the power? And how can the components just disappear. What about the tracker?'

'The tracker on the package was found on the ground a few miles away.'

'I sent a boy to do a man's job. I gave you specific instructions to make sure everything was covered. We can't afford any mistakes.'

'We searched every house and park in a ten-mile radius of where we found the tracker. He couldn't have disappeared.'

'Do you understand how stupid you sound? They could have

taken a bus, a train or driven a car to where are they going? The exorbitant cost of fuel and the hike in transport fares doesn't affect them. You should have done more.'

'Whatever they are building with those components must be found,' I say. 'I have a sick feeling in my stomach that it could end us. Use everything we have, trace where these components came from and find the person who sent them. I need this information now!'

The people we are dealing with managed to steal an impossible amount of money from the organisation. We still can't find that money; yet we own all the banks in the world. This makes me believe the money is hidden in plain sight, which means the fund is in a bank somewhere, but it's not showing up. That is how good they are!

They have managed to stay one step ahead of us. If we are not careful, they will be the force that shuts us down. We are dancing to their tune. I need to change things around; I will not fail like the bosses of other continents. I'm going to make life even more difficult and miserable for them. I am enforcing a curfew, nobody is allowed outside between 8.00 pm and 6.00 am, and we have a new procedure, 'Stop and Search'. We have a right to search anyone, both male or female, if they raise any suspicion. Anyone roaming the streets during curfew, without authorisation, will be shot on sight.

Chapter Seventy-five: New York

Edward

We have been staying in my house in Brooklyn for two weeks working endlessly to catch up for the lost time. We have bought new laptops and monitors. We had to do it discreetly; the economy is at its worst. The irony is that the price of Gamaplug, which retailed at $900 for the basic appliance, is now at an all-time low; $100 with the cost spread over two years. It is the only technology allowed in the whole continent. I know it is a ploy to get people to continue to buy and use it; 97% of the world's population uses Gamaplug, even in remote places where technology is not at its best. Fred Demson donates Gamaplug free to the countries that cannot afford it.

Martin has been able to gather information on Fred, the most reclusive man in the world. Everyone knows his name, but most do not know anything about him. He shies away from the spotlight, only shining a bright light on his achievements. The little we know, Martin got from Jacob White and, even though he worked for him, he had only met him once at the Christmas party. He didn't bring his family to the gathering, but we know he is married to a lady called Jane. We only now this much because his wife comes from the Brown family; the most renowned name in New York. Her father died six months ago, and the multimillion dollar empire collapsed with no record of how that was possible.

The only communication I have had with the team is from Sarah in London informing us about the components being monitored by the organisation. I should have known; if something is too good to be true, it most likely is. They fooled me and almost caught us unawares.

All my work on O-generation was lost in the explosion; I had to begin again. The components needed came via Jamaica, hidden in exported coffee sacks, as advised by Segun. The good thing about a destroyed world is that people are desperate for money; a lot of money was exchanged to smuggle the goods into the US. The three smugglers who risked their lives were only paid when the five coffee sacks containing the components were exchanged and checked. We had to pay them fifty thousand dollars, but these components cost us millions.

I'm glad I have Martin on my side. The goods were smuggled through a tunnel in the Bronx. He drove my 1992 Honda Accord and we left in the middle of the night. We had to change the oil and check the battery before jump-starting the car. We drove back a little before 3.00 am, disguised as older men with dyed grey hair. We have changed the way we look so often that I'm beginning to forget what I used to look like.

The excitement in building O-generation was huge. I smile at my work. I have made tremendous progress. I have been working tirelessly to make up for lost time. We all need to test POWERA next week; this will be the beginning of the end for the organisation.

Andrew Hughes

I stare out of my window overlooking the Hudson River but can't admire the view. All I am thinking about is the limited time I have left as the boss, lamenting how I failed to capture Martin Hills. I chose the wrong people on his team. It was easy to bring Bobby over to our side; he was a greedy man, and all he ever wanted was money and power. The joy I had watching him plead for his life, promising to do better. He had one task, to find Martin Hills, and he failed at every turn. Killing him would have been easy but I choose a slow, agonising death, hearing him scream as the blowtorch was used all over his body. He died a horrible death, disgraced in front of his subordinates, but it served as a warning to the others about what would happen if they should fail me.

I sigh heavily; we all have to face the head next week. I know my time is coming to an end. Fred Demson is a heavily informed man; everything we do is reported to him; he knows about all our failings and we will be punished accordingly.

The scariest thing about the head is that we don't know anything about him. He has all the information on us because he created us. He was a billionaire before he made Gamaplug, so he didn't do it for the money. He was also one of the world's most influential men, so I'm not sure he did it for power either. Why did Fred Demson create this organisation? He certainly doesn't need us to rule the world; every president, prime minister, and head of state consulted him before Gamaplug.

I was delighted when he recruited me over two years ago. I was a young man in my late thirties, thirsty for wealth. I met the other bosses on the isolated island where we were sent, trained in military intelligence, leadership skills, and becoming a killer. As a test, we were tasked with wiping out our own family, which we did without hesitation. We were promised wealth and power; all we had to do was follow a simple instruction; 'protect the organisation', which we have failed to do time and time again.

I gaze around my office, at the opulence, a life I never thought I would live. Millions of people listen to us when we talk. We have brought the world to a standstill. I will not allow a few good men to sabotage everything for me. I'll fight till my last breath; we have a few days to find these people before the big meeting with the head. I gave up too much to be here. I can't go back to obscurity.

I press my intercom. 'Get me the President of the United States; he has work to do.'

I'll make life miserable for you Martin, and your supporters; wherever you are hiding, I'll find you. That is a promise.

Chapter Seventy-six: Lagos

Segun

We have been hiding in the house for the past week, the thirty million naira reward is making people crazy, and the desperation for the money is alarming. I wonder what people think; this organisation caused the country's impoverishment and demoralisation yet want to reward you for what they have masterminded. Everyone has their phones out, trying to film something. Even going to the market is proving to be complicated.

I met with an unknown doctor. I had completely shaved my hair and moustache and was wearing a cap pulled down over my face, and I had to frisk him to ensure he wasn't wearing a wire. We need a dead newborn baby fast, and time is running out. Lola should have given birth by now, and I know the organisation will come calling soon. He has agreed to the sum of five million naira. He will let me know as soon as a dead baby is available. What we are doing is immoral. At least the baby will already be dead, but I feel for the family. We are hoping someone will abandon a baby at the hospital for them to bury.

'Segun, I hope you are not being set-up?' says Lola in concern. 'No one can be trusted. The chance of winning thirty million naira is greater than the five million naira he agreed on.'

'I know! But what choice do we have? We need a dead baby, the only place we can find a newborn is in the hospital. I have to meet him tonight. You'll be my eyes and ears. We will arrive an hour before the stipulated time, 11.55 pm. I will check the perimeter of the hospital to ensure no one is watching. I'll not meet him in person. He will drop the baby in the pushchair I have placed behind the hospital parking lot. We will be able to see what is placed in the pushchair through our binoculars, and then I will transfer the money into his account.

'We must be careful, I am not worried about the cameras; that has been taken care of, but the patrol car that drives around the hospital grounds. I know the organisation is receiving a lot of false information and videos, I am one of the people bombarding them with bogus news. I uploaded an old video of myself into the website they provided, stating I was seen three streets away from the hospital. Hopefully, that will feed into their desperation to catch me, by sending some of their agents to check it out giving us just ten minutes to get everything done.'

'Do you think the doctor will tell the organisation? They might be watching us, with their advanced technology we wouldn't know they are there,' says Lola.

'We must be hopeful; that is all we can do.'

Lola

I don't understand how Segun can be so calm. We are going into a danger zone, not knowing what to expect. We are so close to the finish line; I don't want that to be taken away from us. W-generation is complete with just a few adjustments and testing required. I can't remember the last time I shed tears of joy. The true exhilaration can't be explained when your life has been destroyed and you see a little glimpse of hope. We live in a world without freedom, where every citizen is being monitored and every movement needs to be accounted for.

We arrive at George Thomas Hospital. I'm glad I could remove that horrible fake pregnancy belly. I was starting to feel like I was actually pregnant, wearing it day and night, and all the while not knowing when the organisation might decide to surprise us. We can't be too careful with the hidden security cameras around the area. So far, everywhere looks quiet.

We attempt to gain access to get into the five-storey office building next to the hospital. It is late, all workers have gone home, and the place is deserted. Thanks to Segun, we get into the building using the back entrance without any problem. How he got a key to someone else's building is a question for another day. Right now, I need to concentrate. I wipe the sweat off my face, removing some of the make-up used to disguise my face.

Segun turns to me. 'Stop worrying! Everything will be fine.'

I force myself to breathe deeply, as I follow Segun. He is on the encrypted phone to the doctor instructing him what to do.

We watched as he drops off the baby, looking around anxiously. The pushchair is between two cars in the dimly-lit parking lot. He checks again to ensure the coast is clear.

Segun holds my hand for a brief second. 'I have to pick up the baby; if anything looks suspicious, call me immediately.'

Jesus Christ! I am not good at this. I look all around using my binoculars. I watch as Segun reaches the pushchair, checking the sad package, carefully monitoring his surroundings. He picks up the dead baby and runs. I know he is running towards the car we parked on the road across from the hospital. I leave my hiding place to catch up with him.

The money distributed to us from the team can only be transferred to someone from an encrypted account. Small amounts of money are transferred into our various local accounts so that we can buy food and this was opened online with false information.

Segun wraps the baby in extensive cotton material and places the tiny corpse in the car's boot. I jump into the car, and he drives away. While driving, he picks up his phone to tell the doctor that the money has been transferred into his account. He then provides him with details about his wife and children and their routine. I can hear the doctor asking, 'How do you know my family?'

'It doesn't matter, but I am right, though, aren't I?' says Segun.

'How did you know this?' the doctor asks, in shock.

'This is a warning. I know everything about you, including where you live. Do not discuss what happened today with anyone. Is that understood?'

Segun

I smile, one down, one more to go. The end is getting closer; revenge will be sweet.

I drive as fast as I can, turning to Lola. 'You need to change back to your disguise as a local woman. You have ten minutes before we arrive. We'll park in the usual place and walk the rest of the way.'

We arrived at our house to find five black jeeps parked outside.

'What is happening?' Lola whispers to me. I can hear the fear in her voice.

'Look sad; remember, you just lost a baby. No matter what happens, play your role well. We are about to find out.'

Chapter Seventy-seven: Kabul

Ahmed

'What's the plan?' I ask Jabar.

For days, Mohammed Pir's face has been all over the news, and he is wanted by the International Court of Justice for genocide. The press is having a field day criticising him. To be honest, he is not a good man. Hussain used his weakness against him; Mohammed craved money and power. He was given everything he wanted, thinking he was the most powerful man in Kabul, only to realise he had no real power. It's a sobering moment for him. He has been bitter for days, saying he wants to kill Hussain. Yes, we can use that anger and bitterness to bring Hussain down.

'We need to expose Hussain for who he is,' replies Jabar. 'He has successfully manipulated the people; just look at that.' Jabar switches the television on. It shows Hussain being greeted by a large crowd of people.

He turns to Mohammed. 'He made you into the villain; you need to prove him right. Where is the nuclear bomb?'

'At a power plant in Charikar, less than twenty-five miles from here. It looks like an abandoned building. I was able to buy nuclear weapons from Russia when I came into power. I knew a day would come when it would be my bargaining chip.' Mohammed answers angrily.

'You can't use the bomb; everybody will die. Then what's the point?' I say to Jabar. 'You have worked with Hussain for years. How many people are working for him? What is his weakness, and where does his wealth source come from?'

'We already know that he is part of an organisation intent on destroying the world and distributing the profit among themselves.'

'I don't care about all this!' shouts Mohammed. 'I want my position and reputation back. Nobody will take that away from me. The nuclear bomb is the only thing I have, and believe me, I'll not hesitate to use it.'

'You need to calm down,' I say. 'Nothing will be achieved by killing everyone. Think about it, you would have no people to govern. It would be best if you were rational. No matter how powerful Hussain is, he is still afraid of you. We need to penetrate his base and expose him for who he is. To do this, we need money, and you can't use the money in the bank that has been confiscated.'

He smiles sourly. 'I always have a backup plan.' He stands up and tells us to follow him. He walks down the modest corridor of the four-bedroom bungalow in which we now reside. We are led to a door, and Mohammed enters a code. The keyless digital steel door opens and we enter a secret room. There are large monitors on the walls, and I count about ten computers. Mohammed opens one of the cabinets, and I see stacks of hundred dollar bills. He grins. 'I have about five hundred thousand dollars here, as well as all the latest guns hidden behind the secret wall.' He points to the right side of the room.

'This is good! I have been communicating with some people who are not loyal to Hussain. He has destroyed lives and homes. They will get us concrete evidence of what Hussain is up to; giving them money will ease the risk because their family will be taken care of if anything should happen to them. I know their new location; we'll go next week. We will help them with the raid,' says Jabar.

'We don't have the manpower; this is a suicide mission,' states Latif.

Jabar smiles. 'Yes, you're right; it is a suicide mission. They will grant us access to the facility, and I have intel that Hussain will not be in the country that day. We will bring down his empire before he returns, allowing us easy access to him. What are you afraid of, Latif?'

'I'm not afraid of anything. I just think we should be careful and not set ourselves up for failure.'

'We have five days to plan. We will bring down Hussain's empire; I bet my life on it,' I say. 'He took everything away from me. He deceived me into believing Mohammed was the evil one, not knowing he was the devil himself. In the meantime, Mohammed, we need to use your computers. Is it using satellite for broadband?'

'Yes,' he replies, locking the cabinet containing the money. He leaves the room with Latif following closely behind.

I turn to Jabar. 'I am concerned about Mohammed. I think he is losing it, he is unpredictable, and that is scary.'

'I know! He was a powerful man who has lost his power. We all know what that will do to a dictator. The most important thing now is to communicate with the people helping us with Hussain. Then, we need to connect with the team who told us what is happening worldwide.'

Mohammed

I enter my room, closing the door behind me. I had this bungalow built two years ago and murdered the builders to keep it a secret. Ahmed and Jabar must think I'm stupid. I only allow them to live to serve my purpose. When that is done, I will kill them both. I have worked too hard, killed too many people to get to this place, and I don't mind killing a few more to get back my position of power. I'll play their game, do whatever they tell me to do. I will play the fool. I'll win their trust; I'll dispose of them when the time is right or when their backs are turned. This is just the beginning, I have lost too much, but I'll gain everything back by becoming the most powerful man on the continent.

I need to focus! I want Hussain dead; nobody makes a fool of Mohammed and lives to tell the story. He set me up to fail. He wanted a scapegoat; I was the fool that played into his hands. Hussain, your time in the limelight is ending.

Chapter Seventy-eight: Sydney

Henry

I knew my life would be a living hell, but I couldn't believe it would be worse than I thought. She threatened to report me to the police for the injury I inflicted on her shoulder. I didn't return home for a week. The only reason I went back to that hellhole was that my vacation was over, and I needed to go back to work. The consolation prize is that Tom has made an advanced improvement on E-generation, which they will be testing together next week, and he was able to give me a dossier on Cynthia.

I now understood why the organisation chose her for me; Satan is too a kind word. She was determined to be my wife; I don't know why. She has been following my life and career for years. She has constantly communicated with my mother; I guess they have more in common than I realised. The organisation frowned on me for not living with my wife. We need to keep up appearances. My mother called me endlessly when I refused to come home. I don't know whether she was calling because she cared about me or because of Cynthia. They are just too close.

I am counting down the days until I am free.

After work, I spend most of my time at Tom's house. I don't enjoy being at work anymore with the economy in shambles, and the prime minister being a mouthpiece for the big boss.

I enter my house reluctantly; at 11.00 pm. The lights in the house are switched on. I see Cynthia waiting for me as soon as I open the door. 'I thought you wouldn't come home,' she says. 'I guess I'll have to follow you everywhere since you refuse to see me as your wife.'

'I don't understand your problem, Cynthia. I would never consider a date with you, much less become my wife.'

'You will see me as your wife, whether you like it or not! I'm done playing this game with you.'

'Cynthia, I know you castrated your ex-boyfriend and then murdered him, because he wanted to leave you.'

'I don't care what information you have about me. It doesn't matter; there is nothing you can do with it; everyone works for the organisation. I have something for you; I know your son was taken to a boarding school to keep him away from me. But I'll find him and hurt him to spite you.'

I walked up to her and hold her round the neck; I squeeze tightly. 'Listen to me; I am no longer the Henry you used to know. I'll kill you and the damn the consequence. I'm warning you; stay away from my son!' I release her, and she steps back, holding her neck and coughing.

'Will you murder your pregnant wife?'

'Whatever is in your stomach is not my child; that thing belongs to the organisation. Take it to them.' I quickly climb the stairs to get away from her.

All the information on the organisation's members and the big boss, Sophia Richardson, has been collated. I don't know how a woman became so heartless. They will all be exposed. That is the only thing that keeps me going.

I open the door to my room, and I can hear Cynthia breathing heavily behind me.

'What do you want?' I sigh.

'Why do you hate me so much? What did I do to you? We will soon be the most powerful couple on the continent.'

'You are a heartless bitch. You only care about making it to the top; you don't care whom you step on to get there.'

'Wanting to succeed, there is nothing wrong with that. We are good together.'

She leans into me seductively. I push her away. 'You are a fool! What don't you get? I hate you!' I yell in her face as I enter my room, locking it behind me. I lean against the door. The team have to bring down the organisation and fast. I can't live like this.

Tom

From the hidden camera in my basement, I can see Mia lying on the mattress provided for her. She has been down there for months, poor woman. I have seen her crying several times. I wish I could put her mind at rest, but I need to keep her safe from the people who want her dead.

Having Martin on my team has made things easier for me; all

the components and equipment required for E-generation are ordered in his name. Because he is in the organisation and the Minister for Defence, no one asks any questions.

I look at the almost finished E-generation. The power supply, N60 postnanometer, the frequency receiver and transmitter, the ECTT encoders, and the processors are being assembled. I am almost at the end; the organisation will not know what hit them. We will go to the access point in our country; we need to test it simultaneously. This is where it gets tricky; we must make sure POWERA works when it launches, we will only get one chance.

Sophia Richardson

I close my laptop. I have just finished a conference call with the other bosses. We have a meeting with the head next week; everyone is worried we might be signing our death certificates. We have failed to capture the people working against the organisation. As much as I enjoy destroying people's lives, I don't want mine to be destroyed. I gave up everything to be here. I need to retain it.

Chapter Seventy-nine: Rio de Janeiro

Ana

I don't feel safe after my previous experience; I barely escaped the attack on the warehouse, and I don't know when they will return. I need to finish the assignment given to me; I'm grateful I was able to source all the equipment and components for R-generation before leaving the company on leave. The perks of working in accounting are allocating funds needed for projects. I knew when the heavy equipment ordered for the work in the Amazon rainforest would arrive. I could sneak my orders under the company name without them being aware. I bribed one of the customs officials, who informed me, as soon as the goods arrived, this allowed me to pick up my goods before the company was notified.

The final launch will be next week, where every part of POWERA is put together to obstruct the powerful Gama. I have been working tirelessly to complete my part, but it is not easy. I'm constantly watching my back, afraid I will be caught unawares. The final stages to the big reveal, shit! One of the postnanometer chips falls to the ground. This tiny chip cost two million Brazilian reals. I need to find it; I hope it is not damaged, and this will be a major setback for me. Ana, concentrate. Stop checking the security monitor! My heart is beating fast, please God! Let me find it. I bend down, looking for it desperately.

Adriano Cardoso

I have called an emergency meeting with all the members of Purple Gama. We have one week to eliminate all threats before the meeting with the head. Some of my members have continuously failed me, which is a major setback for the organisation. It's humiliating that my hub was robbed under my supervision, and we haven't yet found those responsible.

I stand on the podium addressing the members of the hub. 'I want everyone out there looking for Ana Santos.' Her picture is displayed on several monitors in the reception room for all to see.

'She is hiding somewhere in Brazil, but we need to find her. We own almost all properties in the country and control the food supply, infrastructure and citizens. She might have disguised herself and not be recognisable, but I want everyone to check on their neighbours. I know we are not liked by the people, but they need us to survive. Offer a reward. We have limited time; I'm seeing the boss next week, counting – three days from now.

'I am sure most of you are aware of what happened to Mr Montes and Mr Ribeiro. I'll inflict the same torture on you if you don't get results. No one will be resting today. I want you to use all your resources to find Ana Santos. I want her brought to me by tomorrow.'

'Sir, Mr Montes was looking for her but to no avail. I honestly think she is dead,' one of my members responded timidly.

'Then I need to see her body. Find her dead or alive!'

Ana

Two people approach the gate of the warehouse. What do they want? It's late at night; no one should be out there.

I lock myself in the building room. They are trying to gain access, but the gate is locked. What am I going to do? They must not find me here. They climb the fence and land on the ground with a slight thud. They take out their guns and walk towards the building. I am in trouble.

Who are these people? The organisation always sends more than two people to conduct a search. Maybe the others are waiting outside. I am not ready for this. There is nowhere to hide R-generation. I just hope that they don't force the door open.

I watch the monitor anxiously. They try to force open the industrial entrance door. They are talking into a two-way radio. Another man jumps over the fence and gives them, what looks like, a key. They try the key in the lock, but the door does not open. When I rented this warehouse, I changed all the locks to be safe.

They survey the entire building looking for a way to enter. My heart is pounding; if they should get in, they will find me for sure. They talk on their two-way radio, but I can't hear what is being said. They head in the direction they came from, and climb back over the fence to get out.

I sigh in relief, but I know they will be back. I need to be ready. I gently move the almost complete R-generation to one of the storage rooms. I lock the industrial roller shutter door. I don't know their mission, but two people cannot search every storage room in this building. I will have to hide in the cardboard box and hope they don't find me this time. The only consolation is that I know it will soon be over. I just hope I can live long enough to achieve that.

A truck parks in front of the gate; they are back. A man climbs over the fence, goes to the entrance gate and breaks the lock. The gate opens, and the truck drives in. I swiftly switch off all the monitors. The room is filthy and still looks unused. I race to the room where I hid the last time and climb inside the extra-large cardboard box, praying I won't not found.

I can hear voices; I know they have entered the building. 'We just need to make sure this facility is empty,' one of the men says. 'The boss said we should search any building in our vicinity. This place looks empty, but we need to be sure.'

I place my hand over my mouth. How long can I go on cheating death?

Chapter Eighty: Hong Kong

Huan

We are to have the final meeting before the big reveal. A lot is happening, and our lives are constantly being threatened. The organisation is not giving up anytime soon. They are ramping up their efforts in the hunt for us, and my greatest fear is that we may be unable to outsmart them any longer. We all have to be at the access point at 1.58 am; my time on Thursday. I have to be at Kwu Tung, in the north of Hong Kong and find where the access point is hidden. I need to set up A-generation, which should be thoroughly tested and working. It will sync with the other generations to make POWERA so powerful it will disrupt Gama transmission. It needs to work. We will not have another opportunity; it will bring down Gamaplug and any technology connected to it.

The only thing pushing me on is the thought that I'm almost at the finish line, I have lost too much, and I have not had time to process all that has happened. I honestly can't allow myself to think too much; I don't think I could live another day if I did. My aunty died because of me. I can't even call my uncle for fear that their calls are being monitored. I mustn't think about it! They will all be exposed soon; there will be nowhere to hide.

Ping Wu – The Organisation

'We have to face the heat in the next couple of days. I have received information from a reliable source that the head will have us eliminated during the meeting,' I tell the other bosses.

'That is what I am afraid of. We have killed members for far less,' says Hussain Atta.

'We need to do something; I don't want to die. The head is watching our every step; I have not slept well; I lock my door, afraid that my men will eliminate me in my sleep. We all know our men work for the head, not for us; they will turn on us at his order,' James Cooper responds. 'How can these people escape us? We have done everything to catch them, but they always find a way to evade us.'

'We need to do something significant to draw them out,' says Andrew Hughes. 'I will not lose my life because of these scumbags. We all know how we got here; through pain and sweat, we lost everything we hold dear to gain this position. We took pride in making people feel the pain we had to suffer, and all to please the head. We fatten his pocket, give him power, and he controls the world. The only setback has been to allow some lousy people to steal a couple of billion.'

'You know it is not about the money,' replies Sophia Richardson 'It's what it represents. This action will give people hope that they can hurt us. We operate on fear, if that is taken away, people will rebel, and we don't want that. Do you think these people can really damage this organisation? There is none like us. We use the most innovative and powerful technology to control people across the globe. We know what they think, their deepest secrets, we have all information in our hands, we can elevate and demote.'.

'Yet we are afraid of them!' Adriano Cardoso laments. 'These people stole one-and-a-half billion dollars. We can't find the stolen money, even with all our advanced technologies. Do you know what else they have stolen that we are unaware of? Let us stop making excuses, agree that we have messed up and find a way to fix it fast.'

'As I said, we need to do something we have never done before. People are already miserable; we need to make them more miserable. We need to stop rewarding them for information. I believe all money deposited in the banks must be seized. They will not have access to their money until the perpetrators are exposed. They will pay for the actions of this handful of people. Our threats are not working. They refuse to cooperate because of their hope in those people for change.' Andrew Hughes laughs. 'So let's squash that idea, and when they have no hope left, they will turn on themselves.'

'People are becoming resilient; look at the people we are fighting against. We took their money, killed their families and put a price on their heads, yet still they resist and fight. I don't think it will work with the citizens,' says Lekan Gbada.

'Well, we need to do something,' I say. 'We can't keep having conference calls and making no progress. We are the leaders, people are afraid of us, but these people make us look like a joke. I think what Andrew said is wise. We need to generate more money for ourselves, the head and the organisation's members, so seizing the little money people have is not a bad idea; they will all be enslaved. We go to their various homes and seize anything of value, and the banks will be closed. The homeless are not exempt, we take the clothes on their backs if necessary. We will tell them the money and valuables seizures are temporary. The faster they find these people and hand them over to us, the quicker their money and valuables will be released. We all know that is a lie. They find the culprits for us, and we keep their money.

'Our days are numbered, and we need to get it done before the final meeting that determines our fate.'

Chapter Eighty-one: London

The Launch

Jude

We had to rent a six-seater vehicle to carry the PG part of POWERA. People are willing to sell their souls just to eat, so we got the car at a bargain price because the owner was desperate for cash. He just wants to feed his family.

The entire country is in a shambles, and the people in power don't care. They have frozen people's bank accounts taking away the little they have saved just because they want to find us. POWERA has to work.

We need to be at Canary Wharf at precisely 5.58 am Wednesday. I'm panicking; it is one of the few busy places in London. The organisation owns most establishments there, just as they control every aspect of the country. Hopefully, we will have finished what we came to do before people started arriving.

I look at Sarah; she is a shadow of her former self. I'm afraid she might collapse soon. She has not been eating well; all she does is work day in, day out, to finish PG. I can see her struggling to help me carry the equipment to the car.

'Sarah, you don't have the strength!. Let me do it.'

'I want to help,' she grunts.

'You have already done so much; you built this equipment. We need to get through the barrier. I need you to charm the security men handling the post.'

I hide beside the equipment while Sarah drives the car. She smiles at the security men and shows them a fake ID indicating she is working in one of the offices.'

'Why are you here so early? It's 3.23 am,' one of the men asks.

'I work for foreign exchange; you know how it is, the early bird catches the worm.' She shrugs.

The men laugh, and one of them presses the button, lifting the barrier so Sarah can drive through.

I carry the equipment, pausing several times to catch my breath.

We hurry to the access point, a renovation site; the PG needs to be placed at 51.5072° N, 0.1276° W. We have our work cut out for us, and we have less than two hours to set everything up. I hope the others are ready! The organisation will not know what has hit them when we are done. Everything they relied upon will be brought down, their safety net taken away from them suddenly, and they will feel what we felt.

I smile at Sarah; it is almost over.

Chapter Eighty-two: New York

Edward

What a day today is; we are going to launch POWERA.

Martin and I have worked tirelessly to complete the O-generation part of POWERA; we do not want to disappoint the other members of the team. We must all be at the access point at 00.58 EST Wednesday. Our clocks are synchronised, and we are all ready. I have tested O-generation many times to make sure it is working, but we have never tested it together.

It's the middle of the night, but the streetlight keeps the darkness at bay. My heart is beating fast; today should be the happiest day of my life. God! Nothing must go wrong; we will never get this opportunity again to bring down Gamaplug.

We arrive a short distance from the access point; we need to draw less attention to ourselves. New York is a city that never sleeps but it is now a city that is angry and disgruntled. This whole situation has been tricky. We spent as much time disguising ourselves as possible. The team members' faces are circulating all over the media; citizens have been left with little choice but to fish us out. All their bank accounts have been frozen, only to be released back to the owners if we are found. People are volunteering their family members to access their money. I don't know how often I have had to stop myself from crying, seeing mothers watching their children begging, people pleading for their lives, knowing they will soon lose them.

The only consolation is that today, we will restore hope to the people; the access point is close to Gama Lab headquarters, about five miles away, and I'm sure they own that building. Martin has been monitoring the area for a week now; we know security men and police officers patrol the building.

We cover the equipment, looking around and trying to look inconspicuous. We arrived five hours ahead of time; we only have a short window to carry the equipment into the empty building to get to the underground. They patrol every thirty minutes to make sure everything is in place. The security cameras have been altered, and we can safely enter the building without being seen.

We have to place O-generation at 40.7128° N, 74.0060° W to sync with others.

I wipe the sweat from my face and look at Martin. 'Do you think this will work?'

He runs his fingers through his hair and looks at the timer. 'We will know in the next twenty-two minutes.'

Chapter Eighty-three: Lagos

Segun

I don't want to think of all that has happened in the last couple of days.

We arrived back at the house to find the organisation waiting for us. The curfew has been lifted, now homes are being raided and anything of value seized. The little money we have is hidden with our gadgets. If food is found in people's homes, it is taken away. How can anyone hope to survive?

I could see the terrified look on Lola's face. Thankfully, we are always prepared. I told Lola to look sad; she had just lost a baby. I cradled the dead baby in my arms, forcing tears to roll down my face. The man I suspect is in charge walked up to us, without talking, and took the baby away from me.

'Give me back my son,' I said. 'I just want to hold him one last time.'

He didn't answer me and took the baby to a waiting car. My heart was pounding; I think they did a blood test. On a dead baby! What kind of people are they?

I looked at Lola. I don't know her blood group; I'm blood group O, very common. Please let the baby be a match for us, or we are dead. 'Lola! You need to keep it together,' I whispered as I held her close, pretending to console her. 'Everything is going to be OK.'

The man in charge, with a stern-looking face, walked up to us and handed us the dead baby. He made a hand gesture, and all the men with him got back into their black jeeps and drove away.

What just happened? I asked myself.

I turned to Lola. I think she was still in shock. 'Are you OK?' I rushed to help when I saw she was about to collapse.

'Segun, I don't think I can do this anymore.'

'We are almost at the end,' I replied. 'You can do this.'

***

'Today, we will finally be free from our oppressors,' I assure Lola. I get into the car, hauling W-generation into the back seat of the vehicle. We need to be very careful. I have padded the back seat; everything must work smoothly today.

We drive to the location in Ikeja, where the access point is. Everything needs to be set up at precisely 6:58 am on Wednesday. The environment is toxic, many people are angry, and most workers have not been paid in months. Now the little money they have has been frozen by the banks.

I tried to locate the exact place days ago; it is empty land we bought from the owners. We erected the W-generation set at 6.5244° N and 3.3792° E to sync with the other parts of POWERA. I touch my chest, close my eyes and pray; please, nothing must go wrong!

Chapter Eighty-four: Kabul

Ahmed

We have been working non-stop for days, planning and double-checking that the attack on the temporary hiding place of the Obedian goes without a hitch. We are just four people, let's say two, because I can see the reluctance in Mohammed, and Latif does anything his boss tells him. We have fifty people on the inside, and you can't be too sure, we may be entering a trap, but Jabar assures me they are loyal.

Hussain pretends to be your friend, makes you promise not to tell your family your whereabouts and leave them behind in a house filled with women and children, not knowing you leave your loved ones in the hands of people worse than the enemies you are fighting.

We were able to reach people from the other side of the world fighting the exact same cause. They are setting up POWERA, which will bring down Gama technology. I know a few people have the privilege to use this technology, including Hussain and the people who work for him; Mohammed is the only one using the technology in the Ahedan Group; he is too paranoid and selfish to share his toys with others. We have warned the people working with us to stop using the Gama technology or the organisation will know what we are planning.

We are ready. Today is the day. I see Mohammed talking to Latif secretly; I hope he doesn't double-cross us. We know we are playing a dangerous game; dining with the devil.

'Yusuf! I'm sure Mohammed is planning something,' I whisper.

'I know! He needs to be killed after this operation. He has provided us with housing, money, and technology, and we know where the nuclear bomb is; he is not helpful to us anymore,' he replies angrily.

'I don't trust him. Do you think he gave us the exact location for the nuclear bomb? I think he is playing us.'

'It doesn't matter; when he dies, the nuclear bomb dies with him.'

'Mohammed, we need to leave now!' I shout.

We must be on-site two hours before the attack. We carry the weapons to the car. We plan to wire the premises with timer bombs. Hopefully, the attack will be over by then, or we will all die. We need to find out where they are keeping our families. We don't even know if they are alive.

Hussain has flown to New York and Yusuf is temporarily in charge, even after his demotion. I want to look into his face when I kill him. The bastard deceived me, and he will pay for it with his blood.

I glance back at the three people following me. We reach their hiding place. One of the men will be waiting for us at the entrance gate to let us in. 'Be safe!' I whisper. We have no idea what we will meet when we enter.

The team will disrupt Gama's transition at precisely 8.58 pm, Thursday, our time. We need to attack at the exact time, and all the technology used by Obedian will shut down.

'When we enter, make sure you set the bombs where I showed you in the layout, the timers are set for 00:58, which means we have two hours to attack and leave the area before the explosion.' I say.

Jabar and I carry the bags filled with guns and explosives on our back. The side door to the entrance opens.

'Hurry!' says the man. 'The guard will be back in two minutes.'

I keep my trusted peshkabz knife with me; I never go anywhere without it. I don't know when it might be useful.

Let the game begin!

Chapter Eighty-five: Sydney

Henry

It will soon be over. I'll be able to get rid of that godforsaken woman and bring my legal wife back home. My mother has been mounting pressure on me to treat my wife right and stop locking her out of my room. The only reason that demon has not broken down the door is that I told my mother I would rather die than sleep with her. She was forced to have a long talk with Cynthia, but that didn't stop her from disturbing my peace. My father is a little confused, wondering why I would marry someone I hate so much and not long after my wife's disappearance. I wish I could confide in him, but I don't want to jeopardise his life with the organisation.

Last night, I slept at Tom's house. I knew Sophia Richardson had travelled to New York, where they will get the shock of their lives. We can't afford any delay; we need the E-generation set up at one of the oldest buildings in the city centre, with three underground floors, at precisely 4.58 am Thursday, facing 33.8688° S, 151.2093° E to sync with the others.

The city is still sleeping; it is sad to see so many homeless people on the roadside. I am ashamed to be a leader in this country at this time. I live in luxury while 90% of the population live in abject poverty. We no longer practise democracy but a dictatorship; the news is monitored to favour the organisation; they determine everything that goes on in the continent. People beg to eat now the little money they have has been taken away from them by the bank. The team told us that the same thing is happening around the world. It must end today.

I have borrowed a pickup truck to carry E-generation; one of the benefits of working with the organisation is that I am not scrutinised. The big boss and my mother think I'm weak like my father, but they are about to get a big shock.

We carry the E-generation carefully to the back of the truck; there is no room for error; we only have this one opportunity. I have already requested access to the building from my office; no one says no to the organisation. I emphasised that no one must be on the premises.

We enter the empty building easily; there are no guards. The access point is on the first floor underground. Tom sets up the E-generation, making sure nothing is out of place and it is working. I turn to him and smile. There are just twenty-eight minutes before the launch; nothing must go wrong.

Chapter Eighty-six: Rio de Janeiro

Ana

How I have managed to escape being captured is a mystery to me; my husband and daughter must be protecting me from beyond. Building R-generation is my last hope of being free from the shackles of the organisation. My reputation has been sullied, and my face is plastered all over the news as one of the most wanted people in the world. I move the R-generation gently to the old truck I have rented. I can never go near my old 2006 Ford, and I know my old home is being monitored. Maybe after today, I will be able to go home.

It will soon be over. I crave my old life. I just want to go home, sleep on my bed and stare at my outdated furniture. I have modified my looks many times. I have dyed my hair red and have now started wearing contact lenses, so I have green eyes.

I cover the R-generation with black cloth; nothing must go wrong. I have tested and retested to ensure it is all working perfectly. I need to get to the central region (downtown), to the old cathedral. I have to be at the underground location at precisely 2.58 am today, which is Wednesday; everything must be set up and ready.

I went to see the parish leader and donated a considerable amount of money to the church; R$250,000. That was before all the banks closed and, as horrible as the organisation is, they allow stipends for a church. There was such joy on their faces when I gave them the money, requesting to use the residence in the middle of the night. I was given the keys and assured no one would disturb me. The organisation has made people desperate for survival, and they are willing to turn a blind eye to questionable situations.

I arrive at my destination, still very cautious; you can't afford to trust anyone. I check everywhere to make sure I haven't been set-up. Everywhere is in darkness, and there are no streetlights. *This is good*, I tell myself. I drag the R-generation into the church, attaching my torchlight to it. Trying to get to the crypt in an old church is a struggle. I look at the dilapidated staircase leading below ground. *It all ends today*, I repeat as I move the R-generation using a platform trolley that I brought from the warehouse. Getting into position is a great struggle; the R-generation almost falls off several times.

I check my watch; there are still one-and-a-half hours before the launch. I need to make sure it is working and syncing with other parts of POWERA. I set up facing 22.9068° S, 43.1729° W; it must work! I can't let the others down.

I will finally go home today, I smiled. I start checking and rechecking just to make sure.

Chapter Eighty-seven: Hong Kong

Huan

I rarely leave my apartment unless I need food. I have been hiding for so long that I am extremely anxious about leaving the house.

I cover the A-generation with black material in case I bump into *them*. It's lucky that I live on the ground floor. I leave in the middle of the night. Everywhere is so quiet, I can hear every sound. I will soon be free; I have had to give up so much to get to this point in my life.

Setting up everything and ensuring it works has taken all my time, but I am determined they need to pay. We can't afford to fail now.

I dress the part to travel to the rural part of Kwu Tung in the north of Hong Kong. I know I will have little or no time to change after the launch, if I hope to escape.

I don't recognise myself; I look like a homeless person pushing what looks like a cart with their worldly belongings. There are homeless people everywhere. I can see the sad and dejected looks on their faces, begging me for alms, when they see me pushing the cart, holding tightly to the little torchlight as I go.

I reach the dilapidated house to set up the A-generation. It is a bleak, black night. I look at my stopwatch. I have one hour and thirty minutes before the launch, which must be done at precisely 1.58 am, facing 22.3193° N, 114.1694° E.

I hope I find my car in one piece when I return. What are the chances? How can the economy of a nation deteriorate this fast? Greed! It is the operative word when certain people's principal concern is themselves and no one else. They have amassed so much wealth, stripping nations of their assets; anyone who dares to challenge them is eliminated. Today is Armageddon; and good will prevail.

Someone taps my back, and I turn around, startled. 'Give me all your money.'

I point to myself. 'Does it look like I have any money?'

'What is that?' He points to the cart. 'Maybe I can sell it!'

Oh no! I can't afford any delay; this will affect everybody else. I glance at my concealed stopwatch before it draws any attention; I have thirty minutes.

'Please don't touch it,' I beg, as the man moves towards the cart. All I have on me is 5 HKD; I knew I was coming to a more dangerous part of Hong Kong, so I brought little money with me. I reluctantly give him the money. I can't see his face. It is so dirty, and his teeth are rotten. 'Just take the money and leave,' I shout. 'it's all I have.'

Thankfully, he grabs the money and walks away. He keeps looking back at the equipment, I know he will return. Hopefully, by then I will have launched A-generation, and I won't have to worry about him anymore.

Today, I break free from the shackles of oppression. I take back my freedom!

There are just five minutes to the launch.

Fred Demson

I narrow my eyes at the seven big bosses I chose carefully and strategically; how could I get it so wrong? They were the best among thousands of people I had secretly monitored for a long time. They had a simple task, take over the world. How hard was that? I'm done! They will all be eliminated today; I have over a hundred enforcers surrounding this secret location. There is no escape route for any of them.

'I don't want to hear any more excuses,' I say, slamming my hand on the conference table. 'I gave you one job. How can you continue to fail me and expect mercy? This organisation does not give second chances, and I have given you many, yet you come back with the same result.'

'Sir! We have searched everywhere for these people, no place was left unturned, yet they can't be found. They must be dead,' says Adriano Cardoso soberly.

'"They must be dead!" Listen to yourself! They stole money from your country and the woman you suspect of being responsible just upped and left. You had security monitoring the building, yet she could still escape, and no one has been able to find her! You think you can deceive me by paying back the money yourselves, you forget that I know everything.'

I turn to James Cooper. 'And some people managed to import questionable equipment and remove it from premises that were being watched, and were able to bring down the country's electricity grid in the process. And you did nothing to stop this from happening on your watch.' He opens his mouth to speak, but I hold up my hand to stop him. His face turns deathly pale.

'I have planned and worked methodically for years to be on top, to dominate the world. For a year, I watched you all; your determination to overcome what life has dealt you at all costs. Now I question myself; I should have chosen them instead of you.'

I upload pictures of Jude Williams, Martin Hills, Segun Gerald, Lola Adeyemo, Ana Santos and Huan Li on the presentation screen. I see the shocked expression on their faces. 'You look surprised, but I know you have been chasing these people for months, but to no avail. They have outsmarted you at every step.'

I have made my decision. I nod at my head of security, and he leaves the room. I can see the panic and anxiety on their faces; they should be afraid. Twenty enforcers enter the conference room. I address the former big bosses. 'You all knew this day would come. You dare to arrive in New York with no updates on these people.' I point at the screen. 'You tried to deceive me by falsely accusing the wrong people, but I have been working closely with your replacements. I know everything. Take them away!'

The enforcers move in the direction of the seven big bosses when all the systems go down. Everything fails at once; the monitors, the computers; all of it. I pull my Gamaplug from my ears; what is that buzzing sound?

'What the hell is happening?' I demand. An IT man runs into the room panting.

'Sir! Gamaplug just went gone down.'

'What! Someone has tampered with my system; find them! How is this possible?'

'They've brought down the whole system, sir. From the reports we are getting, it's happening everywhere in the world.'

I turn to the big bosses. 'Change of plan. This is time for you to redeem yourselves. For Gamaplug to shut down completely everywhere at the same time, they must have built a system more powerful than Gamaplug to obstruct its transmission. This can only be done at the access points. Send your men to the various locations now. I want you out of here and back in your countries. Find these people. If you fail, don't bother coming back if you value your lives.'

I watch them run from the conference room. Everything I have worked so hard for, they want to destroy; they must be stopped and eliminated.

Chapter Eighty-eight: London

Jude

'Go, Sarah, now!' I shout.

We don't have time to cross-check anything; they are coming, and I know it. We can easily be found at this building site. Everywhere is in chaos. This is one of the busiest parts of London, and workers are already up and about in an effort to make ends meets in the shattered economy.

We don't want to be held captive by the organisation. They are blocking the entrance preventing people from getting in and leaving. We are wearing suits, so that we fit in, but we need more than this to escape.

'What are we going to do?' whispers Sarah. I can see fear in her eyes. I am also afraid. They are telling people to go to their respective offices; everyone will have to do fingerprint and facial recognition.

I watched as everyone files in a straight line to their offices. One of the security team tells us to join the queue. I held Sarah's hand and squeeze; they are watching. We need to enter one of the office buildings to figure out what to do next.

There are many buildings. Canary Wharf used to house the largest businesses in the world, but many of them have closed down. We have to reach one of the abandoned buildings without being seen.

The security team is watching the crowd closely, ensuring everyone is following orders. Sarah quickly wipes away a tear, as we follow the man in front of us and enter the building. I can see panic and fear in his expression. I move closer to him. 'Don't be afraid, everything will be OK,' I say, as I pick the wallet from his pocket.

We are inside ADC Bank and the employees have to swipe their employee card to enter. I whisper in Sarah's ear. 'You need to pee yourself; we have to get to the restroom.'

She starts shaking, and one of the agents walks up to her. Tears stream down Sarah's face. She points to her stained skirt, pleading to be allowed to use the restroom. This is the distraction I need. I slip into the restroom as the security agents ridicule her, laughing hysterically.

'Get out of here and use the restroom,' one of the security women says. 'You are embarrassing yourself.'

I wait for Sarah. When she enters, we have less than five minutes before they come looking for her. I open the window, and lift her so she can wriggle through the small window. I follow closely behind, pulling myself up and through. We run to the next building. It is not in use. I open the corporate bag I am carrying and pull out a hammer. I make several attempts before I manage to crack open the double-glazed window without breaking the glass.

'We need to get inside now; they will be looking for you,' I say, pushing the window with all my strength to open it wider.

We enter the abandoned building and I close the window, hoping they haven't seen us. We will have to hide inside the ceiling. We race to the tenth floor, panting badly. I remember seeing an opening when I was checking building structures close to the site. There it is. I point to the faulty ceiling slab. I am able to move it. I can hear voices in the building; we have to hurry.

I help Sarah to climb up into the ceiling, pull myself up behind her and close it gently behind me. 'Hold still and don't move,' I say. 'I'm not sure how long this ceiling can hold us.'

'Find her!' we hear. 'She can't have gone far.'

We keep very still, praying the ceiling will hold our weight, hoping against hope they do not find us.

Chapter Eighty-nine: New York

Martin

'We need to leave here now! They will be here shortly,' Edward says.

Gamaplug is down, but it is not over yet. We race out of the building, but we can already hear people. 'They are here already,' I say.

'How can we escape? This place will be crawling with security in minutes,' Edward says, fearfully.

'We planned for this,' I say, as we run into one of the offices. 'Listen, if everything fails, I'll try to distract them while you escape.'

No! You can't do that.'

'We have no choice; you just have to promise me you will find my wife and kids. Promise me that.'

He nods. 'I promise, but it won't come to that.'

As they start to search the building, we quickly change into the clothes worn by Gama security. We stuff our old clothes into a backpack and hide it behind a door.

'We need to blend in,' I tell Edward. We have all the equipment they carry, from the pistols they wear on the right-hand side, to the earpieces for the submachine guns. 'You need to be bold,' I say, as I open the door.

There are security men and women everywhere. One of them walks up to us. I lift my face. I try to shield Edward, who is trembling beside me. 'All clear here,' I say.

'Did you check that room?' he asks, nodding behind me.

'Yes, sir! It was empty. We've checked everywhere.'

'They couldn't have escaped, we were here immediately after the system went down.'

'We'll find them, sir!' I reply.

He walks away barking orders at some of the others. I turned to Edward. 'Pull yourself together, or they will suspect us.'

'Easy for you to say, I'm not a police officer; I don't even know how to shoot a gun.'

'It is not over until we get out of here alive. They are trying to bring down POWERA.'

One of the men walks up to us and points his gun at my chest. 'I have never seen your faces before. I know all the security personnel that works for the organisation.'

'I think you are mistaken,' I say, pushing Edward forward. 'Run!'

Before the man can fire his gun; I wrestle it away from his hand. I know I will not survive this, but I hope Edward escapes.

The room fills quickly. I am surrounded by security men pointing their guns at me. I close my eyes. I know it's over. I just wish I could have held my family in my arms one last time.

Chapter Ninety: Lagos

Segun

Lola looks around, terrified. 'What are we going to do?' she asks.

The plan was to launch W-generation to sync with others to become POWERA, but we don't have enough of a window to plan an escape route before the organisation locates us. The gate is locked, we own this land, but that has never stopped them before. They are allowed to do whatever they want to whoever they choose. We will climb the ladder we set up to the other side; that will buy us some time; but they are trying to break down the steel gate.

'Hurry!' I yell. We rush to climb to the other side. Everywhere is surrounded.

Security agents swarm everywhere. They use a loudspeaker to announce that everyone must not leave their homes.

It is early morning, and people are already out and about looking for food. I can see people running, looking for shelter. Those who are still in their houses lock their doors. They dare not allow any visitors into their homes.

'What are we going to do, Segun?'

'We are not the only ones stranded on the streets of Ikeja; they won't know who is responsible.'

'Segun, look at us! We don't look like the uneducated people we have been playing for so long; we can't afford to be stopped, and have our identity checked.'

'I knew we would not be able to escape their search, but as much as we don't look like our roles, we still don't look like our former selves. We need to reach our car.'

There are five agents coming in our direction.

'Stay calm!' I mutter.

'I said that everyone must stay indoors and nobody must be found outside,' one of the agents addresses us angrily.

'Sir! We do not live close by; we must get to our car so we can go home.'

He shakes his head. 'I need you to join those people.' He points to the large crowd surrounded by agents. 'We have to carry out facial recognition and take fingerprints.'

'What is going to happen to us?' Lola says quietly, in a scared voice.

Everyone is checked and scanned for recognition; anyone suspected, even a little, was shot on the spot.

All around, people are screaming. No one is allowed to leave. Those who are at home, their houses are searched, and they are also scanned.

Lola is taken to the right, and I am taken to the left to join a group of men. My finger is placed on a machine, and my face scanned. 'Hold still,' the man commands. 'We don't have all day.'

It took me two days to set up our false identity, I need this to work, or we are dead.

I can see my information coming up, stating that my name is Sule Ogunade, my occupation is a professor, my age, and everything from my background to my favourite drinks comes up.

The man looks at me for a long time. 'Your details check out, but I don't trust you. Join those people over there.' I stand in a corner with around thirty terrified people. There is no escape.

I turn around and see that Lola has been cleared to go. I mouth, 'Leave now, don't wait for me!' She walks away, without looking back, and I am left to my fate. I have no idea if I will live or die.

Chapter Ninety-one: Kabul

Ahmed

We are met at the main entrance door by twenty men. 'These are the men who have agreed to work with us,' he says. After placing the explosives on the agreed points, we dash inside and start shooting. People run in all directions trying to escape the onslaught. I'm glad the men who have joined us are also wearing black, as it's difficult to tell anyone apart in the chaos. My main concern is finding Yusuf. He needs to tell me where my family is, that hypocrite!

I begin opening doors in the temporary location. *Where is that bastard?* A man tries to sneak up behind me, but I am too quick. I turn and shoot him. So many men that work for Hussain are trying to stop us, but we have the advantage of surprise and those who have joined us are shooting them from behind. Attacks come from the left and the right. Someone jumps on me, and I slice his throat with my faithful peshkabz knife.

Where is Yusuf? He should be the one leading his army. Suddenly, I am lifted from the ground and slammed into a wall. There is smoke everywhere, and my head is ringing. An explosive device has just detonated in the room. I struggle to my feet, coughing, and I hear Yusuf's voice. 'Kill them all!' I hide behind the debris caused by the explosion; where is he?

He is hiding behind his men; there are five in front of him, holding submachine guns, looking for us. I look around. Where are my semi-automatic firearms? I can make out the outline of my backpack a little to the left; I can't reach it without being seen. I need to trust in the weapons in my gun holsters. I shoot the security man leading the pack, and he falls to the ground. Then I run as fast as my legs will go as bullets rain down on me. Where is everyone else on my side?

'Find him!' Yusuf commands.

I can see him from my hiding place behind a toppled desk; I just need to bring down the two men protecting him. I take out my other gun. The first shot hits the first man in his forehead, and the second bullet hits the second in his chest. I dive and land on Yusuf. I hit him with all my strength.

'Where are my wife and children?' I yell.

I scream as a sharp pain soars through my leg. I turn to see a man about to shoot me again. Before I can respond, he falls to the ground and Jabar comes out of his hiding place.

'Where is my family?' I ask again.

Jabar walks up to me. 'Ahmed, you've been shot in the leg. It is bleeding badly, and you need to take care of it. We don't have much time; it's ten minutes until the explosion, and then we all die.'

Jabar grabs Yusuf and shoves him roughly outside. I tear a strip of material from a dead man's tunic and use it to bind my leg in an attempt to stop the bleeding. I limp outside.

'Hurry,' shouts Jabar as he strikes Yusuf in the face.

We manage to get out of the building. 'Where is everyone?' I ask. I can see some of our men, but there is not sign of Latif or Mohammed.

Yusuf starts laughing. 'You think you can trust Mohammed? He is worse than us.'

'Where are our families?' I yell.

'Kill me now, and you will never find them,' he responds smugly.

'We can't get answers now. We need to get back before Hussain and his men bombard this place; he will be here soon. Hold on to your gun and watch out for Mohammed; he is coming for us next,' says Jabar.

We retreat into the shadows, as the building explodes behind us.

Chapter Ninety-two: Sydney

Henry

'Tom, you need to leave now. I know how the organisation works; the minute Gamaplug went down, they knew the access point had been tampered with. At least Sophia Richardson is not around, but I bet she is on a plane right now, demanding our heads. I need you to punch me hard in the face. Do it! Now!'

Tom throws his fist, and it lands on my right eye. 'Sorry! I'm so sorry!' he mumbles remorsefully, helping me up from the ground.

'Move!' I yell. 'Just go!' I watch as Tom run towards the exit. *You can do this!* I tell myself. I attempt to get up. I can feel that my face is swollen, and I can't see out of my right eye.

This needs to be believable. That is the only way I get out alive. We have done a brilliant job of hacking the security monitors, both in and outside the building, so there is no record of anyone who entered.

Suddenly, there is noise everywhere. I walk slowly, trying to reach the elevator, and someone shouts, 'Stop there!'

I turned around slowly, trying to see with my one good eye. One of the security agents walks up to me. 'I'm so sorry, sir. Mr Graham, what are you doing here?'

'I should be asking you the same question,' I reply. 'I booked the whole building for a function today, and arrived early morning to check on things, but I was attacked!'

The head of security walks up to me. 'I'm sorry, sir, but we have been instructed to arrest anyone found on this premises.'

'What! Can someone please explain what the hell is going on?' I say.

'Sir, Gamaplug is down. Someone built some form of obstruction, and we are finding it difficult to bring it down. It is happening worldwide.'

'And what's that got to do with this location?' I ask.

'It's the access point, sir,' he replies.

'What does that mean? Is that why someone attacked me?'

'Sir, you need to follow us. Someone should look at your eye, it looks awful, and you need to answer some questions to help us identify the culprit.'

'The organisation knew about the booking. I didn't see anything, why question me?'

'Those are the instructions given by the boss. She wants to know why you arrived so early.'

'I need to talk to her; please connect me with her now.'

The head of security picks up his phone, and tries to connect me. 'Sorry, sir. we have been facing major problems since Gama went down. You'll have to wait for her to arrive, she is already on the plane, she will be here shortly. Please follow me, sir!'

I hope Tom was able to escape. Everyone knows about my lousy marriage, and how I'll do anything to get away from my wife. I'll use that as an excuse.

Tom

I watch as Henry is escorted to a black vehicle, holding his face. He did this to distract them so I could escape. I can see security agents pouring in and out of the building from my position in the car we hired. I need to keep my head down. No one must know I am here. There are agents everywhere, checking each building, and every car.

I cover myself with a black cloak and hide on the floor at the back. *They will not find me; Henry will not go through all that for nothing; I'll get away safely,* I tell myself as I sit and await my fate with a pounding heart.

Chapter Ninety-three: Rio de Janeiro

Ana

I am in the secret room. My pulse is racing and my breathing is so rapid, I am struggling for air. I was shown different ways out of the church, but knew I wouldn't have time to get out before the organisation descended on the location; my only hope is that they don't find me.

The cathedral manager is hauled to the basement. I can hear him screaming and begging for his life.

'Who came into the old church? There is no sign of forced entry, so the person responsible was given access to the church. Who was it? Answer me or I will kill you,' yells one of the security men.

'I don't know; someone came here and asked to use the cathedral; I didn't ask questions. No one comes here anymore. We are barely making any money and they made a generous donation. I didn't see the person's face; they had a cap pulled down low with big sunglasses covering half of their face.' He begins to sob loudly.

'You gave someone access to this place without checking their credentials. Is that what you are telling me?'

One of the security men lifts his right hand and wallops the manager across the face. The manager falls backwards.

'He thinks we are joking,' I hear one of the men say. 'I will end you slowly, then go after your family, one by one, if you don't tell me everything you know.'

I hope this man doesn't tell them anything. It is hard to stay strong in the face of such pressure. Every inch of the cathedral is being methodically searched. Where can I hide? I look around frantically. I am in a small room that looks more like a closet. There are old books and manuscripts on the floor and the shelves. I attempt to move the shelves. This is the oldest cathedral in Brazil; there are sure to be secret passages. I bend down and move the small rug to examine the floor and see what looks like a trapdoor. I pull it open. It is stiff and I know it hasn't been used in a long time. I peer down into the unpromising darkness. I have to enter; I don't know what I will find but I have no choice. It is better than staying here knowing they will find me.

The rug is on top of the trapdoor. I lift the trapdoor as much as possible so as not to let the rug slide away. I try to fit my body underneath without it looking like it's been disturbed. It's not easy. I swing into the hole and my leg touches something. I don't know what it is, but it feels steady. I place my other leg. *Don't think, just do!* I close the trapdoor behind me.

I gag as the smell hits my nose, and drop to the ground. My trousers are soaked, as I wade through the dirty water that quickly rises to my stomach. God! I hope it's water because it smells like urine. I'm going to die for sure. I hear a noise and stifle a scream, before continuing into the unknown.

I reach what appears to be a wall and feel my way around, touching everywhere. Something crawls over my body, and I shake it off with my hand. In my panic, I started wading quickly and slam into the wall with force before it opens in front of me. I slow my pace, my head is sore as carefully walk through the space, only to find myself in another underground building. Light shines down from above and I look at myself. My clothes are soaked and covered in mud and slime.

A huge rat scurries over my foot, and he is not alone. They are suddenly everywhere. I stifle a scream and run as fast as my legs can carry me. I have to get out of here.

Chapter Ninety-four: Hong Kong

Huan

We are rounded up. So many people are lying on the street; they can't understand what is happening. This is the only backup plan I have.

The security agents begin questioning us. 'Do you know who set up equipment in that house?' No one answers. The agents become angry. 'We will have to search them all and take fingerprints,' one of them says, looking at the mass of dejected, dirty people. 'I want everywhere searched, all houses, cars, they couldn't have gone far.'

The man who robbed me at knifepoint earlier steps forward; he must be stupid. He doesn't understand that he has just put his life in danger.

'I saw a woman setting up equipment.' He smiles smugly. 'How much will you give me for information?'

My heart is pounding, but I know he can't identify my face. The whole place was dark; the government doesn't provide electricity for areas full of homeless people.

The head security man walks up to him. 'What did you say?'

'I saw the woman who did this, but I need to be paid before I say anything.'

'Follow me; we will provide you with all the money you need,' the agent says, leading him to an awaiting car.

The agent turns to face the rest of us. 'We will provide you with all the provisions you need if anyone can identify the person who set up that equipment.' No one moves. He sighs heavily, and speaks to another agent. 'Take him away, find out what he knows and you know what to do next.' The head agent stares angrily at the crowd. 'Start searching them one by one,' he instructs.

We are made forcefully to stand in a straight line. The agents stand next to us with masks on their faces, After facial recognition and fingerprinting, we are patted down roughly, and our fingernails are checked. My nails are the dirtiest nails you can imagine; I painted my face and ensured my clothes are dirty and smell of rotten eggs.

They carry out a thorough investigation to make sure we are who we say. The agent stands in front of me and holds his nose in disgust when I open my mouth. I haven't cleaned my teeth in days. The odour oozes out, and I cringe at the smell.

The man pats me down wearing gloves. He turns to his partner next to him. 'I don't know what I might catch standing next to these people,' he growls. 'Look at this one standing in front of me, how can this much smell come from one woman.' He carries out the fingerprint and facial recognition checks. I have won so many awards for being smart, but the information that comes up shows that I used to be a janitor. 'I am not surprised,' he says, and they start to laugh. 'What else would she be doing? Get out of my sight; I'm tired of looking at your ugly face.'

I smile as I lower my face. I have to find a way to get out of here without them noticing. I wrap my dirty blanket around me, walking slowly, trying not to attract their attention.

My car is still in one piece, but agents are watching all vehicles closely. I have to wait until the coast is clear, but, first of all, I need to retrieve the car keys from under a dustbin littered with dirt and filth. I approach the bin, pretending to search for food, and pray that I will be able to get away.

Chapter Ninety-five: The Organisation

'This is a big fuck-up. How could we have got it so wrong? All the systems are down; we can't communicate with our inept security agents. They knew what they were doing; someone working in the organisation certainly gave them information. They brought down Gamaplug when none of us were around,' says James Cooper.

All the big bosses are shouting and giving commands to their security teams. This has caused an uproar in the organisation and there is chaos at the airport terminal.

'We need to leave right now!'

'Sir, systems are down; the Gama system is integrated into almost all technologies. We are trying to set up temporary measures, but it will take some hours.'

'We don't have hours,' says James Cooper curtly. 'It's a mess! The only silver lining is that we get to live another day, but I don't think it's for long.'

'How is this possible?' demands Lekan Gbada, placing his hands on his head, pacing back and forth. 'We monitored everything; we knew they imported equipment but how could we miss this? Bring down Gamaplug! That is our source of power and manipulation; if you take that away, we have nothing!'

Sophia Richardson finds it difficult to relax even in the VIP lounge. Wiping a hand across her sticky forehead, she picks up her phone, trying but failing to connect to the agents on the ground in Sydney. Being selected as one of the two female bosses is a big deal. She was challenged and pulled beyond breaking point to prove that she deserves her position, and no one was going to take it away from her.

Andrew Hughes

I head to the access point, grateful that I don't have to take a plane out of the country. I have limited time to find and eliminate the perpetrators. My men race to me, and we identify the suspect, after filtering through his many identities. Martin Hills! An ex-cop. I enter the building, my heart pounding.

'What is the hell is this?'

I look at the equipment; it is a sophisticated set-up and seems to connect with other equipment.

'Sir, we have never seen anything like this before; even if we close it down, Gamaplug is destroyed, and all signals are entirely blocked.'

'There has to be something we can do.' I look at the team hired by the organisation, supposedly the best in their field. 'Are you trying to tell me that a bunch of punks has outsmarted you? Fix this now! I don't want to hear excuses. Now, show me the dead man!'

'This way, sir,' one of the agents responds.

I stare at the body of Martin Hills, but feel no elation at his death; it has come too late. His group have accomplished what they set out to do, stop the organisation. I turn to the head of security furiously. I fist my hand and throw a punch, and he staggers backwards. 'This man was a New York cop; he did not have the expertise to build that equipment. Where are the others?'

***

The remainder of the big bosses are finally allowed to get into their luxurious private jets after waiting for an hour and a half to board. Fidgeting in their seats, they can't enjoy the wine and meal placed in front of them. They have no idea what awaits them when they arrive in their respective countries.

Adriano Cardoso turns to his head of security. 'Anything?'

'No sir! I have been trying to reach the temporary team on the ground. We are lucky to be able to get on the plane as almost all equipment is down.'

'This is a disaster! I need to know what is happening in Rio de Janeiro! Why can't they fix the problem, it has been hours, and still the issue hasn't been resolved. This doesn't look good for us. Our way of life has made us billions. If the citizens find out they will rebel against us, there is nothing we can do to prevent it.'

Hussain Atta

I sit back in my seat, and try to relax. Gamaplug is not widely used in Kabul and the other countries I control. It is used only by the elite. This situation should not affect me, but I am uneasy that something is wrong. I left the organisation's management to Yusuf, and his sole job before I arrive was to eliminate Ahmed, Jabar and Mohammed. I shake my head uneasily. Why did I leave it to him? I was too distracted; scared about the fate waiting for us from the head. I know I'm about to come home to a disaster, and I can't reach anyone to tell me what is happening.

I fluff the pillow, and try not to worry. I can feel a headache forming; this is a bad sign. What fate awaits me when we arrive back in Kabul?

Chapter Ninety-six: London

Jude

We drop down on the floor in exhaustion.

'We did it!' Sarah screams. But we don't have time to celebrate; those responsible now need to be exposed. The world needs to know that they have hidden in the shadows for too long; they must be in the public light.

'Everything is already in place,' she says. 'All I need to do is press a button on my computer.'

'Do it now!' I whisper weakly. 'After this, we don't have to fight alone; people will fight for their freedom.'

Sarah drags herself across the room. She is on the point of collapse, but this needs to be over today. She presses 'enter' on her computer and releases the information, revealing the personal details of all those connected to Red Gama and responsible for the European hub.

I watch as the information takes over the news. The newscasters are confused; they have no control over what is happening. The face of every member is being shown on screen, their home address, their secret locations and all the atrocities they have committed. It is being shown everywhere.

I pull my curtain across, and watch as the many homeless people, forced into this situation, get up from where they lay to watch the billboards.

There is an uprising on the continent, from little children to adults, as people come out of their homes and pour into the streets, declaring that they will be free from oppression. They pick up whatever weapons they can find, little kids holding tightly to little stones. The nation has suffered enough!

***

James Cooper turns to his men. 'Hide me! They are coming for me,' he yells, but his men do not move. 'Why are you not doing anything?' he shouts furiously.

His forty security men slowly turn around, walk out of the secret cave and lock the door behind them.

'He will not be able to escape,' says the head security man. 'He needs to pay for all he has done to us and our families. We mustn't kill him. That will be too easy, let the people deal with him.'

The mob arrives at the secret location. The security team open the door and allow them to enter, the look of anger on their faces speaks volumes.

James Cooper is quivering when he is pulled forcefully out onto the street.

'You will join the other members soon,' one of the men says.

'You cannot do this to me!' James shouts. 'Do you know who I am?'

'Oh we know exactly who you are; you are the monster that has been terrorising our nation for months.'

'Kill him! Kill him!' the mob chants.

The head of security stands in front of his former boss and shoots him in both legs. He falls to the floor, screaming. 'This is for all the lives that you destroyed,' he says, before walking away and leaving him at the mercy of the baying mob.

Chapter Ninety-seven: New York

Edward

No! Why would Martin do this? He gave up his life to save me when he has a family he loves. I am burdened with guilt and regret. *Focus, Edward! You have to make Martin proud. His sacrifice will not be for nothing.*

I knew launching POWERA would be risky, but I never thought this would happen. The cocky security man was so focused eliminating Martin, that I was able to escape without being seen. Everything we have done is to get to this moment. Everyone in the organisation will soon be exposed, and people will know how they plundered nations of all their resources.

I can see the confusion on people's faces. They have come to rely entirely on Gamaplug; it is the only technology that the owner sold to users, and at low prices. It was painful to watch people rushing to get this technology not realising they had signed away their freedom.

I wipe away the continuous tears that refuse to stop. His last words to me were 'find my family', and that is what I am going to do. I hope the others have made it, because this is the first step; the next is exposure.

I sit in front of my computer with all the information gathered on the organisation; it is time for phase two. Those in charge will hide because their manipulation will no longer work. I connect to all the television networks, digital screens and social platforms. I send all the names of the organisation's members, and details of how they were able to manipulate everyone. It is time we rise as a nation and fight against them. All their atrocities and crimes would boomerang back, and they will be the ones being afraid for a change. We created POWERA, and they can't stop it; the information is out there.

I walk out of my house. People are leaving their homes in droves with a determined look on their faces. More and more people gather. I can feel their frustration as they march and chant, 'Enough is enough!'

Fred Demson

I knew it was the end when Gamaplug went down. There was no point in killing the bosses because I wanted them to see what their failure had caused. No amount of security will prevent the stampede of people that will be heading to my home. All information was provided, including our names and our addresses. I try to call the head of the bank and Andrew Hughes, but no one picks up. That would not have happened an hour ago. I need to ensure my family is taken care of. I tell them to hide in the secret security room and not to come out until I say.

'Where is James Cooper?' I demand to know.

The head of security laughs. 'Mr Cooper is dead. The building he bought for himself, the pompous bastard, has been burned down with him inside.'

I see that some of my security men have joined the mob, and the noise is getting closer. We could have still won if we had remained united. I guess you can't force people to follow you.

I lock myself in my study and hold my handgun; I will never give up without a fight. I press a button on my left side. There is an explosion, and the whole building vibrates. This should slow them down, but it won't stop them for long. The noise gets ever closer.

I smile, the end has come, but I am Fred Demson. No one wins against me.

Chapter Ninety-eight: Lagos

Lola

There is commotion everywhere. The sound of uncontrollable grief follows me as loved ones are killed just because they are suspected of being involved with building W-generation.

I move away swiftly, without looking back, and wait at a safe distance, hoping Segun will join me soon. I cannot allow myself to wallow in sorrow; all our work to get to this point will be for nothing. I still have work to do. I reach the car and drive to our home. I am not as knowledgeable as Segun, but I have learnt a lot through working with him, and he has made contingency plans in case he doesn't return. I need to save him, and the only way to do that is to expose those bastards who have continually tormented our lives.

I sit in front of the computer, hoping that this will work. Our spirits have been broken, we live daily in hopelessness, and people disappear or are murdered because they stood against the organisation.

I download the information into the system and press the 'enter' key. It will be displayed everywhere; on people's phones, computers, televisions, every device. The only thing that will be showing are the names of all the members of Green Gama, their addresses and how they were able to take over. Details of corruption, murder and brutality. I place my hands over my face and sigh heavily. This is my last hope.

Segun

I am told to get on my knees. 'I'm still not sure about you,' says one of the agents, laughing maliciously and pulling out his gun.

I close my eyes, waiting for the shot, but nothing happens.

I open my eyes again. The agents are running away. Crowds of people run after them. Some of the agents are shooting, but that does not deter the angry mob. There are just too many people, and the agents can't handle it. Some of those caught plead for their lives, saying they were only doing their jobs. 'You showed us no mercy, we will show no mercy,' shouts someone in the crowd, before the men are stabbed multiple times.

I have never seen anything like this; the people are united, both young and old, overcoming their oppressors.

I smile, finally! When you push people to the limit, don't be surprised when they rise up and fight.

Lekan Gbada

I arrived at my house an hour ago; I want to know what is happening now! What is taking too long?

'Sir! People are on the streets, most of our men have been killed, and some have joined the mob. They have been given ammunition, and from the information I have gathered they are heading this way.'

'Get me out of here!' I say.

The head of security shakes his head. 'The roads are blocked, everything is on fire, and everywhere, and they are burning members' houses.'

'I don't care. Just get me away from here.'

Two agents enter the security room. One of them shoots the head of security.

'What are you doing?' I yell.

'What we should have done a long time ago. You murdered our families; you took everything away from us. We are handing you over to the mob; they will kill you slowly.'

My blood freezes in my veins. 'You can't do that to me. Do you know whom you are dealing with?'

One of the agents slams into me and I fall. I curl up to shield myself as I am kicked in the stomach and face. The crowd force their way inside the security room, as my men retreat, leaving me to face the people who are armed with sticks, stones and knives. I cover my head and start to pray.

Chapter Ninety-nine: Kabul

Ahmed

Is it safe to return to Mohammed's house? We have no idea what is waiting for us. Mohammed's main focus is to bring down Hussain; we need to expose him before he lands. We don't have enough time; he is on his way back and arriving shortly.

'We shouldn't have killed Yusuf; he could have been helpful to us,' I say to Jabar.

'He is useless,' Jabar sneers. 'He would have wasted our time.'

We arrive at the house. It seems to be deserted. Where is Mohammed hiding?

We enter the technology room. We need to send the information on Hussain Atta to all media houses. He has been hailed a hero for too long, convincing people he is a good man.

With all the information we have compiled with the help of our allies from other continents, we have solid evidence against him. We have uncovered the source of his wealth from extorting other nations, the manipulation of Mohammed Pir who was used as a puppet, his overall goals to destroy the country and anyone who opposes him. The information is streamed in all media outlets. I can see the surprise in the eyes of the newscaster as all other news is halted as our broadcast is streamed. The nation is in shock; the man they considered their hero was the one who enslaved them.

***

Hussain lands with his security team of about fifteen men.

'Where is everyone? Why is no one waiting to pick me up from the airport?' he says.

He saunters into the airport and sees the people waiting for him. His men raise their weapons, but Hussain can see that the crowd, led by Jabar, is also armed.

'Why are you here?' Hussain asks Jabar.

'Your days of manipulation are over; all your men have been killed, including Yusuf.'

He turns to Hussain's men and tells them that if they don't want to die today, they must change their allegiance. The men join the mob.

'Now kill him,' Jabar commands.

Ahmed

I wait anxiously in the house while Jabar leads the angry crowd to the airport.

I feel the barrel of a gun at the back of my head. Then Mohammed's voice. 'It's time to die! I have been watching you and Jabar. When you are both gone, I will lead Kabul the way I want.' He laughs maliciously.

I raise my hands, and attempt to stand up.

'Don't even try it!' Mohammed shouts angrily.

'Why? Are you ashamed of your height?' I laugh. 'You must be a weak man to be so short!'

I can see his reaction in the mirror mounted on the wall. He is blinded by rage, an insecure man. His anger distracts him and I turn suddenly and dive for his weapon. We wrestle on the ground and I twist the gun out of his hand. A shot rings out and he falls, a shocked expression on his face.

The men working for Hussain are stripped of their guns and instructed to take us to our families. So many people whose loved ones were forcefully taken from them in the pretence that it was all instigated by Mohammed.

We are taken to an underground cave on the outskirts of Kabul.

I see my wife's face, as tears fall unchecked down her face. And then I see my children; I hardly recognise them, they are so malnourished. I run towards them and hold them tightly, weeping as I whisper, 'I'm so sorry.'

Chapter One Hundred: Sydney

Henry

'Why are you still keeping me here?' I yell at the man in charge of security.

'I'm sorry, sir, I'm just following instructions. We have not been able to reach the big boss; the mobile phones are acting up, and we don't know what to do.'

I stare at him with hatred. 'You have kept me here without my consent, and I'm a respected member of the organisation.' I look at my watch. 'It's been over two hours, and I'm tired.'

One of the agents rushes into the room and whispers to the head of security. He runs outside in a panic without locking the door. God! I hope Tom has exposed members of the organisation. My name and mother's will be removed from the list; I'll deal with her myself.

'Can someone please tell me what is happening?' I shout after him, but no one answers. There is so much commotion. I open the door and step outside. All of the agents have gone. Everywhere looks empty. Where is everyone?

I walked out of the building, and I see some of the agents trying to change out of their black suits to blend with the crowds heading this way. 'What is happening?' I shout again. One of the men points to a screen on the side of the building.

As I suspected, all information on the organisation is being broadcast to the public. I need to get home; I must deal with my folks. The crowds block all the roads. I know all organisation members will not escape, and the leader, Sophia Richardson, is air-bound. She will receive an unpleasant welcome at the airport.

I walk for a long time and progress is slow. Everyone, it seems, has taken to the streets. So many people have had enough, and are targeting the luxurious homes of people from the organisation. I know they will be heading to my house because Cynthia was one of the first names mentioned.

I enter my parents' home by the back entrance. The mob has not yet reached them. My mother is trembling with fear, and my father is continually asking her what is going on. I touch him gently on the arm and say, 'I'm so sorry, Dad. Mum ordered Mia's execution.' His face falls. I squeeze his arm. 'It's OK, fortunately, she is still alive.'

My father moves away from my mother in shock. 'Did you do that?'

Tears fall down her face. 'I had no choice; I did it to save you and Henry. Everything I have done is to protect you.'

I shake my head sadly. 'This is the last time you will ever see me; my father is the only person allowed to visit. You are still alive today because you are my mother, but you will spend your life without your grandson and me. If Dad wants to stay with a woman who will not hesitate to take a life, that is his choice.'

I walk out of my parents' house for the last time, the emotional pleas of my mother ringing in my ears.

When I finally reach home, the main gate is open. I walk around cautiously. Some windows are broken, and the entrance door is damaged, but I have never felt so much peace. She has gone.

There is blood all over the floor, and some items of furniture have been broken. My fancy chandelier is on the ground, shattered in pieces. I bend down and start laughing uncontrollably, holding my stomach. I have not laughed like this in months. It's time to bring my family home.

Chapter One Hundred and One: Rio de Janeiro

Ana

I stink so badly that people avoid me and stare as I pass. I honestly don't know how I look; but it must be bad. I get into the old rented truck and drive away. The next step is to expose the members of the organisation, then I'll be home and free. I cannot even dare to hope.

Some time later, I arrive at the rented warehouse. I am so tired I nearly fell asleep at the wheel several times. My hands are sore and my body is itching, but I have little time to clean myself up. I need to get to my computer. I quickly wash my hands and gulp down mouthfuls of water. That will have to do.

The group has done a fantastic job compiling all the information I need. Those responsible can run, but they can no longer hide. We have suffered so much at the hands of this organisation. Amassing great wealth while the rest of the population suffers; it is time for them to be afraid. We have lived in fear for too long. I press 'enter', and, finally, I can breathe. The day of reckoning has come. I hope this information pushes people to fight for their freedom. No one should be enslaved in their own country.

***

The head of Brazilian City Bank is having a management meeting in his conference room, content with the way he has become a billionaire in such a short period.

The door to the conference room bursts open, and he sees his employees and some faces he doesn't recognise. 'What in God's name… How dare you disrupt my meeting!'

One of his female employees walks up to him and gives him a head-turning slap across his face. He is too astonished to speak.

He is pushed forward forcefully by a member of his management team, who says, 'Today will be your last day on earth.'

Then he is surrounded by a large crowd, who punch, kick, and stab at him with knives. He cowers on the floor, blood pouring out of his wounds, praying for his end to come quickly.

Adriano Cardoso

I know something is wrong when the pilot finds it difficult to land; no one seems to be responding to give us clearance to land.

'We have a problem, sir. We are unable to land the plane, and we don't have enough fuel to continue flying for long.'

'Such insolence! They knew about my arrival days before I left the country.'

'It's radio silence; but we have to land, sir. We have no choice.' The seat belt sign is activated. 'We commence descent in five minutes.'

I hold on to my seat, my heart pounding; someone will pay for this!

Minutes later, the plane plummets and overshoots the runway. It slides a short distance and comes to an abrupt halt to the sound of screeching, twisting metal. I am pushed forward by the force but held in place by the seat belt. There is smoke everywhere. I have to get out before I am trapped in the plane.

I struggle to get up and make my way, with some difficulty and a handful of men, to the emergency exit. The door opens automatically, but a vast crowd is waiting for us. They have come prepared and pointing their guns at us. We are instructed not to step down from the aircraft.

'It's on fire,' I shout needlessly.

'Yes! So it is,' one of them laughs. 'You get to die slowly.'

The crowd is forced back by the heat, as the fire slowly engulfs the plane.

If we jump out, we will be shot, if we stay in the plane, we will die anyway.

I step back on the plane, sit down, close my eyes and wait for the end.

Chapter One Hundred and Two:
Hong Kong

Huan

I watch anxiously as the agents conduct their search. Many people are arrested and taken away.

Finally, the place looks deserted. I change immediately and dispose of my old clothes. I then get in my car, driving cautiously and making sure I'm not being followed. I keep my head down as I enter my building and open the door to the apartment. I place my hands over my mouth as I slide to the floor. I have never felt this emotional; everything I have gone through comes rushing back to me. I shake my head vigorously; you can't think about this now; you still have work to do.

I get up from the floor. I open my computer. *I must do this!* The continent needs to know what their leaders and members of the organisation are up to. All the information has been gathered for Asia_1 and Asia_2. I know our friend and contact in Kabul will handle Hussain Atta, but they have members all over Asia, and they need to know what is going on. This will be the first time they have to bond together without thoughts of religion, ethnicity, or language, to face the thing we have in common; oppression. Our rights have been taken from us by power-drunk and money-greedy humans.

I download the information and press 'enter'. The resulting broadcast will take over all mobile phones, television screens, billboards, everything. Everyone will be able to identify their oppressors. My eyes are swimming with tears; as I cover my face with my hands, laughing and crying hysterically.

I must find Lan Song. He set-up my husband with his mistress, and he must pay for his sins. I open the door. People are streaming out of their apartments, shock on their faces as they digest the information, slowly turning into rage. They take out their Gamaplugs and set them on fire.

The crowd is increasing by the minute, marching to the homes of the organisation's members. I join them, holding my bread knife.

I have one goal; Lan Song must die by my hands in the same way he killed Chun and Feng.

***

The smile leaves his face as he tries to flee. Lan Song heads towards his car, leaving his family behind, as he tries to escape the crowd. He doesn't realise that some of his security team have turned against him and show them his whereabouts.

He can't outrun them, so he stops and kneels, pleading for his life, promising to pay them whatever they want. I push my way through the throngs of angry people and walk up to him.

'Lan Song!' He looks up as I slowly remove my hood so he can clearly see my face.

I stab him repeatedly in the stomach with the bread knife, refusing to let him go.

'This is for my husband,' I say in his ear.

Stabbing continuously, I am pulled back forcefully.

'He's dead,' says one of the women. I fall to my knees and start crying.

Ping Wu

The plane lands on the private hangar. To my relief everything is still how I left it. Four black sedan cars are waiting to transport me and ten of my security agents.

I enter one of the cars confidently, and relax in the back seat. We have been driving for a few minutes when I look out of the window.

'Where are you taking me?' I ask the chauffeur. 'This is not the way to my house.'

There is no response. I turn to my bodyguard, wondering what can be happening, but he looks just as confused. I try the door, but it is locked.

We are taken to a secluded place. The door is opened from the outside and I stumble out of the car.

I am pulled into the middle of a large, waiting crowd, with my bodyguard. I smile but the faces in the crowd are hostile. Someone spits at me and my legs buckle underneath me. We are pulled to our feet and my hands are tied behind my back. I am then dragged to a pole and tied securely. I look up to see a line of people, armed with machine guns, a firing squad. I open my mouth to scream, but then they start shooting…

Chapter One Hundred and Three:
The Unity Team

Edward

I can't believe I am able to connect and communicate with other group members after the ordeal we have been through; it feels bittersweet. The world will never be the same again; the effect of the devastation cannot be comprehended. The great leaders the world looked up were nothing but wolves in sheep's clothing. Now we are forced to face the truth that the only way forward is by working together as one world, united in honesty and transparency. It's a pity that we had to experience such pain before humans could look past themselves to work together to build a better future. It will take years to restore the economy. The pain and agony people suffered at the hands of Gama will last forever.

The world was plunged into impoverishment and nations need to start from scratch to rebuild and restructure. People need guidance and counselling; they have lost their homes, loved ones and finances. Where do they start?

The secret cells run by the organisation used to perpetuate their evil by arresting family members to force their subjects into submission have released all prisoners.

I was the first in line to welcome Leah Hills and her daughter. That day will forever be stamped in my memory. I watched tearfully as families were reunited with loved ones after months of separation, their tears of joy, hugging each other as if they would never again let go. Others were met with anguish, knowing they would never again see their loved ones.

It was difficult for me to tell her the news. I remember holding her tightly because she felt light-headed and almost fainted. I understood her pain and regret for not believing in him when it mattered. 'It was not your fault they had overwhelming evidence against him,' I told her.

'I have known him for over two decades and still didn't believe him when he repeatedly told me he didn't do it. I chose to believe his partner; Oh God! What have I done?'

It was good to hear the news from other team members, like Ana Santos, in Rio de Janeiro, who got to see her sister and her sister's children again. They were able to bury the hatchet realising they had been exploited. They are trying to rebuild their lives. Ana has returned the money she received from Gama back to the people.

Sarah Philips, in London, was able to restart her family distribution business from scratch.

Henry Graham brought his wife and son to his new home, their old home held too many terrible memories. He has not spoken to his mother in a while. His father chose to walk away from his marriage.

Lola has been reunited with her family. They have a lot of animosity towards her, it is going to take years of counselling to try and heal from the loss and not blame herself for her father's demise.

For the first time in years, leaders are chosen not by party but credibility and accountability. Society needs to push away greed, this is the genesis of all problems. It is good to see people opening their doors to help and shelter those who have lost more. The greatest necessity is food, the government is distributing foods to its citizens. This new world is not about your connections, how you look, how you dress, your education or background. People just want to survive.

All funds stolen by the Gama group have been frozen, and the money will be distributed to all nations to help people rebuild, with utmost transparency. New credible leaders have been selected, as we purge the old, corrupt regimes.

Healing will take time. The only way we were able to defeat the organisation was by working together, putting our differences aside, and focusing solely on the goal; it came at a high cost and we lost loved ones, but we gained our freedom.

Character/Place List

<table>
<tr><td>

A
Adriano Cardoso, big boss of Purple Gama (South America)
Ahmed Nazar (Kabul)
Ana Santos, accountant, widow (Rio de Janeiro)
Andrew Hughes, big boss of Blue Gama (Europe)
Aisha, Ahmed's wife (Kabul)
Abdul, Ahmed's son (Kabul) Abdul and Leila

</td></tr>
<tr><td>

B
Bobby, a New York cop, and Martin's ex-partner in the force
Blue Gama (North American hub)

</td></tr>
<tr><td>

C
Carl, Henry's son (Sydney)
Chun, Huan's husband
Cynthia Coleman, old friend of Henry's (Sydney)
Carlos Ribeiro, Ana's immediate boss
Chyou, female bodyguard (HK)
Carlton, Fred Demson's PA (NY)

</td></tr>
<tr><td>

D
Dan Campbell, president of US

</td></tr>
<tr><td>

E
Edward, Martin's friend and hacker (NY)

</td></tr>
<tr><td>

F
Fred Demson, founder of Gama (the master)
Fernanda, bank manager (Rio)

</td></tr>
<tr><td>

G
Gama Hub Deputies:
James Cooper, Red Gama (Europe)
Andrew Hughes, Blue Gama (North America)
Lekan Gbada, Green Gama (Africa)

</td></tr>
</table>

Hussain Atta, Yellow Gama_1 (Asia 1)
Sophia Richardson, White Gama (Australia)
Adriano Cardoso, Purple Gama (South America)
Ping Wu, Yellow-Gama_2 (Asia 2)

H
Hussain Atta, Yusuf's boss (Kabul), big boss of Yellow Gama_1 (Asia 1)
Henry Graham, Minister for Defence (Sydney)
Huan Li (Hong Kong), former Chief Technical Officer of Yamson Telecommunications
Mr Hunan, current CEO of Yamson Telecommunications

I

J
Jude Williams (London), successful chef
Jabar, Ahmed's contact in the compound (Lagos)
Jacob White, Gama Lab technical specialist
James Cooper, big boss of Red Gama (North America)
Jane Brown, Fred Demson's wife (the Browns are a monied family)

K

L
Lola Adeyemo, journalist (Lagos)
Leah, Martin's wife (NY)
Latif, Mohammed's bodyguard, Kabul
Lekan Gbada, big boss of Green Gama (Africa)

M
Martin Hills, New York, cop (has a wife and two daughters)
Mohammed Pir, Ahedan Group leader (Kabul)
Mia, Henry's wife (Sydney)
Mr Montes, CEO of Ana's company (Rio)
Maria, Ana's sister (Rio)

N
Nader, one of Mohammed's inner circle of trusted henchmen (Kabul)

N60 postnanometer, new technology being developed by the Unity team

O Overland Investments, Fred Demson's company Obedian, opposition group to the militants (Kabul)

P Pedro, Ana's sister's husband (Rio) Ping Wu, big boss of Yellow Gama_2 (Asia 2)

Q

R Roger Smith (London), police sergeant promoted to inspector Rob, Henry's assistant, Sydney

S Sam Philips the founder and CEO of Sam Wholesale Sam Wholesale, competitor in food chain (London) Sarah Philips (London), daughter of the above Segun, Lola's helper (Lagos) Sophia Richardson, big boss of White Gama (Australia)

T Tom, Mrs Graham's security man helping Henry (Sydney)

Y Yusuf, Ahmed's former friend, who recruited him to work for Mohammed (Kabul) Yamson Telecommunications

OTHER P-generation for the European hub (PG) O-generation for the North American hub (OG) W-generation for the African hub (WG) E-generation for the Australian hub EG) R-generation for the South American hub (RG) A-generation for the Asian hub (AG)

About the Author

Josephine Ronk lives in England with her husband and children. Her life is spent multitasking, writing her books and raising her kids.

She developed a passion for reading at a young age, but did not start writing until later in life after being encouraged by her loved ones. Once she started, she became hooked. She loves to create powerful characters that are mysterious and allow you to unlock your imagination to infinite possibilities. When not writing in her favourite library, she spends most of her time reading, cooking, and travelling the world with her family.

Be sure to follow Josephine Ronk on Amazon, Facebook, Twitter, and Instagram. Sign up for her newsletter to receive information about upcoming releases.

Website: http://www.josephineronkauthor.com
Instagram: http://www.instagram.com/iamjosephineronk
Twitter: http://www.twitter.com/josephineronk
Facebook: https://www.facebook.com/JosephineRonkAuthor

By the same author:

Gama Generation
Seven Heroes Searching for a Common Enemy

www.ingramcontent.com/pod-product-compliance
Lightning Source LLC
Chambersburg PA
CBHW061144210726
48294CB00006B/1579